D0789249

WE'LL MEET
Again

Center Point
Large Print

Also by Melody Carlson and available from Center Point Large Print:

Once Upon a Winter's Heart
Your Heart's Desire
I'll Be Seeing You
As Time Goes By

Melody Carlson

Center Point Large Print
Thorndike, Maine

This Center Point Large Print edition
is published in the year 2019 by arrangement with
WhiteFire Publishing.

The text of this Large Print edition is unabridged.
In other aspects, this book may vary
from the original edition.
Printed in the United States of America
on permanent paper.
Set in 16-point Times New Roman type.

ISBN: 978-1-64358-362-4

The Library of Congress has cataloged this record under
Library of Congress Control Number: 2019944735

One

Late April 1944

Margaret knew it was irrational, but she still felt somewhat responsible for Brian's war injury. Oh, she knew she hadn't actually thrown the grenade that cost her husband his right leg while leading his troops through Italy, but she felt guilty all the same. If only she'd attended Mass more faithfully, lit more prayer candles, recited the rosary more often—or, most troubling, if only she'd been a more faithful wife—perhaps poor Brian would still be whole.

Despite going to confession weekly and doing the penance imposed by Father McMurphey, Margaret still couldn't shake the idea that God wanted to punish her. And why not? Didn't she deserve punishment? Yet it seemed unfair that Brian was the one to suffer . . . all because of her.

As Margaret drove through the morning fog to Letterman, she tried to redirect her mind to more positive thoughts—like Father McMurphey, who had been encouraging. She reminded herself of how little Peter was saying more words and how helpful old Mrs. Bartley had been at the store these past few months. And it was so great that

Colleen was home—and expecting her first baby. Those were all good things.

Yet as she turned into the visitors' parking lot at the imposing military hospital, all her happy thoughts evaporated. All she could think about was packing her wounded serviceman into the backseat of this car and transporting him home. Her stomach knotted as she pulled into an empty space, and her hands trembled as she removed the key from the ignition. She wanted to be strong, wanted to be upbeat, wanted to be like Mrs. Miniver from the Greer Garson movie. But it was so hard.

Just last night, when she held an emergency planning meeting with the family to discuss how to handle Brian's unexpected discharge, Margaret had put on a brave front, assuring her family and Brian's that she could handle this. But now she could barely hold back the tears—she wanted to run away and let someone else deal with it.

"Put your best foot forward," Colleen had advised this morning as she adjusted Margaret's headpiece. The latest fashion, straight from Hollywood, was a gorgeous teal blue beaded fascinator that Margaret hoped would help conceal how distraught she really felt.

Margaret checked her image in the rearview mirror, retouching the lipstick that she must've chewed off during the short drive here. "God give me strength," she prayed aloud as she snapped her handbag closed and got out of the car. Various family members had offered to accompany her this morning, but Margaret knew this was her cross to bear. She also knew that everyone was busier than ever these days. Mam was caring for Margaret's toddler Peter today, and Molly had university classes as well as her internship at the newspaper. Colleen, despite her morning sickness, was working at the store, and Dad, well, he was supposed to avoid all forms of stress and strain. As if that were possible. All one had to do was turn on the radio or pick up a newspaper and blood pressure was certain to rise. This horrible war . . . would it ever end?

It wasn't just her family that was busy. Brian's dad was trying to round up a wheelchair, and his mom was busily getting their house ready for their wounded hero's homecoming. It had been decided last night at their emergency meeting that Brian could be best cared for at his parents' home since they had a spare bedroom on the first floor. And Mrs. Hammond had seemed comfortable with the unexpected chore of caring for her disabled son. That was a relief.

The family member Margaret truly longed for as she walked through the parking lot was her sister Bridget—well, besides her big brother Peter, but there was no bringing him back from the dead. As a trained army nurse, no one would be more skilled than Bridget to help with Brian's recovery. But Bridget was God-knew-where in the South Pacific right now, caring for other wounded soldiers . . . some who would be sent back to the battlefield, some who would come home to better-equipped hospitals, and some who would not survive.

"Thank God that Brian's alive," Margaret said beneath her breath as she entered the lobby of the busy military hospital. By now she was fairly used to Letterman and barely shuddered to see a pair of severely wounded servicemen sitting in wheelchairs parked in a nearby hallway. The facility was filled to nearly overflowing. That was why Brian was being discharged this early, even though, according to the doctor, he was still in the healing process. Not only with the leg, but his cracked ribs and some of the other injuries would take time. But to be fair, most of the patients here were in worse shape than Brian—and space was limited.

Holding her head high, Margaret stopped at the nurses' station, where the head nurse greeted her. Before long, she was signing discharge papers and listening as the head nurse explained about future outpatient treatment and therapy, mostly reiterating what the doctor had told Margaret yesterday when she'd been informed that Brian could go home.

"These pills are for pain." The nurse handed Margaret an amber prescription bottle. "Just follow the directions." A pamphlet joined the bottle. "And this has some helpful hints for caring for an amputee."

Margaret placed the items into her purse and thanked her.

"Well, then, I guess we're set." The nurse nodded toward Brian's ward. "Unless you have any questions for the doctor. Although he's quite busy this morning. A new shipment of patients is expected to arrive soon."

Margaret just shook her head then, bracing herself, followed the nurse into Brian's ward. She felt slightly relieved to see Brian fully dressed and seated in a wheelchair. She smiled as she greeted him. "You look like you're ready to go."

He nodded with what was clearly a forced smile, and before long, with the help of a sturdy orderly and the supervision of the head nurse, they were loading him into the backseat of the car. She clumsily attempted to arrange the pillows she'd brought along, hoping she could make him comfortable but fearing she was only making it worse. If Brian was in pain at the jostling and bumping, he didn't say a word. But, of course, he was probably used to pain by now.

"Here's a blanket." She offered him the woolen lap robe as the hospital staff departed.

"I'm fine." He pushed it away. "It's not cold. Let's just get out of here."

"Yes, of course." She hurried into the driver's

seat, trying not to tremble as she started the engine. She did not want to cry. *Please, don't cry!*

"So . . . where are you taking me?" he asked in a flat tone. "Or perhaps you'd like to simply toss my carcass into the bay."

"Brian!" She stopped at the edge of the parking lot, turning to stare. To her relief his lips were curved slightly up . . . but his eyes were dark and somber.

"I'm sorry, honey." He grimaced. "I guess I just feel a bit useless at the moment."

"You are *not* useless," she declared, but before she could elaborate, the sound of a car horn made her jump.

"Keep moving," Brian commanded. "Someone back there sounds impatient."

Margaret returned her focus to driving, reminding herself that she was transporting a seriously injured man and needed to proceed carefully. As she drove, she tried to think of a gentle way to inform him of where he'd be staying during his continued recuperation. She felt certain he wouldn't be pleased with the news.

"We all met last night," she began carefully, stopping for a traffic light. "Everyone agreed that it's best for you to stay at your parents'. You know, because they have a first-floor bedroom and your mom—"

He released a loud groan.

"I really wanted to bring you home to the

apartment above the store, but they all talked me out of it. There's the stairs . . . and the bathroom's downstairs and—"

"Yes, I know. I understand. But being back at Mom and Dad's . . ." He let out a loud sigh. "Well, it figures."

"I can start looking for a place," she said suddenly. "Something that's on one level and where we can be—"

"Don't bother," he snapped. "From what I've heard, there's a shortage on housing in this town. Probably will be until the war is over. Maybe longer."

"Well, we don't have to live in the city. We could move out—"

"You've got the store, Margaret. Our families are here. Of course, we want to live in the city. Don't be ridiculous."

"That's all true, but what if—"

"The light's green," he declared in a sharp tone.

Tears burned in Margaret's eyes as she passed through the intersection. She knew he wasn't trying to be harsh and that she should have thicker skin, but none of this was like anything she'd ever expected of their lives together. But why should that surprise her? When had anything in her life ever gone as planned?

"Are you comfortable?" she asked meekly as she turned onto a bumpy street, instantly wishing she'd chosen a smoother route.

"As much as I can be," he said stiffly.

"I'm sorry." She blinked to hold back her tears.

"It's my fault. The nurse tried to get me to take pain meds, but I refused. I didn't want to be doped up for the ride."

She considered offering to stop so he could take a pill but figured it was too late. Instead, she kept her mouth closed and concentrated on avoiding the worst bumps. But by the time she reached his parents' house, she felt like a bundle of raw nerves.

"Here we are," she said as she parked the car. "I'll run inside and tell them." She hurried up to the house where Mr. Hammond was already emerging with an old wooden wheelchair, his wife just steps behind him with an anxious expression.

"How's he doing?" Mrs. Hammond asked with wide eyes.

"I think he might be in some pain." Maggie quickly explained about the missed pain medication then reiterated the orderly's instructions for easing Brian out of the car and into a wheelchair. It was an awkward process, but at least they didn't drop him in the street. Still, Margaret could see by the firm line of his jaw and the paleness of his lips that he was in pain. As soon as they got into the house, she ran for a glass of water and immediately offered him one of the pain pills. He didn't protest.

"Dad managed to find you a hospital bed," Mrs. Hammond said pleasantly as they wheeled him into his old childhood room—the same room Margaret had occupied after Peter was born. To her relief, all the childish décor and dusty school pennants were gone. It smelled as if Mrs. Hammond had done some thorough cleaning, but the stripped-down space now had a rather stark and clinical appearance.

"Where is Margaret going to stay?" Brian demanded.

"Margaret?" Mrs. Hammond's brows arched.

"Yes, she's my wife. Shouldn't she be here with me?"

"But we all decided that it was best for Margaret and little Peter to remain in their apartment above the store," Mrs. Hammond explained. "Didn't she tell you?"

Brian frowned darkly.

"I meant to tell you, but—"

"If Brian would like to have his family here," Mr. Hammond intervened, "I don't see why we can't accommodate that. Right, Louise?"

"Well, if everyone thinks that's for the best." Mrs. Hammond sounded uncertain.

"I think that's best," Brian said firmly.

Mrs. Hammond glanced at Margaret. "Is that going to work for you, dear? I must say I would love having little Peter here full time. And I can help with him."

"We'll let you use Patrick's room too," Mr. Hammond declared.

"I'll have to relocate my sewing and we'll need to get a—"

"We need to get Brian into bed," Mr. Hammond said with authority. "I'm sure he's worn out from the trip home. You ladies can discuss the living arrangements later."

Both Margaret and Mr. Hammond managed to hoist Brian into the bed, but seeing the beads of sweat on Brian's forehead told Margaret that he was in pain. "Hopefully that pill will start to work soon," she quietly told him as his parents exited the small room.

"I should've taken it earlier," he muttered between his teeth.

She went around the bed, gently tucking in the blankets, taking extra care on his right side . . . where the lower half of his leg was missing. "Can I get you anything else?"

He shook his head. "Just need to rest."

"Yes." She leaned over to kiss his smoothly shaved cheek. "Welcome home, darling."

"Thanks." His voice sounded flat and dull, mechanical.

"You'll feel better soon." She slowly backed out of the room. "Just give yourself time, Brian."

He simply stared blankly at her, as if doubting her words. Then he closed his eyes, and she closed the door. *Time* . . . They would all need lots of time to get beyond this. And even if the old adage were true, that time could heal all wounds, she knew all the time in the world would never replace Brian's missing leg. Or anything else that they'd lost since this stupid war began.

Two

As Colleen unloaded a case of canned peas, it hit her—this was nothing like Hollywood. She chuckled to herself as she set the last can on top of the pyramid. If only her fans could see her now. Of course, some of them could, and did, see her. The older customers had quickly gotten over her, limiting their trips to the store after her first week of filling in for Margaret. But it was her second week and star-struck teenagers were still flocking in after school. Sure, they'd buy an apple or orange, but it was clear that they hoped to make small talk, get signatures, or even take a photograph with her. It wasn't bad for business, but it did get old after a while.

So they decided a few days ago that Margaret, who was still helping Mrs. Hammond with Brian's care, would work afternoons at the store. And Colleen would go upstairs and put her feet up. The baby wasn't due until August, but Colleen's waistline had already expanded enough to make maternity clothes a must. For now she was borrowing some things from Margaret, but she eventually planned to look for something more fashionable.

"Time for the changing of the guard," Margaret

announced as she came into the store. “How’s it going?”

“It’s been steady.” Colleen removed her apron and reached for her purse. “And Mrs. Bartley had to leave early for a doctor’s appointment.”

“Is she unwell?” Margaret asked.

“I think it was just a routine checkup.” Colleen suddenly noticed dark circles beneath her sister’s eyes. “How about you?” She peered curiously at Margaret. “You look worn out. Are you okay?”

Margaret shrugged as she picked up the grocer’s apron. “I’m fine.”

Colleen frowned with real concern. “You don’t look fine to me.” She hooked her arm into Margaret’s then led her into the back room, calling out to Dirk, who was cleaning vegetables. “You watch the front for a few minutes.”

“The autograph seekers already here?” he teased as he laid down his knife.

“Not yet. But I need to talk to Margaret.” Colleen led Margaret into the office then pointed to one of the chairs. “Now tell me what’s going on.”

“Nothing is going on.” Margaret sighed as she sat down. “I’m just a little tired.”

“You look more than just a little tired.” Colleen leaned forward, looking intently into her sister’s eyes. “What’s wrong?”

Margaret blinked then looked away.

“Is it Brian?”

She barely shrugged. "It's just so hard."

"Of course it's hard." Colleen reached for Margaret's hand, clasping it in hers. "You've been such a trouper too. I'm really proud of you."

Margaret shook her head.

"But I can tell it's getting to you, Margaret. Tell me what's going on."

A tear streaked down Margaret's cheek, and she reached for her handkerchief. "I—I'm afraid if I talk about it—I'll start crying—and I won't be able to stop."

"Go ahead," Colleen encouraged. "I promise you, you'll be able to stop when you need to. Besides, you'll feel better after a good cry."

"Well, you're right—it *is* about Brian." She blotted the tear. "He . . . he's so unhappy. And who can blame him? He's half a man, Colleen. And . . . and he doesn't want to live." She choked on a sob.

"Doesn't want to live?"

"That's right. He . . . he wants to die." Margaret's tear-filled eyes grew big. "He—he was hiding his pain pills under his pillow, Colleen! Every time I gave him one, he pretended to take it, but he was storing them up. He planned to take them all at once. He planned to kill himself."

"Oh, honey." Colleen wrapped her arms around Margaret, holding her as she sobbed for a couple of minutes. "I'm so sorry."

"It's just so—so hard. And I don't—don't even know what to do."

Colleen smoothed Margaret's hair, peering into her tear-streaked face. "Did you tell Brian's parents?"

"Oh, how could I? They would be devastated. And besides, Brian made me swear not to."

Colleen pursed her lips. "Well, Brian isn't thinking clearly right now, Margaret. You don't have to agree with everything he says."

"I know. But now I'm scared. What if he tries to kill himself in some other way?"

"You need to call the hospital, Margaret."

"I—I did. The nurse there told me this wasn't uncommon. She just said to make sure that all firearms and sharp objects and medications were locked up."

"That's all?"

"She said it was something most amputees went through and that it was all in the pamphlet they gave me when he got discharged from the hospital."

"So they can't put him back in the hospital?"

"Letterman is already overly full. Casualties just keep pouring in."

"This blasted war." Colleen felt a rush of concern for Geoff. She knew that being a navy pilot was one of the most dangerous jobs in the military—something she tried not to dwell on too much. Although it was easier said than done, she knew it was better to pray than worry.

Margaret blew her nose. "So last night—after I discovered the handkerchief holding his stash of pills—we had a fight. He confessed his plan. But it was so late, and I didn't know what to do. I was afraid to go to sleep . . . afraid he might do something to harm himself." She shuddered. "I sat in a hard chair, like the night watchman. I actually dozed off a couple of times but not for long. And then Peter woke up early." She closed her eyes and sighed. "I'm just so tired."

"I can see that."

"I haven't had a good night's sleep since I moved in there. I sleep on the little cot in Brian's room, but I'm constantly waking up. Sometimes he's groaning in pain. Or he's had a bad dream. I'm always jumping up, making sure he's okay, giving him his pills to help him rest better." She shook a fist. "The pills he wasn't even taking."

"That sounds like pure torture."

"I'd sleep in Peter's room, but we decided that Brian needs someone nearby. Even more so now that I know what he was planning."

"Is he safe now?"

"His mother is there with him. I hinted to her that he wasn't doing too well, and I insisted on leaving Peter with Mam for the afternoon. I made it seem like she was missing him. And I made sure Brian took a pain pill before I left. I watched him actually swallow it. The pill will make him drowsy. And, really, I don't think he'd attempt anything with his mother around. But at night . . . when everyone is asleep . . . and if he had access to the pills or something else, well, I just don't know." She let out a sob. "I feel like I'm never going to be able to sleep again."

"You're going upstairs," Colleen insisted. "To have a nice long nap."

"What about the store? It'll get busy soon."

"I'll stay." Colleen pulled Margaret to her feet. "Come on."

Colleen led Margaret up to the apartment. "I'm sorry it's not very tidy." She kicked a pair of shoes out of the way. "I guess I've been tired too. Not like you though. Just morning sickness. You know how that goes."

"I'm surprised you want to stay here." Margaret looked around the apartment that she'd worked so hard to carve out of an attic storage area. "You could be in your old room with Mam and Dad."

"I know. But this is handy for helping out in the store. Besides, I'm used to my independence. And I think they're enjoying having their home to themselves for a change." She peeled the bedspread back from the bed. "Less stress for Dad too."

"I guess." Margaret sank down on the bed, and Colleen knelt down to pull off her shoes.

"And I've been thinking that, if you don't mind, I might do some improvements to the place."

"Improvements?" Margaret asked sleepily.

"Maybe get a plumber to install a bathroom up here. And a real kitchenette." Colleen plumped the pillow.

"That'd be nice." Margaret lay back with a tired sigh.

"Just close your eyes and don't think about a single thing." Colleen pulled the blanket up over her. "Everyone will be fine. Just rest." She tiptoed out and down the stairs just in time to hear the chattering noise of girls coming into the store. Instead of going out to wait on them, Colleen picked up the big produce knife and proceeded to clean the pile of cabbages that Dirk had been working on. Just like she used to complain about doing when she was a teenage girl, back when she used to dream about being a famous movie star.

"You're not in Hollywood anymore." She gave the stemmed end of a cabbage a hard whack with the knife. But the truth was she was relieved to have this forced break from the limelight. She reached down to touch her slightly rounded midsection and smiled. A piece of her and Geoff was growing down there. Maybe it wasn't exactly what she'd planned on, but she was happy about it. And, although she'd assured her agents that she wasn't quitting Hollywood for good, promising not to burn any bridges, she seriously doubted that she'd be back. Hopefully this war would soon end, Geoff would come home, and the three of them would live happily ever after.

May 1944

Mrs. Bartley told Molly that after the hard work of soil preparation and planting was complete, she would be happy to tend their shared victory garden. "You've already got plenty on your plate," Mrs. Bartley had reassured her. "Just stay on top of your studies and your internship at the paper, and I'll see to the garden."

But Molly got so much comfort from seedlings growing into sturdy plants that she didn't mind popping over on the weekend to check on things. Not only was it peaceful here, but it allowed her to catch up with her parents and whatever other family members or friends might be around. Molly wasn't ready to admit it to her family, but she wasn't particularly enjoying sorority life. Oh, most of the girls, other than her roommate, were nice enough—for "rich girls." But many of them seemed slightly shallow and distracted. Molly felt they wasted too much time husband hunting. Or else they'd complain about the lack of available men. So much so that, as the school year drew to an end, Molly grew weary of hearing them. Weren't they there to get an education?

"Good morning," Mrs. Bartley called out as she

came into the garden where Molly was sitting with a book. "You're an early bird today."

"So are you." Molly stood to greet her, giving her old friend a big hug. "It's such a glorious day, I couldn't bear to stay inside." She wrinkled her nose. "And my roommate was sleeping in so I would've had to be as quiet as a mouse anyway."

"Is she still as cantankerous as ever?"

"Greta will not win any congeniality awards. I try to keep out of her way." Molly stooped to pull a weed.

"Oh, I must've missed that one."

Molly tossed the weed into the composting pile then smiled. "The garden looks spectacular, Mrs. Bartley. I can tell you've been taking good care of it."

"Well, I do my best." Her smile seemed to fade a little.

Molly studied the old woman, noticing something different . . . or perhaps she was simply tired. "How are *you* doing?"

"Oh, I'm fine. Just old." She rubbed her back. "Old and achy, but that's nothing new."

"I know how helpful you've been at the store. I hope you're not overdoing it."

"I thoroughly enjoy my time there. Much better than holing up in my house and listening for more bad news on the radio." Mrs. Bartley sat on the garden bench. "It makes me feel younger to be helping out . . . more alive."

"I'm so glad." Molly reached for her hand. "You've become like one of the family. Everyone says so."

"Thanks to you." Mrs. Bartley squeezed Molly's fingers. "And how are you doing, dear girl? Any news from your sweetheart?"

Molly felt her cheeks grow warm. She still wasn't quite used to having her relationship with Patrick out in the open like this. "I did receive a letter shortly after his leave ended. A couple months ago. Patrick wrote it while en route and sent it from Hawaii. But he did sound quite happy." She smiled to remember his affectionate words. How many times had she read that letter? So much that she practically knew it by heart.

"But nothing since then?"

Molly sadly shook her head. "It's hard to post letters from a submarine."

"Of course it is." Mrs. Bartley turned her face up toward the sun with a sigh. "And how is our Bridget? What do you hear from her?"

"Well, she was very pleasantly surprised recently. Her old doctor friend, Cliff Stafford, has been reassigned to her unit. And it sounds like they're striking up their friendship again."

"A romantic friendship?" Mrs. Bartley's thin brows arched.

"I think Bridget hopes he'll become her beau. But she doesn't say as much. And according to Bridget, a handsome young unmarried doctor is quite a popular commodity among all the nurses."

"Oh, let's hope that romance blossoms. Bridget is such a dear girl. Serving her country like she's doing. I keep her in my prayers, always. Just like I do for all the boys serving over there. Speaking of that, how Brian is doing? I don't see Margaret anymore. Not since she's coming to work later in the day. We're like ships in the night."

"I barely see her myself. But Colleen told me that caring for Brian has been hard on her. Poor Brian is not in very good spirits."

"Understandably so. When will he get his, uh, his . . . what did you say it was called, dear?"

"A prosthesis. From what I've read, they usually give the wound six months to heal before fitting for a prosthesis. That won't be until mid-July."

"That must be discouraging for him."

"Yes. And Margaret is discouraged too. She's so worried about Brian. According to Colleen, it's not only about his physical condition. He has bad dreams about the battlefield and his spirits are low." Of course, this was an understatement. Molly knew that Brian had wanted to end his life. She'd been praying for him daily.

"You know what that boy needs?" Mrs. Bartley said suddenly.

"What?" Molly waited.

"Brian needs to finish his schooling," the old woman declared. "If he had his law degree, he could start a practice. That would get his mind off of other things."

"I think you're absolutely right." Molly nodded eagerly. "Although I'm not sure that Brian would agree with you. At least not right now. He's been very negative about pretty much everything lately."

"I'm sure it's terribly difficult for him. A grown man suddenly dependent on others. He probably feels rather helpless . . . perhaps even useless. So sad."

"And according to Margaret, living with his parents isn't easy." Molly shook her head. "I think the Hammonds are lovely people, but I don't think I'd want to live with them."

"Hopefully you and Patrick will never have to."

Molly blushed. "Patrick and I aren't even engaged, Mrs. Bartley."

"Not yet anyway." She winked slyly.

Molly picked a pale pink peony, spinning it around. "Well, if I were married to Patrick . . ." She sighed happily. "I think I could live almost anywhere—and with anyone. I mean, if we had to."

"Could you live with your roommate Greta the Grouch?" Mrs. Bartley chuckled.

Molly grimaced. Had she been mistaken to confide in Mrs. Bartley about her cantankerous roommate? "I can't imagine how that would ever be necessary. But I suppose, if I had Patrick around to buffer Greta's meanness, I could do it."

"So, she's still picking on you?"

"Let's just say the girl has a very sour disposition." Molly frowned. "The harder I try to be nice to her, the more she seems to hate me."

Mrs. Bartley patted her hand. "Maybe you should just move back home."

Molly considered this. "Well, besides having a longer commute to my classes, which are nearly done anyway, I suspect that Mam and Dad have been enjoying their calm, quiet house. Besides I'll be home soon enough . . . in June."

"Then why don't you live with me, Molly? I have plenty of room. And I would appreciate the company."

Molly considered this. "Really?"

"Absolutely."

"Well, the school year is nearly over, but I suppose I could move in with you after finals."

"Then it's settled." Mrs. Bartley clapped her hands.

"And I would be closer to the newspaper here. Did I tell you that I've been offered a full-time job for the summer?"

"That's wonderful news."

"You're sure you want me?" Molly peered into her old friend's pale blue eyes. "I'd hate to impose."

"Believe you me, I am thrilled at the idea of having you here." Mrs. Bartley started to stand.

"You know me, Molly, this is not an offer I would make lightly. Certainly not to just anyone, but I gladly make it to you."

"And I gladly accept it." Molly helped Mrs. Bartley to her feet.

"I'll start getting things ready for you."

"Please, don't go to any trouble." Molly walked with her to the back door. "I can help with any moving or cleaning or whatever."

"Perhaps you'd like to occupy the second floor," Mrs. Bartley told her. "I rarely go up there anymore. The stairs are hard on my knees."

"That'd be fabulous. And you just let me know what you want done up there and I will gladly do it," Molly assured her. "And if there are chores I can help with in the house, you let me know that too. Perhaps you could make a list for me."

Mrs. Bartley nodded as she opened the door. "I think we will be very happy together, dear."

Molly knew that most people her age wouldn't want to live with an old lady, but Molly and Mrs. Bartley had been good friends for several years. Living with her would make life better all around. Molly would be close to her parents without imposing on them. She could tend the garden, and Margaret and Brian were just a few blocks down the street. Plus, it was a short trolley ride to the newspaper. It was perfect.

Three

Early June 1944

This past month had been the longest, most trying one of Margaret's life and, as far as she could see, it was not getting any better. Brian seemed determined to be miserable. Oh, he could act like he was fine—when other people were around to witness it, which was less and less of the time. But when it was just her, he didn't bother to hide his bad disposition. Today was no different.

"Mam and Dad really want us to join them for dinner tonight." Margaret repeated the invitation that she'd already given to him several times over the past few days.

"I already told you, I *don't* want to go."

She pursed her lips as she helped him to slip into his shirt. He really didn't need her help to get dressed each morning, but unless she did this, he would remain in his pajamas and never get out of bed. She glanced at the crutches leaning against the wall. It had been recommended he start using them after his last physical therapy session, but Brian claimed that his ribs still hurt too much for crutches. And maybe they did, but Margaret didn't think so.

"Your parents plan to go tonight. And Molly and Colleen will be there—and there's supposed to be some good news—"

"I said I'm *not going,* Margaret!"

"You don't have to yell." She pulled her hands away. Let him button up his own shirt.

"I only yelled because you don't seem to hear me." His voice was lower but just as intense. "Or you refuse to listen."

"I *hear* you," she hissed back. "It's just that I don't agree with your choices."

"My choices?" He glared at her. "Do you think I chose this?" He pointed to the stump where she'd just folded up his trouser leg, neatly tucking it behind and securing it with one of Peter's diaper pins.

"Of course not. You know that's not what I mean." She stooped down to put his shoe on his left foot.

She'd been ready to toss out all of his seemingly useless right shoes, but the therapist had asked her to bring one for Brian's next appointment. "To send to the prosthesis company so they can fit it onto the prosthesis," he'd explained. "We'll do all the measurements for that next week too."

"Then what do you mean?" Brian growled at her. "What choices do you not agree with?"

She nodded toward the crutches as she tied his shoe lace. "Your therapist said to start using those, yet you choose to remain in this wheelchair."

"I'm still convalescing. I don't know why you can't understand that."

"But you're not getting better," she persisted. "It's like you're stuck, Brian."

"Stuck in this blasted chair with an aching body and only one leg," he grumbled.

"Maybe you'd feel better if you got out more and—"

"I don't want to get out more." He shook a fist at her. "Can't you understand? I don't like being out there where people look at me with pity. Do you know what that feels like?"

"Not exactly—not like you do anyway—but I do know a little bit about it. Customers at the store look at me in a similar way."

"The poor wife who's stuck with half a man?"

"You're not half a man." She turned away from him, staring out the window and wishing for answers. "You just need to try harder," she said firmly. "Your doctor said it's good for you to get out and socialize, that it'll help you get better faster."

"Look, Margaret, if you want to get out and *socialize,* knock yourself out. But don't think you need to drag me along for the ride."

She spun around, locking eyes with him. She was sorely tempted to declare that she could not go out and socialize—not if he selfishly insisted on staying home. She wanted to yell at him that he could not be left alone and that he was her ball and chain and, if he refused to go out, she was stuck here too. Instead, she turned her attention to making his hospital bed. "Well," she huffed as she yanked up the sheet, "if you're not going, I'll stay home too."

"Oh, Margaret, Margaret." He sounded genuinely disgusted. "You don't think I can see through your little ploy? Trying to guilt me into going with you tonight? Really, I am not a child."

She wanted to dispute his claim. In some ways Brian was very much a child. And not so different than his toddler son, although Peter's disposition was usually much sunnier. But they both required diligent watching. She didn't dare leave either one of them alone for fear they might come to harm. Peter's would be accidental, but Brian's would not. Still, she knew it was pointless to argue with him. Brian always managed to win their arguments—or so it seemed.

"What are you stewing on now?" he demanded as she finished making his bed.

"Stewing?" She turned to glare at him. "What makes you think I'm stewing?"

"The way you're snapping those sheets, pounding that pillow. It's rather obvious." Although his lips curved in a smile, his eyes were steely. "I really do believe you'd be relieved if you could be free of me, Margaret."

"That's not true." She planted her fists on her hips, staring down at him in frustration. "If you really must know what I was thinking—I was wondering why on earth you refuse to go back to school and—"

"I already told you that I—"

"You made some sorry excuses, but you didn't give me one logical explanation. Lots of injured veterans are returning to school. Good grief, the government will pay your tuition now. And if you applied yourself, you could be done in one or two terms and—"

"Look at me, Margaret. Can you imagine me wheeling around on campus, trying to get up stairs and into classrooms? In this thing?" He slapped his hands on the armrests of his wheelchair. "Really?"

"You could have your prosthesis by then. Perhaps a cane to help—"

"So I'd be limping around campus, garnering pitiful glances from young healthy students? And what if something happened? What if I tripped and fell? Or my prosthesis failed me? Can you imagine the pathetic scene? Half a man spilled out across the front steps of the law school?"

"What of it?" She threw her hands in the air. "You'd pick yourself up and put yourself back together and keep going. That's what people do."

He ran his fingers through his hair. "You just don't understand."

"I understand *this,* Brian. You're my husband and Peter's father." She knelt down to look into his face. "And we *need* you. If you finished law school and passed your boards, you could be practicing law in less than a year from now. You could be supporting your family and—"

"So that's it? You think I can't support my family? You're worried you'll be working at the store for the rest of your life? Is that what's troubling—"

"That is not it," she declared. "I just believe that you have more to live for. I believe you'd find fulfillment in practicing law. It would challenge your mind. It would ignite you. It's what you worked for and dreamed of, and I hate for that dream to die just because you've lost a piece of your leg." She felt tears filling her eyes. "You'd make a truly great attorney, Brian. No one can argue like you."

His eyes lit up, ever so slightly, and that tiny glimpse of tenderness broke Margaret. Laying her head in his lap, she let the tears flow.

"I'm sorry, Margaret." He stroked her hair. "I know how hard I am on you. I'm sorry."

She looked up through teary eyes. "Why? Why are you so hard on me?"

He pursed his lips with a creased brow. "The truth?"

She nodded, fumbling a handkerchief from her pocket.

"I think I want to drive you away. I want to make you leave me."

She blinked. "You . . . you don't love me anymore?"

"That's not it." He shook his head. "I do love you . . . but I—I don't deserve you."

"Oh, Brian." She choked back a sob. "That's not true. If anything, I don't deserve you."

For the first time since Brian had come home they *really* embraced and, holding tightly to each other for several minutes, they both cried.

"Oh, Margaret." Brian shook his head. "It's really true. I mean it. I don't deserve you."

Margaret was tempted to tell Brian everything. To tell him how she'd betrayed him—not physically, but in her heart. She wanted to confess how she'd flirted with the idea of an affair with Howard Moore. She could barely stand to think of that man now. How could she have ever been so foolish? But in the same instant, she knew that her admission would only hurt Brian. And he was already hurting. No, this wasn't the time.

"I love you," she told him. "No matter what you do to me or how hard you try to turn me away, I love you, Brian. I always have and I always will."

He kissed her. "I love you too, Margaret."

She jumped when a knock sounded on the door, followed by a cheery greeting. "I have Brian's breakfast," his mother called out.

Margaret sprang to her feet and, wiping her tears away, opened the door. "Good morning," she murmured.

Brian wheeled over to his mom. "You don't need to bring food in here to me anymore. I can come out and eat my meals with the rest of you."

Mrs. Hammond's brows lifted. "Are you sure?"

He nodded grimly. "It's about time."

Mrs. Hammond exchanged relieved glances with Margaret, but before she could say anything, Peter, still in his pajamas, rushed into the room, jumping into Margaret's arms. "Mommy, Mommy, Mommy!" She hugged him close, pressing her face into his sweet- smelling hair. And then she held him out to Brian. "Want to ride in Daddy's chair?" she asked.

Peter looked slightly uncertain, but when Brian extended his arms, Peter went to him and then, as Brian made motorized sound effects while wheeling out of the room, Peter giggled. Soon all five of them were seated at the breakfast table.

"I've made a decision," Brian announced after Mr. Hammond asked a blessing.

"What's that?" Mr. Hammond passed the plate of pancakes to Margaret.

"I'm going to see about returning to school," he declared. "Hopefully I can be enrolled by fall."

"That's wonderful," Mrs. Hammond gushed. "I'm so happy for you, son."

Brian glanced at Margaret. "My wise wife has managed to convince me that it's a good idea."

"Well, I'm glad to hear it." Mr. Hammond reached for his coffee. "I've been looking forward to the day when I could brag about my son, *the attorney at law.*" He winked at Brian.

"He'll make a fine lawyer." Margaret wiped jam from Peter's chin then smiled at her husband.

"Where will you go?" Mr. Hammond asked.

"We have several good law schools nearby," Margaret said hopefully.

"I want to go back to Gould," Brian said.

Margaret's heart sank. "But the University of Southern California is so far away."

"I know. But it's where I started and I'd like to finish down there."

"Are you sure?" his mother asked. "Wouldn't it be less expensive to attend in San Francisco and live at home?"

"I want to graduate from Gould," he said firmly. "And if I live on campus, I can focus all of my energy on school and hopefully finish my degree in just a term. Two if necessary."

Margaret knew she needed to be supportive. "That makes sense to me. As much as I'll miss you, I understand."

"Thank you." Brian turned to his mother. "So, I hear we're invited to the Mulligans for dinner tonight."

"And I hear they have some big announcement to make." Mrs. Hammond frowned. "Do you suppose that Patrick has proposed to Molly?"

Brian looked shocked. "But Molly's just a kid."

"That just shows how much you know,"

Margaret teased him as she helped Peter with his sippy cup. "Molly did some growing up while you were away." She didn't want to mention that although Brian had been home for a couple of months, he hadn't been fully back. Not really. Although she'd attempted to include him, to share news with him, he'd never shown real interest or made any inquiries about her family members. Sometimes she'd wondered if he'd even heard her.

"Molly is a college girl now," Mr. Hammond informed his son. "And she works for the *San Francisco Chronicle* too."

Brian nodded. "Impressive."

As they continued to eat, they conversed about various family members. Margaret suspected they were all attempting to brief Brian on some of the things he'd missed out on in the past year. To her relief, Brian seemed to pay close attention—appearing truly interested, nodding and commenting . . . just like the old Brian.

But Margaret's relief was short-lived when she remembered something from an army booklet about suicide prevention. One warning sign was an abrupt change in attitude. Someone intent on taking his life could suddenly appear positive and engaged. Everyone would feel hopeful and then be shocked to discover their loved one had ended his life. She studied Brian closely . . .

Was that what this really was? Was he just preparing them for his exit?

Four

Colleen was surprised to see Margaret and the Hammonds wheeling Brian into her parents' home that evening. But Brian, with Peter in his lap, appeared happy and more like his old self. Colleen hugged Margaret. "Things seem to be looking up," she whispered in her ear.

"I'm not so sure." Margaret frowned as she removed her hat.

As others exchanged greetings, Colleen whisked Margaret into the dining room on the pretext of setting the table. "What's wrong?" she asked as she removed the good dinner plates from the sideboard.

Margaret quickly explained Brian's sudden change of behavior and what she'd read about suicide. "Now I'm more worried than ever."

"What if he's simply turned a corner?" Colleen laid out the silver.

"I hope and pray that's what this is, but I'm on pins and needles now."

Colleen listened to the conversation coming from the living room for a moment. "He certainly sounds cheerful," she said quietly to Margaret. "Like he used to be. What brought about the change?"

Margaret explained about their confrontation and the challenge to return to school. "And he actually decided he wants to finish his law degree."

"Well, that doesn't sound like he's getting ready to buy the farm." Colleen folded a napkin. "It sounds more like he's truly turning a corner, Margaret. Why not just hope for the best?"

Margaret attempted a smile. "I'd like to."

"In the meantime, just keep an eye on him." Colleen patted her back. "Until you know for sure."

Before long they were all seated at the table—the Hammonds and the Mulligans and Mrs. Bartley from next door. Everyone waited impatiently while Dad said a rather longwinded grace, and then they all demanded to know what the good news was all about.

"Well, this is Molly's doing," Dad explained, as if enjoying the drama. "She got a mysterious letter this week, and she has refused to tell anyone what was in it or who it was from until we were all gathered together." He turned to Molly. "I hand this off to you."

Molly slowly reached into her skirt pocket.

Mrs. Hammond gasped to see the V-mail letter. "Is that from Patrick?"

Molly looked surprised then laughed. "No. It's from Bridget."

Mrs. Hammond was visibly relieved. "Oh . . . of course."

"Bridget wrote to me of her good news, but she insisted that I must tell everyone at the same time. She wanted to feel as if she were making the announcement herself right here at the dinner table. And I am trying to honor her wishes by—"

"What is it?" Mam demanded.

"Do you want me to read her whole letter or just spill the beans?"

Everyone insisted on hearing the news—now.

"Okay then." Molly grinned. "Doctor Cliff Stafford has asked Bridget to marry him." She waved the letter like it was evidence. "And Bridget has told him yes."

Everyone let out cheers and exclamations of joy, and Dad lifted his water glass in a group toast to Bridget and Doctor Cliff. And then Molly read the letter. Cliff, it seemed, wanted to marry right away, but Bridget was inclined to wait until the war ended.

"Why wait?" Colleen asked.

"Because Bridget is being sensible," Margaret said.

"Sensible?" Colleen frowned. "Or scared?"

"Bridget is the bravest woman I know," Molly declared. "She's over there in harm's way doing one of the hardest jobs—"

"That's not what I meant," Colleen said. "I mean that Bridget has always been overly cautious when it comes to relationships with guys.

She's scared. She even told me that very thing once."

"Oh." Molly nodded.

"It's understandable that she would be a little nervous about getting married," Margaret said. "But I still think she's being sensible. It's not easy being married while there's a war on."

"But if you love each other?" Colleen lifted her chin.

"Then won't you still love each other *after* the war is over?" Margaret challenged.

"But, Margaret, you didn't wait," Molly pointed out. "You were eager to wed. Remember?"

Margaret pursed her lips.

"Perhaps she wishes she'd waited," Brian said somberly.

Margaret turned to him with wide eyes. "I do not." She pointed to Peter, who sat in his high-chair with smashed peas all over his cherub face. "We wouldn't have our lovely son if we'd waited."

Brian smiled. "That's true."

"But you have to admit that it's been a little difficult," Mam said quietly. "It's not easy to be newly married and apart. Maybe Bridget understands that."

"But Bridget and Doctor Cliff wouldn't have to be apart," Molly said. "They work in the same hospital."

"They do for now," Brian said. "But one or

both of them could be transferred at any time. For all we know, they might've been moved by now. When you're in the army, you go where you're told to go. They could be married one day and sent to opposite sides of the globe the next."

"Even so," Colleen continued, "if they know they love each other, I think they should marry right away. I remember how much I regretted that I didn't marry Geoff when he first asked me. And even though he's far away, I'm so thankful we're married now. I wouldn't change a thing."

"I'm sure Geoff would agree with you," Molly added. "And it must be a comfort for him to know he has a wife—and will soon have a child—waiting at home for him." She sighed. "I've heard that married servicemen have a better chance at survival."

"So you think these wartime marriages are a good thing?" Mrs. Hammond focused on Molly. "Tell me, dear, would you want to be married to a serviceman who's stationed overseas?"

Colleen watched as her little sister's cheeks glowed pink. She seemed to be carefully considering her answer, and Colleen was tempted to intervene, but before she could Molly spoke up. "I would be honored to marry a serviceman . . . if we loved each other, and if we both felt it was the right thing to do."

"Ah-ha." Mrs. Hammond's brows arched with interest.

"But I would be just as honored to wait for the war to end . . . if that's what my, uh, my beau wished. But since he would be the one serving overseas, laying his life on the line for his country, I would defer this decision to him."

"That's a lot of wisdom coming from the youngest person at the table." Mr. Hammond patted Molly on the back.

Molly laughed then pointed to Peter. "Excuse me, Mr. Hammond, but your grandson is the youngest person at this table." Now everyone laughed.

"And in a couple of months there will be an even younger one." Margaret nodded to Colleen.

Colleen touched the rounding bulge that had eclipsed her waistline. "But back to Bridget," she said, "why don't you read us her letter again, Molly?"

"And while she's reading, let's eat," Mam said.

"Before the food gets cold." Dad passed the potatoes to Mrs. Hammond.

As Molly started the letter from the beginning again, it indeed seemed clear that Bridget felt it best to wait. She fully understood the complications of war and the possibility of army transfers. As much as Colleen wanted her sister happily married to a man she loved, she could see that in this situation, it simply made sense to wait. Besides that, Bridget wanted to have a wedding at home with her family.

"I'd love to help her plan that wedding," Colleen said dreamily.

"And the ceremony will be held at Old Saint Mary's." Dad brandished his loaded fork.

Margaret nodded. "As soon as the war is over."

"Let's just pray the war ends soon," Mam said solemnly. "Let's pray that God gives us the victory and that all our children come safely home . . . and that life returns to normal." Everyone said a hearty amen, and then they continued to eat and talk and laugh, just like old times. Colleen sighed happily. It was good to be home.

"I feel guilty," Molly said quietly as Colleen drove her back to campus after the family dinner party.

"Guilty? You? Whatever for?"

"I got a letter from Patrick today."

"But that's nice, Molly. Why should that make you feel guilty?"

"Because I never breathed a word of it to the Hammonds."

Colleen chuckled. "I'm surprised Mrs. Hammond didn't squeeze it out of you. The way she grilled you about your thoughts on marriage was almost comical."

"Sometimes it feels like she really dislikes me," Molly confessed.

"Oh, that's not it. I know she likes you, Molly. Everyone likes you."

"But she's always so worried. As if she thinks Patrick and I plan to run off to Las Vegas on his next leave."

Colleen chuckled. "You wouldn't, would you?"

"For starters, although Patrick made his feelings toward me fairly clear . . ." Molly fingered the string of pearls he'd given her for her eighteenth birthday and smiled. "He didn't officially propose."

"Well, no, but he is definitely courting you."

"Perhaps. But he's courting me from the other side of the world."

"And knowing Patrick and how he's the responsible type—so much like Peter." She glanced at Molly as she waited for the traffic light to change. "Will we ever stop missing our big brother?"

Molly sighed. "I don't think so. But at least it doesn't hurt so much."

"That's true. Time does help. But back to you and Patrick and the likelihood of you two eloping to Vegas. I think Patrick's a fine, sensible fellow, and I suspect he wants to wait for the war to end before he commits to matrimony. Would you agree?"

Molly considered the passionate kisses she and Patrick had exchanged during that brief time he'd been here in March and some of the things he'd said to her both then and in today's letter. "I'd agree with you . . . in theory," she said cautiously.

"Oh . . . ?" Colleen's tone grew suspicious as she parked in front of the sorority house. "So perhaps you two really might run off and get hitched on his next leave?"

Molly giggled. "I honestly don't think so, Colleen. But like I declared before God and everyone tonight, if that is what Patrick wanted, I would not object."

"But would that be what *you* want?" Colleen demanded.

Molly couldn't suppress a big smile. "Like I said, I would not object."

"My darling baby sister! You never fail to amaze me." Colleen threw back her head and laughed loudly. She pointed to the sorority house. "Have you told any of your sorority sisters about your romance?"

Molly wrinkled her nose. "I don't think that's a very good idea." Already she was picked on for being the youngest sorority sister and for taking the heaviest load of classes, plus interning at the paper. If they knew she was in love with a naval officer, they would probably really go after her.

"Do you even like living in there, Molly?"

Molly confessed her plan to live with Mrs. Bartley. "I didn't tell anyone because I didn't want to hurt Mam and Dad's feelings. I'm worried they'll think I should live at home with them, but at the same time, I know they've enjoyed having less chaos in their house. It's tricky, you know?"

"I know." Colleen nodded. "Mam still questions why I want to stay in the apartment above the store. Especially after the baby comes."

"How is your remodeling plan coming?" Molly reached for the car door handle but was reluctant to go.

"I have a builder giving me a bid for everything this week. If it looks okay, he says he can start next week. And then I'll have to move back home while the place is all torn up."

"I wonder how long it'll take for him to finish it."

"He said it should only be a couple of weeks. Three at the most. So I could easily be back there before the baby comes."

"And you don't think you'd want to be home after the baby comes? I mean, so Mam could be around to help?"

"I honestly don't know. Geoff's mom has been begging me to come stay on the farm with them, but I've told her that I want my independence, so it may seem hypocritical if I run home to Mam and Dad."

"I suppose so." Molly glanced at her watch. "I better get inside before I get in trouble for breaking curfew." She thanked Colleen for the ride then scurried up to the front door of the pitch-black house. Of course, it was only darkened because of the blackout curtains, but it still looked foreboding and unfriendly to her.

Even as she opened the door to the dimly lit foyer, she knew she was done. When she left the sorority house for summer break, just a couple of weeks from now, she would leave it for good. With no regrets.

Five

Margaret was relieved to see Brian getting stronger each day, and he was even practicing getting around on his crutches. It seemed that his intent to rejoin the human race was in earnest. So much so that she began to let her guard down and sleep better at night. But when she came home to see him actually dancing around his parents' front room and singing out loud, she was somewhat taken aback. "Brian?" she asked cautiously.

"We've liberated Rome!" he announced happily as she set down her handbag.

"What?" She unpinned her hat. "What does that mean?"

"It means we are within bombing distance of Germany!" He hopped over to hug her. "This is big news, honey. This could be a turning point for taking out Hitler and ending the war."

"Really?" She felt her hopes soar. "The war could be over?"

"Well, on the European front. And it won't happen quickly. But taking Italy is an important strategic step." He hopped over to turn down the radio. "I just hope that my troops are okay."

Margaret had nearly forgotten that Brian had

been officer in charge of a number of men. She'd almost assumed that when he'd been injured and come home, they had all done likewise. Now she realized that was foolishness. But hopefully they were all right. "Do you remain in contact with any of them?" she asked cautiously.

"I haven't. But, you know, that's not a bad idea. A few of my men never received letters from home. It was rather sad." He rubbed his chin. "Perhaps I could write to them. I've certainly got plenty of time on my hands." He leaned over to kiss Margaret. "How was the store?"

"Fairly busy for a Monday." She sank into an easy chair. "But that was nice because it makes the time pass more quickly." She glanced around the room. "Where's Peter? And your parents?"

"Mom took Peter for a stroll and Dad's still at work."

Margaret leaned back in the chair and sighed. "This is rather nice, being home alone, just the two of us."

"Uh-huh." Brian was still hobbling around, practicing his turns and balancing.

"You're getting pretty good on those things."

"Well, I told Dad that I'd like to get handy enough that I can go to work with him, help him in his store."

"That's a great idea." She nodded eagerly. "He was just telling me that since he started carrying clothing—after the leather and shoe business became so impaired from rationing—he's starting to get pretty busy."

"Yes. So I hoped I could lighten his load some." He did a quick turn. "Watch this." He sat down one crutch, hobbled across the floor then picked up the phone with his free hand. "Hello?" he said brightly, although no one had called.

Margaret clapped her hands with glee. "That's wonderful, Brian." She watched him moving about the room, acting so much like his old self that she nearly forgot about his injury. And so much like his old self that Margaret got an idea—a slightly romantic idea. She raised the volume of the radio and tuned it to a music program.

"Would you like to dance with me?" She held her arms open.

"With you?" He suddenly looked uneasy.

"Yes." She nodded. "Give it a try. Just set down your crutches and hold onto me."

"But I—"

"Come on," she urged. "Just pretend I'm your crutch."

He looked skeptical but leaned his crutches against the wall then slipped one arm around her waist, grasping her hand with the other. "I don't know about this."

For a moment they swayed to the music together, but when Brian attempted to make a move, she went the wrong way and they were both caught off balance. Suddenly Margaret could feel them tipping sideways. She tried to keep them from going over, but it was too late. They tumbled to the floor in an awkward heap. "Oh, Brian," she cried. "I'm so sorry. Are you okay?"

He didn't appear to be in pain, but his expression was grim. "I don't think I'm ready for the ballroom, Margaret. I might never be."

She clumsily got to her feet and, feeling embarrassed, helped him to stand as well, apologizing again.

"I realize you've missed out on a lot in life." He pushed a curly strand away from his forehead. "And you're probably missing the, uh, the romantic part of our relationship. But you need to understand, Margaret, you can't rush these things." He reached for his crutches. "I'm sorry to disappoint you." Without another word, he hobbled off toward the bedroom. She was about to call out and ask him to wait, but the front door was opening and Peter, followed by his grandmother, skipped toward Margaret with a happy smile and a fistful of dandelion blooms. As she greeted them, Margaret heard the solid click of the bedroom door's lock snapping into place. Brian's signal. He wanted to be alone.

It was finals week and Molly had informed Mick Blackstone that she planned to take a few days off from the paper. Since her internship ended with the spring term, she didn't actually need to report anyway, but when she got wind of the Normandy invasion, she knew the best place to hear the whole story was the newspaper. Hearing news that was literally hot off the press was one of her favorite perks of working at the *Chronicle*—and the Normandy invasion was the hottest news around.

By the time she arrived, Mick had already gathered the staff in his department. "It was an amazing feat," he told the small group. "We don't have all the facts yet, but it's reported that around 150,000 troops landed on Normandy's beaches earlier today." He described the boats launching into rough seas, the dismal weather, and the bravery of the men who invaded the European shores, then he grimly shook his head. "But reports of casualties are coming in too . . . many men died."

"How many?" a young secretary with a husband serving on the European front asked with concern.

"We don't know yet. But the number of lives lost will be great and the wounded number probably greater." He sighed. "The cost of war is high."

For a long moment no one spoke, and only the sound of the presses coming from downstairs interrupted the silence.

"Let's pray for them," Molly said suddenly. "For the ones who are standing up to Hitler's forces, for the ones who've been injured, and for the loved ones of those who have fallen. Let's all pray, right now." To her surprise, no one questioned her suggestion. Just like that all heads were bowed and Molly, followed by a number of them, prayed for the soldiers on the European front.

"Amen." Mick then attempted to put a more positive spin on the big story. "This will be the big turning point of the war," he reassured everyone. "With so many Allied troops on European soil and air forces within bombing distance of Germany . . . well, it won't be long before the Nazis are backed into a corner. And hopefully the rumors are true that Russia will soon press in from the east. God willing, we will end this nightmare—maybe before next year." He waved his hands. "Now, everyone back to work. Our department may not be directly covering the war stories, but we do have a paper to get out."

As Molly went to her desk, she couldn't stop thinking about all the young men who'd bravely taken the Normandy beaches—the ones who were probably in the midst of battle right now, the ones who were wounded, and the loved ones of those who would never come home.

"Hey." Mick came over to her desk. "I thought you weren't coming in until after finals week. And then as an official employee."

She smiled sheepishly. "When I heard about Normandy, I just wanted to be here. Actually I wanted to be anywhere other than my sorority house."

"Why's that?"

"Because the hottest topic there seems to be about what to wear for the Good-bye Dance on Friday."

He chuckled. "Don't forget to stop and smell the roses, Molly."

"Huh?" She laid down her pencil to stare at him.

"Don't forget that you're only eighteen," he said gently.

She rolled her eyes. "Thanks for the reminder."

"It's just that you have the rest of your life to be a grown-up. It's okay to enjoy being a kid for now."

She made a tolerant smile. "I'm well aware of that. But I can only be who I am, right? If I don't get giddy over the latest fashions or a new shade of nail polish, it's my choice, right? If I don't want to go to a silly dance, I don't have to, right?"

He held up his hand as if to surrender. "Right, right."

"Thank you."

"Anyway, I'm glad you're here, Molly. I want to talk to you about something." He nodded toward his office. "Got a minute?"

Suddenly she felt nervous. It wasn't that long ago that Mick had shown signs of romantic interest—before Patrick showed up. But she'd explained all about Patrick to Mick. She felt sure that he understood. This must be something else.

"Take a seat." He pointed to the chair across from his desk with a grim expression.

"I feel like I'm in the principal's office," she said jokingly. "Did I do something wrong?"

He chuckled. "No, not at all. You know that everyone here loves you. You're smart and a hard worker. No complaints."

"Oh, good." She grinned. "So I'm getting a raise then?"

He laughed. "Being that you haven't even started your actual job, I'd say that's a little premature."

"Oh, right." She waited.

"Here's the deal. I realize that, although you're a very good writer, your main interest in journalism is photography."

She nodded. "Although I do love to write too."

"But if you had to choose?"

She shrugged. "I could never give up photography."

"Yes . . . but you haven't gotten to utilize your photography skills around here. Not much anyway."

"I've been down in the photography department a few times," she said, "but I know Jim and Mazzie are pretty busy, and I'm still so inexperienced."

"As you know, the paper's been shorthanded by the war. There's always too much to do and not enough hands to do it."

"I wish I could be more helpful with Jim and Mazzie." She sighed. "At least I'll be taking some photography classes next year in college."

"And that's good." He rubbed his chin. "But I happen to have a friend who runs a photography studio. Have you ever heard of Bernard's?"

"Of course. Everyone knows Bernard's. It's the best studio in town."

"Well, Archie Bernard is one of my best friends and his dad is Simon Bernard and—"

"You know Simon Bernard?" Molly had long been an admirer of his work.

"I do. And it so happens that Simon is looking for a good assistant."

Molly sat up straighter. "Do you really think . . . Would I have a chance?"

"I think he'd hire you in a heartbeat, Molly. I'm sure of it. The problem is that I'm not eager to see you leave the paper."

She frowned.

"But Studio Bernard would be a great place for you to learn more about photography—and from a real pro."

She nodded eagerly. "That would be amazing."

"You'd learn more working one summer with

Simon than you'd learn in a whole year at college or interning here."

"I'm sure you're right."

"And you'll get paid."

Molly felt torn now. "But I do hate to leave the *Chronicle*. . . ."

"You'll always be welcome back here."

"Thank you."

"You have to ask yourself, Molly, where would you rather work? The newspaper or the photography studio? They're both great opportunities. Which is best for you?"

She smiled. "As much as I love the newspaper, I'd welcome the chance to learn more about photography from someone like Simon Bernard."

He nodded. "That's what I thought." He slid a business card across his desk. "Give Simon a call as soon as you can. I already told him about you. He said he needs someone right away. Summer is a busy season for him."

"Well, that would be amazing if he hired me." Still Molly wavered a bit. "But I'll be sad to leave this place."

"Maybe you'll get enough experience with Simon that you'll be useful in the photography department by next year. I'm sure they'd love to have you for an intern." Mick smiled, but his eyes were serious. "So tell me, how's that sailor of yours doing?"

"I just got a letter." She gave him the latest

updates, as much as she could anyway. "I'm not really sure where his submarine is," she admitted. "Patrick says they've been all over, from the New Hebrides clear up to the Aleutians. He never mentions location, but he writes a lot about his men. It sounds like he's got a good crew with him. That's worth a lot."

"And he's got a good girl waiting for him back home," Mick said somberly. "That's worth a lot too."

She smiled with some embarrassment. "I hope so."

"I want to thank you for leading us in that prayer for our troops in Normandy, Molly. I know the staff appreciated it too."

"Sometimes it seems like that's about all we have," she admitted. "I mean prayer. It's hard knowing how many young men are out there in harm's way, hearing stories of bravery . . . and loss. Anyway, prayer has been a big comfort to me."

"It can be hard hearing the unadulterated news here at the paper—the cold hard facts, real numbers of wounded . . . and the dead. It almost makes me understand why we put a positive spin on these stories for the public."

"Yes . . . it's not easy to read headlines and be reminded of a loved one serving overseas." How many times had she read of a naval attack and immediately thought of Patrick? She wasn't naïve. She knew his submarine was an underwater target for a Japanese torpedo—and if one hit, there would likely be no survivors. She didn't know where she would be without prayer, and she hoped the rest of the country was praying too.

Six

Mid-July 1944

After nearly four weeks, Colleen had grown more than a little weary of staying in her parents' home—so much so that she even visited Geoff's family out on the farm. She spent several days there and was even invited to stay indefinitely, but she explained her need to attend to the project she was supervising above the store. Unfortunately, the remodeling was taking longer than expected. Her builder had discovered more to do than she'd initially anticipated. Besides making the bathroom and kitchenette, he'd improved the electrical wiring, reinforced floor joists, put in a couple more windows, and even created two separate bedroom spaces. One small one for her and a tiny one that would serve as a baby nursery.

But as quickly as Colleen's waistline had expanded, her old childhood bedroom had shrunk. Even though she'd turned Margaret's old bedroom into a closet and had utilized Peter's old room to store her small stockpile of furnishings and goods for the apartment, Colleen had felt more and more cramped. Molly had invited her to stay in one of Mrs. Bartley's rooms on the second floor, but the idea of relocating over there and then moving again when it was time to return to the apartment just made her feel more tired.

"But you don't have to move back to the apartment," Mam had told Colleen last night while she'd been packing to go. "You could just stay here with us. After all, the baby will be here in less than two months. Wouldn't you like to be home for that?"

"I want to stay in the apartment," Colleen insisted. "It will make it easier for me to help out at the store." And Colleen really didn't mind working at the store. It was a good distraction from other things . . . like this never-ending war. Even when Mam had put her foot down when Colleen entered her seventh month of pregnancy, Colleen had talked her into just a few hours a day, promising no heavy lifting.

Colleen wasn't comfortable with too much free time. More and more, she found herself thinking about—and missing—Geoff. She tried not to worry about him, but every time she turned on the radio or picked up a newspaper, it seemed that the battles in the Pacific were growing fiercer than ever. Every victory came with a price.

Although the Marianas Turkey Shoot had been good news a couple of weeks ago, since 220 Japanese planes were shot down, Colleen had later learned that twenty US planes had been lost in that same fight. She'd immediately written to Geoff, expressing concerns for his safety, but in the two weeks since she still hadn't heard a word from him. Was it possible that his plane was one of the twenty? Had he been shot down, or forced down? Had he been captured again? Or worse? She prayed for him, but it was hard to quiet the doubts that stirred within her in the middle of the night.

Colleen couldn't imagine her life without Geoff or raising their child alone. And yet she knew that he'd barely escaped death's jaws once before. How many more times would he be that lucky? Even though she knew it was a waste of time to worry and not usually something she gave into, it was hard not to fret. She blamed this new compulsion on her pregnancy. Being "large with child" wasn't just hard on her self-esteem—it played havoc with her emotions too. Colleen remembered a time when she was required to cry on set, and it had been so difficult that they'd eventually resorted to glycerin tears. Now she could cry at the drop of a hat. And it could be embarrassing.

But today wasn't a day for crying. Today, Colleen was finally moving into her "new" apartment. With Margaret and Molly's help, she hoped to be settled in by the end of the day.

"I've got yours and Mrs. Bartley's car all

loaded," Molly announced as Colleen started down the stairs with a bundle of clothes in her arms.

"Colleen Maureen! We told you not to do any carrying." Margaret hurried to take the clothes from her.

"It's not heavy."

"Yes, but you're coming down the stairs," Margaret reminded her.

"Why don't you follow me over to the store," Molly told Colleen as they gathered below. "Margaret can finish loading the car and come later."

"Just make sure Colleen doesn't try to carry anything up to the apartment," Margaret told Molly. "Those stairs are even steeper than these."

"I already asked the guys to handle the unloading," Molly said. "They'll get everything up the stairs for us."

"As for you." Margaret pointed to Colleen. "You will remain upstairs and simply tell everyone where to put everything."

Colleen grinned. "Like the queen."

"Why not," Molly told her. "After all, it is your birthday tomorrow."

"Your birthday?" Margaret seemed surprised. "I completely forgot."

"That's okay," Colleen said. "I sort of forgot too." But as she drove to the store, Colleen thought about her birthday. Tomorrow she would turn twenty-one. And although she knew that she'd accomplished quite a lot for her age—married to her true love, about to have a baby, and a semi-famous film star—she also had a feeling that the best part of her life was behind her. As she parked her car behind the family store, she wasn't sure how she felt about that. As happy as she was about having Geoff's baby, it wasn't something she'd planned. And the idea of never returning to the screen was a bit dismaying. Of course, she'd promised her agents that she wasn't done yet . . . but she felt done. As she struggled to get out of the car, looking down at her swollen midsection, she could not imagine how she would ever be fit for film again.

"Hi there," Jimmy said cheerfully as he set a wooden apple crate outside the back door. "You ready to move back in?"

She smiled. "You better believe it."

He pointed to the car now pulling in. "And Molly told me not to let you carry anything."

She nodded toward her car. "That's fine with me. I'll leave you to it." Eager to see the finished apartment, Colleen hurried inside and up the stairs. The last time she'd been up here, it had been a mess. But her builder had called her yesterday, informing her it was finished. She cautiously opened the door and walked into what smelled like a freshly painted room. Margaret had felt her choice of off-white for the living space was boring, but it looked fresh and clean against the hardwood floors. Colleen had hoped to get carpeting, but due to rationing, carpet was hard to come by. Still the gleaming floors looked pretty, and she'd found a couple of secondhand rugs to warm it up. As well as some secondhand furniture that was more to her taste than the odd bits and pieces that Margaret had been using.

She was just inspecting the sweet little kitchenette when Molly came in. "Oh, Colleen, it's beautiful," she exclaimed. "Everything looks so fresh and new."

Colleen ran her hand over a painted kitchen cabinet. Buttery yellow just like she'd requested. She opened the small fridge to see it was cold then tested the faucet on the sink to find both hot and cold running water. "So far so good."

"Hello?" Jimmy appeared at the door with a large box of bedding. "Where does this go?"

"Right this way." Colleen led them to her bedroom, opening the door to a closet tucked into the eaves and turning on the light. "Just set it here for now."

Jimmy peered into the closet. "That's almost as big as your bedroom."

She grinned. "A girl needs a good closet." She went back into the room, going over to the window. "I'm so glad my builder insisted on putting this here."

"The light is nice. And I love this pale blue on you walls. Very elegant." Molly walked around the small room. "When will your furniture arrive?"

"Hopefully this morning." Colleen turned away from the window. "Let's go see the bathroom and baby's room."

The bathroom, like her bedroom, was pale blue, but the baby's room was a sunny yellow, which would be good for a boy or a girl. "This is pretty small," she conceded, "but big enough for a baby." Hopefully she and Geoff would have a real house by the time their child needed more space.

Before long Margaret joined them. She'd just finished gushing about the miraculous transformation when the apartment suddenly got very busy with the furniture movers and Jimmy and Dirk carrying up boxes. Colleen did her best to direct traffic, but by the time everyone left several hours later, there was still much to be done. Fortunately, she convinced everyone that she could handle it, promising again not to lift anything heavy.

But first she turned her radio to a music program and sat down to eat an apple. It felt good to be in her own space. As much as she loved her parents and appreciated their hospitality, she'd felt the need to tiptoe around and keep her radio turned down low. She could relax and do as she pleased here. It would be truly perfect if Geoff was with her.

Colleen went back to work unpacking boxes and putting things away, determined to keep busy—which kept her from worrying about Geoff. Sure, she hadn't heard from him for more than two weeks, but that happened sometimes. At least she hadn't received any telegrams, so really she should be thankful.

As much as she wanted to pace herself and not overdo it, she was determined to have everything in its place before she went to bed. As a result, she didn't get to bed until well after midnight, but she was so exhausted she expected to enjoy a good night's sleep. And one of the perks of being in her own apartment—she could sleep in as long as she liked too. And since it would be Sunday, the store would be quiet downstairs.

So she was surprised to wake to the sound of knocking the next morning. It was barely eight o'clock when she opened the door to see Mam standing there with a grim expression.

"Is something wrong?" Colleen attempted to tie her robe around her wide middle but was unable to make it reach across.

Mam held out a yellow envelope. "A telegram arrived at home . . . for you."

Colleen felt her heart lurch. "Is it—who's it—"

"I don't know what it is or who it's from." Mam came into the room, closing the door.

Colleen's knees felt weak as she led Mam to the sitting area, slowly easing herself onto the small gray sofa she'd found at the secondhand store. "Do you . . . do you think . . . ?" her voice trailed off as she stared at the envelope.

"We won't know until you open it." Mam sat next to her, wrapping a comforting arm around Colleen's shoulders. "Go ahead, dear."

"Yes." Colleen used her fingernail to carefully slit it open and with trembling hands unfolded the paper and began to read aloud. *"Happy Birthday, darling—stop. I wish I were there—stop. All my love—stop. Your husband, Geoff—stop."*

"Thank God." Mam let out a loud sigh.

"Yes, yes, *thank God!*" Colleen clutched the telegram to her chest with a sob. The tears flowed freely. Of course, they were tears of relief, but they came like a flood just the same.

"Go ahead and have a good cry." Mam patted her on the back. "Like I've told all you girls before, tears wash the soul."

"I've been so worried about him," Colleen confessed as she fished a hanky from the pocket of her dressing robe. "These past two weeks. I didn't want to tell anyone, but I had such a bad feeling."

"And all for nothing."

Colleen nodded as she wiped her tears. "Thankfully."

Mam blinked suddenly, as if seeing the room for the first time. "Oh my, Colleen."

"What?" Colleen wasn't sure that Mam would approve of her changes. Especially since Colleen's tastes were much more modern than Mam and Dad's. And, after all, they owned this space.

"It's absolutely beautiful!"

"Really?" Colleen looked around with satisfaction. The room, she felt, was a lot like some of the movie sets she'd watched being arranged. The gray sofa on one side, a pair of matching burgundy chairs on the other side. A coffee table and matching end tables with a pair of modern table lamps. So unlike her parents' home of comfortably mismatched furnishing and crocheted lace doilies everywhere.

"It looks like something out of a magazine."

"Thank you."

"Very modern." Mam stood and walked around, taking it all in.

"I'll give you the full tour," Colleen offered. "It takes about a minute."

Mam seemed to approve of everything, marveling at all that had been fitted into what had once been a storage attic. "It's just lovely, dear. I'm sure you'll be very comfortable here." She pointed to the telephone table by the door. "Does that work?"

Colleen explained about having a new line installed. "Separate from the store's phone. I hope you don't mind."

"That's a relief, dear. I worried about Margaret having an emergency and needing to go downstairs in the middle of the night to use the phone."

"It seemed a good idea."

Mam hugged Colleen. "You've grown into such a fine, responsible young woman, Colleen." She chuckled. "Remember when we all used to call you our flibbertigibbet?"

Colleen smiled. "Yes, but it seemed to fit."

"We were wrong." She patted Colleen on the cheek. "Well, I need to go if I want to make it to Mass, but I wanted to invite you for dinner today."

Colleen was tempted to make an excuse to remain in her sweet apartment, but since it was her birthday, Mam probably wanted to bake a cake or something, so she agreed. "Three o'clock?"

"Sounds good."

After Mam left, Colleen fixed herself a small breakfast and sat down to read Geoff's telegram again. There was no birthday gift anyone could've given to her that would've been better than this. Well, unless, Geoff himself showed up. But she felt fairly certain that wasn't going to happen. Although she hoped and prayed he'd get a leave when the baby came.

Seven

Margaret and Molly had been planning Colleen's surprise birthday party/baby shower for more than a month now. As far as she could tell, Colleen was clueless. Mam had done her part, inviting Colleen to dinner at the house, but when Colleen arrived, she would find the house empty and no food on the table. Then Molly would appear to wander over and invite Colleen to Mrs. Bartley's for a sandwich. That's when everyone—family and friends—would leap out yelling, "Surprise!"

Margaret's only concern this morning was that Brian was out of sorts. He hadn't slept well last night and had refused to go to Mass this morning. Although it wasn't unusual for him to be moody sometimes, she'd really hoped that he could be more helpful today. She tried to humor him at breakfast, hoping to enjoy having the house to themselves while his parents attended Mass, but he seemed sulky and sullen.

"You're not using your leg," she said as she helped Peter down from his highchair. She'd taken to using the word *leg* instead of *prosthetic* because it sounded gentler.

"No, I'm not," he said crisply.

"Why not?"

"It aggravates my stump." He got up, balancing himself on his crutches. "Is that a problem for you? Are you embarrassed to be seen with a man on crutches?"

"No, of course not." She started to gather the breakfast dishes. "I just thought that—"

"Well, maybe you shouldn't think so much, Margaret. At least not for me. Let me do my own thinking, okay?" He clumsily folded the newspaper, tucking it under his arm. She knew what was up, could see the writing on the wall. Brian was trying to pick a fight with her. Then he could lock himself in his room and just mope. But she was determined to keep him from it.

"I wasn't trying to think for you, Brian." She glared at him. "I was merely trying to *converse* with you."

He looked down at the floor.

"I didn't realize the prosthetic leg bothered you so much. Do you need to have it refitted or—"

"See!" He looked up with angry eyes. "There you go again, trying to think for me. Sometimes you treat me like a child."

"Sometimes you act like a child," she snapped then instantly regretted it. But instead of apologizing, she turned and carried the dishes to the kitchen. But hearing him hobbling off to barricade himself in the bedroom, she set the dishes in the sink then hurried out to waylay him.

“Look,” she said, catching him before he opened the bedroom door. “You can’t just keep running away from everything.”

“I’m not running from everything, Margaret. I’m running from you.”

She stood between him and the door. “Why?”

“I get tired of your nagging.” He gave her a weary look.

“Nagging?” She noticed Peter watching them with curiosity. A reminder to keep this from going into a full-blown argument. “Asking you about your leg is nagging?”

He simply shrugged.

“I don’t understand you. I’m trying to understand, but sometimes it seems like you want to push me away. You get in these moods and no matter what I say or do, it’s wrong. How am I supposed to know what—”

“You should know that I need you to leave me alone sometimes.” His tone was slightly softer. “You need to give me room, Margaret . . . and time.”

“I try to do that, but it seems like it’s never enough. It seems like you’re never going to really get well or get over this, whatever it is. Like you’ll never be the same man you were before . . . the man I married.” She felt her eyes misting up, but she didn’t want to cry. Especially with Peter watching with such interest.

“You’re probably right about that,” he said

solemnly. "I will never be the man I was before. That was over and done with when I lost this." He kicked out his stump for emphasis.

She was flustered now. "That's not what I meant."

"Hello?" called Brian's mother cheerfully.

"Get out of the way," Brian growled at Margaret.

"No," she said firmly.

"I'm sorry you missed Mass," Brian's mother chirped as she removed her hat. "It was very good today. Don't you think so, Jack?"

"It was all right." He peered at Margaret and Brian with a slight frown.

"We were, uh, just having a conversation." Margaret forced a smile but continued to block the bedroom door.

"Well, don't let us interrupt." Jack swooped up Peter. "In fact, we were just saying it's a nice morning to take this fellow to the park. What do you think, Louise? Want to take our grandson down to the park? Maybe we can stop by the donut shop."

Louise gave her husband a curious glance then looked at Margaret and Brian before she nodded and reached for her hat. "Sounds like a good idea, Jack."

Just like that they were gone, and now Margaret locked eyes with Brian. "Why are you treating me like this?" she asked in a gentle but firm tone.

"I'm not your enemy. If I ask you about your leg or about how you slept, it's simply because I care . . . because I love you. Why can't you just talk to me . . . like you used to?"

Brian hobbled over to the living room, collapsing into his dad's easy chair and, leaning over, held his head in his hands. "Because I'm not that same guy, Margaret. Can't you understand that?"

She went over to sit across from him. "You are the same guy," she insisted. "You lost a part of your leg and you've been through some hard things, but underneath all that, you are still Brian Hammond. I know that."

He looked up at her with moist eyes. "You don't know everything."

"Of course not. No one knows everything. Well, except for God."

"I mean you don't know everything about me, Margaret."

"I'm aware of that." She was about to add that he didn't know everything about her either but stopped herself. Something in his eyes made her want to just listen. "What is it?" she prodded. "What are you trying to tell me?"

There was a long moment where neither of them spoke. All Margaret could hear was the ticking of the clock and the sound of an occasional car on the street. But instead of questioning him, like she wanted to do, she simply waited.

"Something happened over there. . . ." He ran

his fingers through his hair then shook his head. "Something that changed me."

She frowned, wanting to say that she was well aware of that, but instead she waited.

"Something I'm deeply ashamed of, Margaret. Something I deeply regret."

A shock of realization went through her. This was not about losing his leg.

"But I don't want to hurt you with it." He sighed. "I feel like I've already hurt you enough."

"Go ahead," she said in a voice that sounded wooden to her. "I can take it."

There was another long pause and then he began to speak. "We were stationed in a village outside of Rome. The people there—mostly women and children—were so poor and downtrodden, I felt sorry for them. I tried to help out when I could." He stared off into space as if someplace else. "There was a young woman with a small child. Vittoria. I tried to help her—her and her son. They were homeless and hungry."

"Was she . . . was she pretty?" Margaret felt a hard lump in her throat.

"Oh, I suppose she was, in that Italian way. But mostly she was desperate. She had nothing, and her little boy was skin and bones."

"Oh." Margaret felt her world crumbling, like the very breath inside of her was being snuffed out. She didn't know what to say or do, and her stomach felt sick.

"I never intended for it to go where it did," he continued, as if oblivious to her pain. "I found Vittoria a place to live. Just a room in a rundown house. I paid the rent—it was cheap—and I got them some food. It really wasn't much, but Vittoria was grateful."

"And she showed her appreciation?" Margaret stared at Brian as if seeing him for the first time, absorbing this shocking image of him in the arms of another woman. Her stomach twisted and she wanted to throw up.

He nodded, looking down at the floor. "She fixed me a meal, which seemed innocent enough, but then there was a bottle of wine and . . ."

"Do you—do you love her?" she asked in a raspy voice.

His head jerked up. "No, of course not."

"Are you certain?" she asked.

"Yes. I'm certain." He nodded vigorously. "I love you, Margaret. And Peter. You're the only ones I want. It's just that—" His voice cracked. "I've been eaten alive with guilt about this. That's why I keep trying to push you away. I thought if I kept you at arm's length, I wouldn't have to tell you." He sighed. "But I feel better having it out into the open. It's as if a heavy stone has been lifted from my back."

And placed on mine, she wanted to say. But she couldn't speak. The words were stuck inside of her. And so she stood and avoiding his eyes, she went into their room, closed and locked the door, and just cried.

"What's wrong with Margaret?" Molly quietly asked Colleen as her sister's surprise birthday party/baby shower wound down. Only a few of their immediate family members still lingered at Mrs. Bartley's house, and Margaret had already started to clean up.

"I don't know," Colleen whispered. "I've never seen her so quiet."

"And Brian never did make it," Molly pointed out.

"Do you think she told him?"

"You mean about Howard?" Molly glanced over to where Margaret was carrying a load of dishes to the kitchen.

"I hope you enjoyed your party," Mam said to Colleen. "Your sisters worked so hard to get it all put together."

"Margaret did most of the work," Molly clarified as Margaret joined them. "She had us all collecting sugar rations for weeks."

"Well, it was truly lovely," Colleen declared. "And what a surprise." She hugged her sisters and mother. "Thank you all so much."

"I'm glad you enjoyed it," Margaret said without enthusiasm. "If you'll excuse me, I'd like to help Mrs. Bartley in the kitchen." She frowned.

"I told her not to start on the dishes, but she's already running water."

"Did Peter go home with the Hammonds?" Molly quietly asked Mam after Margaret left.

Mam shook her head. "Dad took him home for a nap. You probably heard him getting fussy earlier." She checked her watch. "I should go check on them. Peter might be waking up by now. I don't want your father having to chase him around the house."

"I'll finish loading your gifts into Mrs. Bartley's car," Molly told Colleen. "If you don't mind, I'll help out here a bit more then bring them over to your apartment." She grinned. "I can't wait to see it."

"Why don't you spend the night with me?" Colleen offered. "We can keep celebrating my birthday."

Molly finished loading the car and tried to make herself useful in the kitchen, but Margaret just shooed her—and Mrs. Bartley—away. "Go ahead and take Colleen's things to her," she finally said with irritation. "I can take care of this myself."

"But you should probably go get Peter," Molly protested. "I can finish up in—"

"Just go, Molly. Peter is fine. Mam said not to worry."

Molly felt uneasy as she drove. Something was troubling Margaret. Something big. Only yesterday, she'd been so excited for today's festivities. It was all she'd talked about when they'd put out the decorations last night. And then today, she was as deflated as a couple of the balloons they'd blown up. Whatever was wrong, Molly hoped and prayed it wasn't too serious.

Molly was soon carrying load after load of gifts up the stairs in back of the store. And then she got a quick tour of Colleen's remodeled apartment. The transformation was truly amazing. Before long, she and Colleen were in the tiny baby nursery, putting all the sweet baby things away. "These shirts are so little." Molly held up a doll-sized nightie with embroidery around the neckline. "Can you believe that in less than two months you'll have a new baby filling this?"

Colleen laughed. "It's hard to imagine, but the bigger I get, the more eager I am to meet this child." She patted her stomach. "I think it must be a boy. Probably a football player, it's been kicking so much."

"Oh, I hope it's a girl," Molly told her.

"I honestly don't care what it is, as long as it gets here on time—and in good condition." Colleen hung a pink and blue crocheted baby afghan over the side of the crib.

"Do you think Geoff will get much leave when the baby comes?"

"I sure hope so. But there are no guarantees." Colleen turned to look at Molly. "How did

Margaret seem before you left? Did you get a chance to find out what's wrong?"

Molly described how eager Margaret had been to get rid of her. "She didn't seem the least bit inclined to chat with anyone."

"I wonder if she might be expecting? I remember how she'd been out of sorts the last time. Although I think it would be sweet for Peter to have a younger sibling. You know he'll be two this fall."

"I actually wondered the same thing, but yesterday evening Margaret was in good spirits while we put up decorations for your party. She was going on about how much fun it would be to have a new baby around when yours arrives. It really didn't sound like she was expecting to me."

"Do you think it's her marriage?"

Molly frowned. "I sure hope not. But I must admit that the Hammonds didn't seem their usual jovial selves today. They seemed nearly as troubled as Margaret."

"And they left early."

"I know. And they didn't even offer to take Peter home with them. And that was when he was starting to get fussy too."

"She must've told Brian about Howard." Colleen set a small stack of diapers on the changing table. "That's the only thing that makes sense. She confessed her transgressions and

Brian probably got mad. He seems easily angered these days."

"I'm sure it would be painful to hear something like that." Molly had been dreading the idea of Brian finding out about Margaret's indiscretions.

"And they probably got into a big fight." Colleen closed a drawer with finality. "And when he decided to stay home, Margaret probably got mad."

"I'm sure they'll get over it." Molly set a bunny shaped baby rattle in the cradle that had been from when her parents' first child, Peter, had been born. Hopefully she would get to use it herself . . . someday.

"Brian shouldn't hold it against Margaret for too long." Colleen sighed as she moved to the door. "After all, she was never actually unfaithful."

"But I can understand how that could still hurt Brian." Molly felt slightly defensive of her brother-in-law. "I mean, he was over in Europe, risking his life for his country, and in the meantime . . ." She couldn't finish the sentence.

"In the meantime, his wife was over here flirting very seriously with disaster." Colleen turned off the light. "I don't like it either, Molly."

"It's just so sad." Molly slowly shook her head. "But I do think it's for the best to get it out into the open. Don't you?"

Colleen nodded. "Hopefully we can all put

it behind us now." She led Molly out to the kitchenette. "Want a cup of tea?"

"Sounds lovely." Molly reached for the kettle. "Why don't you let me fix it? You go put your feet up. You've had a long day."

Colleen reached around to rub her back. "That's an offer I won't refuse."

Molly continued to chatter at Colleen as she puttered around the sweet little kitchenette. "I really love what you've done to this place." She carried the loaded tea tray. "If you and Geoff ever go back to Hollywood or your beach house in San Diego, I want to put first dibs on this place." She set down the tray then handed Colleen a cup.

"How do you like living with Mrs. Bartley?"

"It's actually very nice." Molly sat down. "She doesn't treat me like a child. Just lets me come and go as needed."

"You mean she doesn't question you like Mam and Dad?" Colleen teased.

"I know it's only because they love us." She sighed. "They worry about us, especially when we're living under their roof. But it's different with Mrs. Bartley."

"And how's the job at the photo studio going?"

"Simon Bernard is a dear." Molly laughed. "Well, he can be a cantankerous dear at times. But the things I'm learning from him—well, it's a fabulous opportunity."

"But you still plan to go back to school in the fall?"

Molly's brow creased. "I'm not sure. Mrs. Bartley keeps telling me I should continue, but I can't help but wonder . . . Is the experience I'm getting with Simon Bernard better than taking classes? It was like that at the newspaper."

"But maybe it's important to have a college degree." Colleen looked uncertain.

"Maybe . . . but I'm not completely convinced." She pointed to Colleen. "You've done quite well without one."

Colleen laughed. "I'm an actress, silly. That does not require a college education."

"I know." Molly shrugged. "Anyway, I'm thinking about it. Praying about it."

"Well, if you're worried about tuition money, I can still help you."

"Thank you, Colleen. That's so very sweet. And Mrs. Bartley has offered to help too. But, really, that's not it. Not all of it anyway. I just don't know." She pointed to Colleen. "And not to change the subject, but I keep forgetting to ask you about something."

"What's that?"

"I actually wanted to offer you my help."

"Your help?"

"When the baby comes. If you don't want to move back home with Mam and Dad, I thought I could come stay with you. You know, to help with the baby . . . and whatever. I mean, if Geoff doesn't get a lot of leave time. I can fill in the gap. I already mentioned it to Mr. Bernard, and he seemed okay with me taking a few days off."

Colleen's eyes lit up. "Oh, Molly, that would be wonderful. I was wondering what I'd do when the time came. Mam keeps pestering me to bring the baby home so that she can help me, but I know Dad doesn't need that kind of stress. We all know how much noise a baby can make. Peter made that obvious when he threw that little fit today."

"And yet Dad was the one to take him home." Molly set down her empty teacup and slowly stood. "But Peter probably just needed a nap." She suddenly noticed a vase of red roses on a table by the window. "Oh, Colleen, those are beautiful." She walked over to sniff the blooms. "Where on earth did you get them?"

"They're from Geoff. For my birthday. They came right before I left this afternoon. He must've wired his family to have them sent." She rose and picked up a large silver box. "Because this came too." She chuckled as she opened it. "I think it's a cigarette box, which is pretty amusing since Geoff's mother does not approve of smoking." She closed the lid. "And I haven't had a cigarette in months." She patted her rounded midsection. "I don't think junior cares for it. But Geoff still smokes. I'll stock it for him."

Now Colleen told Molly about how her birthday had started, how she'd been shocked when Mam showed up with a telegram. "I immediately thought the worst," she confessed. "And it shook me to the core." She sat back down, refilling her teacup. "I don't know what I would do if I lost Geoff now. I mean, it was hard enough when I was alone and thought he'd been killed, but with a child to raise . . . by myself . . . well, it was very, very scary."

"But you wouldn't be by yourself, Colleen. You'd have all of us. Your family would help you. You know that."

Colleen nodded somberly. "Yes, I know that. But it would still be hard."

Molly understood. She hadn't heard from Patrick for several weeks. Although they weren't married or even engaged, she knew that a part of her would die if he didn't make it home. She could hardly bear to think of such a thing. Really, it was better to just pray.

Eight

It was just getting dark when Margaret quietly slipped out of Mrs. Bartley's back door, pausing to lock it before she closed it. Mrs. Bartley had gone to bed—under protest—an hour ago. Meanwhile, Margaret had put down the blackout curtains then scrubbed and cleaned and straightened. She was determined to leave the house spotless as a thank you to Mrs. Bartley.

At least that was what she would tell Mam and Dad as her explanation for coming home so late. The truth was Margaret had simply wanted to procrastinate. She hoped that Mam would've put Peter to bed by now. And, not wanting to disturb him, Margaret would ask to spend the night there too. Anyway, that was her plan.

She made her way through the victory garden, pausing to admire the plants in the moonlight. Molly was really a marvel when it came to growing things. Margaret didn't like feeling jealous of her youngest sister, but sometimes she just couldn't help herself. Molly's life, compared to Margaret's, seemed abundantly blessed. She was the golden girl. And Margaret, well, she seemed destined for troubles.

Margaret let herself in the back door and,

seeing the kitchen was dark, hoped that her parents had gone to bed. But when she reached the living room, a single table lamp glowed and Mam was sitting in her rocker with knitting in her lap. But the needles were still and Mam's eyes were closed, and so Margaret attempted to sneak past her.

"Mary Margaret," Mam quietly called out just as Margaret's foot touched the first stair.

"Oh?"

Margaret turned to see Mam patting the chair beside her. "Come here, dear."

Margaret prepared her excuses as she went to sit down. "I'm surprised you're still up, Mam."

"I'm surprised you stayed so long at Mrs. Bartley's."

Margaret started to explain how she'd wanted to leave the house spick-and-span, but Mam stopped her. "What's troubling you, dear?"

"Troubling me?" Margaret attempted to look surprised.

"Is there trouble between you and Brian? We all noticed he didn't come today. And Jack and Louise seemed a bit out of sorts."

Margaret knew it was no use. "Mam, you must promise not to tell anyone."

"You know you can trust me."

"Not even Dad."

Mam's brow creased slightly, but she nodded.

The story came pouring out of Margaret, along

with the tears. "I can't go back to him, Mam," she said finally. "I will never forgive him for this. Never."

"Oh, Margaret." Mam sadly shook her head. "I'm so sorry. For both of you."

"For both of us? After what Brian did?" Margaret's hands balled into fists.

"I know it hurt you deeply, but you must be able to see that Brian is hurting too."

"You mean because of his leg?" Margaret scowled. "He can't use that as his excuse for everything, Mam. And, just for the record, Brian still had his leg when he got involved with *Vittoria*." She spat out the name.

"Do you think he loves this woman?"

"Oh, he says he doesn't. He says that she was desperate—and he was lonely. And Vittoria seemed helpless. She had a child and they were hungry and homeless. He helped them get settled and Vittoria was grateful. She fixed him a meal, and they shared a bottle of wine . . . and well, you know how it went after that."

Mam's brow creased as if carefully considering this. "It's not an unusual story, Margaret. It's happened over and over, from the beginning of time. Men . . . well, men will be men."

"Mam?" Margaret felt like throwing something. "Are you defending Brian?"

"No, I'm just stating a fact." She looked down at her knitting.

Margaret felt a stab of concern. "You're not suggesting that Dad ever did anything like that, are you?" Margaret couldn't imagine her father dishonoring his marriage like that.

"No, no. Not that I know of anyway." She looked up. "But I do know of such instances. Your father told me stories of other men's infidelities during the previous war. Stories very similar to Brian's. Although I don't know of any who confessed such things to their wives. I'm actually rather surprised that Brian made such an admission to you."

"It's because he's so guilt-ridden. He believes that's the reason he lost his leg . . . because he was unfaithful. He is certain it's God's punishment."

"Oh." Mam pursed her lips. "What do you think?"

Margaret shrugged. "Maybe he's right. Maybe it was God's judgment."

"Do you honestly believe that?"

"I don't know."

"Because if that were true, don't you think there would be an awful lot of people walking around with missing limbs?"

Margaret considered this. Mam probably had something there.

"I believe in a loving God who is quick to forgive. And I suspect that Brian confessed his transgressions to you because he loves you."

"It sure didn't feel like it. That's a strange way to show love." Margaret cringed to remember the horrible, hateful words they'd exchanged while Brian's parents took Peter to the park.

"So what now?" Mam asked in a weary voice. "I assume you'll spend the night here. I put Peter in your old room."

"Yes, I hoped you would, Mam. And if you don't mind, I'd like to stay here awhile. I plan to make it sound like Mr. and Mrs. Hammond need a break from my rambunctious son."

Mam's brows arched.

"And I'll do my best to keep him quiet, Mam. I don't want him to disturb Dad."

"As long as you understand this is only temporary. My hope is that you'll iron things out with Brian."

"Iron things out?"

"Well, you did make marriage vows, Margaret. You promised—"

"Brian broke his vows," Margaret said in anger.

"That's true. But you both promised before God that you'd stay together. For better or worse, richer or poorer, in sickness and in health. Remember? And besides that, you two have a child together."

"I'm well aware of that, Mam."

Mam set her knitting aside and slowly stood. "I realize you're in pain right now, Margaret, but you'll have to move past it . . . in time."

As Mam said good night and shuffled to her room, Margaret felt certain she would never move past this. The mere idea of Brian with another woman burned like a hot fire-poker in her chest. It seemed a pain she would bear forever. How could a wound this deep ever heal? A part of her had wanted to die when she'd heard Brian's confession this morning. Another part of her wanted to kill him. How could they ever go back to living as husband and wife? She wasn't sure that Brian even wanted to be married. Perhaps that was why he'd confessed his sordid affair to her. It was a surefire way to end their marriage, once and for all. And the truth was, she did not care.

Nine

Although Molly loved her job at Bernard's and was learning so much about photography, there was a serious fly in the ointment—and her name was Lulu. Molly honestly didn't understand why Simon kept Lulu as his receptionist. Well, except that she was his only niece. But when it came to customer service, Lulu was a lost cause. She did a fairly satisfactory job with the rest of the office work, but with such a bad attitude that Molly went out of her way to avoid her. Until she overheard Lulu while helping a customer to select photos. Molly was just returning from her lunch break but had paused to straighten the mat by the door.

"My uncle is a photographer," Lulu told the customer, "*not* a miracle worker."

Even though the young woman's back was to Molly, she could tell by her tense posture that she was uneasy.

"Please, make your selection," Lulu said with impatience.

As Molly went around the front desk, she recognized the woman from a photoshoot a couple of weeks ago. Her name was Donna and she'd called herself a "plain Jane" and was uncomfortable being photographed, but she was eager for a good picture to send to her husband, who was serving overseas in the navy. Molly had done all she could to befriend her and help her relax in front of the camera.

"Donna," Molly said in a friendly tone. "How are you doing?"

Donna looked up then smiled. "Oh, Molly. I'm, uh, just fine. Thank you."

"Your photos turned out great." Molly pointed at one lying on the counter. "I think that one is my favorite. Your eyes look so bright and your smile is relaxed and pretty and I like the tilt of your head."

Donna picked up the portrait, nodding slightly. "You really like it?"

"I do." Molly picked up another one. "This is nice too, but I like the other one better." She glanced at Lulu, who was now glowering at her. "Which do you like best?" she asked Donna.

"I agree with you." Donna picked up Molly's favorite then turned to Lulu. "I'll have this one in the midsized portrait."

"Fine." Lulu wrote down the order.

"Only one?" Molly asked Donna. "The smallest package doesn't cost much more than a single portrait, and it comes with some wallet-sized photos. Your husband may appreciate one that he could keep on him. Plus, you'd have a spare photo for him when he comes home. And what about giving a framed photo to your parents or grandparents for Christmas? We have some nice frames over there." She pointed to the shelf of picture frames for sale.

Donna nodded. "Yes, that's a good idea. Thank you so much."

Molly smiled. "You're welcome. And I'm sure your husband will be pleased." As Molly went into the back, she could feel Lulu watching her. She was obviously angry. But Molly was irritated. Donna might not have been their most beautiful subject, but that was a rotten way to treat anyone, especially a customer. As Molly headed down the hall, she knew it was pointless to complain to Simon. He was aware that Lulu wasn't an ideal employee, but as he'd pointed out, Lulu was, after all, family. Well, at least Molly didn't have to work directly with her. And that suited her just fine.

Molly still felt aggravated when she went into the darkroom. Fortunately, she had plenty to distract herself with today. An afternoon's worth of negatives was waiting to be developed. She flicked on the door light to signal that she was busy in here then put on her heavy apron and went to work. She loved this space, the glow of the red light, and the process of watching photographs come to life in the developing solution. It always seemed slightly magical. And, according to Simon, she was getting quite good at it. She was just removing a gorgeous wedding portrait when the door flew open, flooding the darkroom with bright light and spoiling the portrait. "What is going—"

"I want to talk to you!" Lulu's dark brown eyes were fiery.

"You just ruined this." Molly held up the dripping photo then pointed to another tray where several others were likewise ruined.

"I don't care. You interfered with my customer, Molly. And I will not put up with it. The reception area is mine. You have no right to stick your oar in."

"I was simply helping Donna to select a portrait." Molly tried to keep her tone calm. "Something you should've been doing."

"I'd already tried to help her." Lulu scowled darkly. "She was hopeless."

"She was a customer, Lulu." Molly's patience, like the photos she'd been developing, had just vanished. "My family owns a store, and I have worked there since I was tall enough to look over the counter, and I happen to know a thing or two about customer service. You, apparently, do not."

"You can't talk to me that way. I'm going to tell Uncle Simon that you're—"

"What are you going to tell Uncle Simon?" He poked his head into the darkroom with a puzzled expression.

“Molly wants to take over my job,” Lulu told him.

“I was simply trying to help a customer.” Molly dropped the ruined photo in the trash can.

“I was already helping her, thank you very much.” Lulu glared at Molly then turned to Simon with a more pleasant expression. “Molly interfered when I was—”

“You made Donna uncomfortable.” Molly untied her apron. “You made her feel like she wasn’t worth your time.” She hung up the apron then shook her head. “I simply felt sorry for her.” Molly locked eyes with Simon. “And if you approve of your customers being treated like that, then perhaps I shouldn’t be working for you. Because my family taught me that customer service was vital for the—”

“That’s enough.” Simon’s brow was furrowed as he held up both hands, and Molly braced herself for being fired. As horrible as it would feel, it might be a relief. But then she realized that, for the sake of future employment, she should be the one to call it quits.

“I’m sorry,” Molly somberly told him. “I’ve loved working with you and all that I’ve learned, but maybe it’d be best for me to go—”

“No, no, no.” He grimly shook his head. “That’s not what I want.” He turned to Lulu. “Please, return to the reception area right now. And I expect you to do a better job of dealing with customers. Molly is absolutely right. Everyone who comes through our door must be treated with respect and kindness."

"But I—"

"Lulu." His tone was firm. "Go now."

After she was gone, Simon peered down to the tray of ruined photos. "Is Lulu responsible for those?"

"She came in while I was working." Molly pointed to the warning light which was still on.

"I'm sorry about that." He shook his head. "Lulu, as I'm sure you noticed, has a sizable chip on her shoulder. But I never told you much about her, did I?"

"I know she's your niece." Molly reached for her apron.

"My brother's only child. He passed away when she was quite young. Her mother remarried, but Lulu doesn't get along very well with her stepfather."

Or anyone, Molly was tempted to add.

"So I've tried to be a father to her and, for the most part, we've had a very good relationship. But last winter, her beau was killed overseas, and she took it very hard."

"I'm sorry. I didn't know that."

"I probably should've said something. I had hoped that you two would become friends. Mick told me that you lost your brother in the Pearl

Harbor attack, and I hoped that would help you to understand her better."

"I've never really had much of a conversation with her," Molly admitted. "I attempted to engage with her early on . . ." Molly remembered how rude Lulu had been when Molly had mentioned her relationship with Patrick. Now it made some sense. "But maybe I need to try again."

"You're such a positive person," Simon told her. "I feel that you could be a good influence on Lulu. To be honest, that was one of the reasons I hired you. Mick spoke so glowingly of you, so I thought you might be just what we needed here." He smiled. "And you have been a ray of sunshine. So I beg you, please, don't quit. And don't give up on Lulu."

"Well, it helps to know more about her history. And I'll do what I can to befriend her."

"Be sure to give her a chance to cool off. One thing I know about my niece is that it takes time for her to get over a grudge. Give her a day or two."

Molly nodded. That wouldn't be a problem since she wasn't eager to engage with Lulu. Besides that, she had a lot of work to do. Especially since those spoiled photos needed to be redone. But at least she understood now. Lulu had been through some hardships. And even though many people were going through difficulties, as a result of this war, Molly knew that people reacted differently. Her own family was proof enough of that.

Colleen knew that Margaret and Peter had moved back home, but she wasn't sure why. Mam had made it sound as if it had gotten too crowded at the Hammonds', but Colleen wasn't buying it. So, after more than a week of Margaret's glum silence, Colleen was determined to get to the bottom of it.

"Would you mind caring for Peter tonight?" Colleen asked Mam.

Mam frowned. "I suppose I could . . . but why?"

"I'd like to invite Margaret to join me for dinner. I want to talk to her. I plan to find out what is troubling her." With Colleen's shift over, she was now filling a grocery basket to take up to her apartment.

Mam's eyes lit up. "Oh, yes, that's a fine idea. I think Margaret needs someone to talk to. I'd be happy to watch Peter."

"Can you tell her about my invitation?" Colleen put a head of lettuce on top of her basket. "You don't have to tell her about my intentions, just say I'd enjoy her companionship. Make it seem that I want to talk about this." She patted her rotund middle. "You know, baby talk."

Mam nodded. "Yes, that's a good plan."

As Colleen carried her basket of groceries up the stairs, she wondered how she could possibly go through another month of what felt like a never-ending pregnancy. Already she felt as big as a house. In some ways, she was grateful that Geoff wasn't around to see her like this. And she seriously doubted she'd ever get back into film-making shape. Oh, her agent Georgina seemed certain that it could be done. She'd reminded Colleen of Jane Wyman, Lana Turner, Rosalind Russell and a few other actresses who'd returned to their careers after giving birth. She'd even shared a rumor that Hedy Lamarr was currently expecting.

Several months ago, Georgina had sent a package of pregnancy beauty products—creams and oils and ointments that Colleen faithfully lathered on before bed each night. Even so, as Colleen put her groceries away, it seemed a losing battle. And right now, she felt so tired, she wondered why she'd even thought it a good idea to invite Margaret for dinner. Colleen had never been a good cook, but besides that, she was too tired. Maybe she'd call out for Chinese. She'd just heard that Ming's now delivered. Margaret would probably like that better than Colleen's cooking anyway. And, in the meantime, Colleen could grab a nice long nap.

It was just a little past six when Margaret, bearing two white bags, showed up at Colleen's door. "Delivery for *Miss Maureen Mulligan.*" Margaret's tone was slightly mocking.

Colleen laughed as she removed cartons from the bags. "I figured I'd get better service if I used my stage name." She pulled out a handful of fortune cookies. "Looks like it worked."

They were soon seated at the little plastic topped table, but Colleen could see that it was up to her to keep the conversation going. And since they were eating, she decided to keep it light. She would ask the hard questions later. She chatted on about some of the latest Hollywood news—not that Margaret seemed very interested.

"Have you seen Molly lately?" Colleen asked as they were finishing up. "I mean, since you're neighbors and all."

"I saw her a few days ago."

"Has she heard much from Patrick? Or Bridget?"

"We didn't really talk much. Just said hello."

"Oh."

"This was good." Margaret picked up their empty plates, taking them to the sink. "Thanks for inviting me." She started to run water to wash up, but Colleen stopped her.

"Let's leave that for later." Colleen reached for the tea kettle. "How about some tea with our fortune cookies."

When they were seated in the living room area, Colleen asked how Dad was doing. "Has he enjoyed having his grandson around more?"

Margaret frowned. "Well, he loves him, but

Peter can be pretty rambunctious. I try to keep him quiet in the evenings, but sometimes it's hard." She opened her fortune cookie then frowned as she looked at the message.

"What does it say?" Colleen asked.

"After a hard year, good news will come your way."

"Oh? Well, who doesn't want good news?" Colleen opened her cookie, reading her fortune aloud. "Your smile brings sunshine to many." She grinned at Margaret then realized her sister was crying. "Oh, Margaret, what is it? What's wrong?"

Margaret held up the strip of paper. "It's already been a hard year—it's been a hard few years—but I don't think it's ever going to get any better. It never gets better. Not for me." And now she was sobbing.

Colleen went to sit by her on the sofa, wrapping an arm around her as Margaret continued to sob. "Tell me what's going on, Margaret. I know you've been miserable lately. Something is wrong. Please, tell me." She handed her a fresh hanky and waited.

"I didn't want to tell anyone," Margaret finally said. "I told Mam, but I made her swear not to repeat it."

"I'm your sister, Margaret, and I'm Peter's godmother. You have a responsibility to tell me what's wrong in your life. Whatever you're going through, it's not good to go through it alone."

Margaret took in a deep breath. "It's Brian."

Colleen nodded. "I suspected as much."

"Oh, Colleen, my marriage is over!" Margaret told her about Brian's involvement with a woman named Vittoria in Italy. "I've never been hurt so deeply," she finally said. "And as much as I wish I could forgive him, I'm not sure that I can. And I'm not sure that he even cares."

"Oh, Margaret." Colleen didn't know what to say. "I'm so sorry."

"It's this blasted war!" Margaret shook a fist. "It's ruining everything." She looked at Colleen with teary eyes. "And it could happen to you too. I don't want to say anything bad about Geoff, but he's out there in the South Pacific and a pilot gets around a lot. It's possible that he's having relationships with those island women. I hear about it all the time."

"Oh, I don't think Geoff would—"

"He's a very handsome man, Colleen. Women are attracted. It's just a fact of life. A terrible, horrible fact of life." And now she started to cry all over again.

Colleen slowly stood, going to her room on the pretense of getting a fresh handkerchief, but Margaret's words cut deeply. Even more so as Colleen caught a glimpse of herself in her full length cheval mirror. She stared at the rounded image there, taking in the dowdy gray maternity dress and frumpy shoes. Even her hair looked dull and listless. It would be no wonder if Geoff preferred an island girl to *this*. Of course, that was ridiculous. He couldn't see Colleen right now. Well, unless he saw her on the screen, and her latest movie was about to release with the armed forces. But besides all that, Geoff loved her. She knew it. Still . . . hadn't Brian loved Margaret?

"I'm sorry," Margaret said as she joined Colleen. "I shouldn't have said that about Geoff. Of course he won't cheat on you like that."

"I don't know." Colleen turned to look at her. "I suppose it's possible." She held out her arms. "And seeing me like this, well, I wouldn't blame him."

Margaret hugged Colleen. "Geoff isn't going to do anything like that. I never should've suggested such a thing. I'm sorry. Please, forgive me. And forget I said that." She stepped back, her face wet with tears again. "It's just that I'm so unhappy. I don't think I'll ever be happy again."

"You will, Margaret." Colleen handed her the fresh hanky, leading them back out to the living room. "If only for Peter's sake, you'll be happy again. But I'm afraid to be truly happy, you'll have to forgive Brian." Colleen wasn't sure how hard to press this, but she couldn't help but consider Margaret's flirtation with Howard. "And, all things considered, I would think you'd understand the temptation . . . you know?"

Margaret sat down with a dark frown. "I know what you're suggesting, Colleen. That because I enjoyed a friendship with Howard, I should have more compassion toward Brian. But I did not do what Brian did. And I honestly believe, even though I enjoyed Howard's attention, I never would've let it go that far."

"But you knew it was wrong," Colleen reminded her. "You felt guilty."

"That's true. But we're still talking about two very different things."

"Different, yes . . . but similar." Colleen weighed her words carefully. "Do you think Brian's confession may be your opportunity to come clean with him, Margaret?"

"Except that we're not exactly speaking to each other right now."

"But maybe in time you'd consider telling him the truth. I mean, think about it. Wouldn't it have been hard for him to confess his indiscretion to you? I'm actually a bit surprised he even did. It's not as if he had to. You never would've found out."

Margaret's eyes suddenly grew wide. "What if Vittoria is . . . is *with child?*"

"Oh, Margaret, I don't think—"

"It happens, Colleen. I've heard that some foreign women purposely get pregnant with

American GIs. It's their ticket to the United States or a payoff."

"Well, everyone's heard those stories and, sure, they make for great films, but I suspect they're exaggerated for drama's sake. You shouldn't assume this woman— Vittoria—has done such a thing. Really, Margaret, it doesn't do you any good to go there."

For the next hour, Colleen did her best to convince her sister not to give up hope or think the worst. In a way, it was almost like playing a role in a movie. Because, truth be told, Colleen didn't fully believe some of the things she was saying. But she hoped that Margaret would believe her because somehow her sister needed to find hope in her situation. As hard as it might be, she needed to forgive Brian and give him a second chance. Would it save her marriage? Colleen had no idea. But Margaret couldn't go on like this. Not only was it unhealthy for her, it would surely affect her young son too. And since Colleen was Peter's godmother, she felt responsible to see Margaret move past this.

Ten

As far as she could tell, Molly was not making any headway with her relationship with Lulu, and she was getting tired of trying. She'd told Lulu about losing her brother and how her dad had nearly died from tuberculosis and how his health was still impaired. She told her about her concerns for Patrick's submarine being hit by a Japanese torpedo and how her brother-in-law had lost his leg in Italy. But nothing seemed to make any difference to Lulu. The sulky young woman seemed determined to play the female version of Sad Sack.

It wasn't until the end of the work day when Molly was picking out a frame for a recent photo of Colleen that Lulu initiated a conversation. "Is that Maureen Mulligan?" Lulu asked with curiosity.

Molly nodded as she tried the picture in a brass frame, holding it up to see if it looked right. She'd taken photos at Colleen's baby shower, thinking she'd send some to Geoff, but this one had turned out so well that she'd decided to enlarge it as a gift for her sister. She hoped it might help Colleen to see herself in a different light and accept that she was still beautiful, even if she was pregnant.

"Is she expecting a baby?" Lulu asked with even more curiosity.

"Yes. She's due in a few weeks."

"How'd you get this photo?" Lulu reached for the picture and Molly let her. "Did my uncle take it? He never told *me* about it."

"He didn't take this." Molly had never talked to Lulu about Colleen, but she'd assumed that Lulu knew "Maureen Mulligan" was her sister. "Do you remember my last name?" Molly asked.

Lulu's forehead creased.

"Mulligan," Molly told her.

"Oh? Is Maureen related to *you?*"

"My sister."

"Really?" Lulu looked doubtful.

"Did you see her in *Stardust in the Moonlight*?"

Lulu nodded but still looked skeptical.

"I got to be on set while she was making it." Molly described some of her Hollywood experiences.

"You're really Maureen Mulligan's sister?" Lulu held the photo up next to Molly, looking from one to the other.

"Her name is Colleen Maureen. We call her Colleen."

Lulu still looked slightly perplexed. "Well, you do sort of look like her."

"Would you like to meet her?" Molly said suddenly.

Lulu's eyes grew wide. "Doesn't she live in Hollywood?"

"She did while she was filming, but she came home to have her baby."

"Do you think she'd really want to meet me?"

"She would if I asked her to." Molly picked up the phone and called Colleen's apartment, explaining that her coworker would like to meet her.

"Is this that witch you told me about?" Colleen asked.

Molly giggled. "Uh, yes. But it seems she's a fan."

"Is she being nicer to you?"

"I think it could happen." Molly glanced at Lulu. "I'd like to see it happen."

"Well, if it would help you, Molly, I'll do it. But only for your sake. And I'll warn you, I'm not having a very good day."

"What's wrong?"

"Just tired . . . missing Geoff . . . and Margaret's been giving me the cold shoulder lately."

"You're not the only one."

"So when are you coming?"

"Well, we're just quitting here at the studio. Is now a bad time?"

"I guess it's as good as any time. Just don't expect me to put on the dog."

Molly told her that was fine and that they'd be there in about an hour then turned to Lulu. "Okay, we're set." She held up the brass frame. "And I'd like to buy this. I'll give her this photo as a thank you for meeting you. Especially considering she's not terribly happy with her appearance right now."

"I'll pay for the frame," Lulu declared.

Molly was surprised but didn't stop her. After they got off the trolley and were walking up the hill toward the store, she explained about Colleen living in the apartment while Geoff was serving as a navy pilot. "She has a really nice beach house in San Diego, but she wanted to be around her family."

"I remember reading about how her fiancé's plane was shot down. I felt so sad for her. That was before my Rich was killed."

"How long has it been since he died?"

"About eight months."

Molly nodded. "It took me a long time to get over losing my brother. To be honest, I don't think I'll ever get completely over it." She sighed. "And I can't imagine how hard it would be to lose Patrick . . . although I know it could happen." For a moment, neither of them said anything. Then, hoping to lighten up their conversation, Molly asked Lulu if she'd heard the latest news. "Allied troops have reached Paris," she said eagerly. "I actually saw the headline on the trolley. I was tempted to grab the evening paper from the man to read the details, but I didn't think he'd appreciate it." She chuckled as she used her key to open the front door of the store. "I'll get one in here."

Molly grabbed a newspaper then turned on the light by the stairway and led Lulu up the stairs. Before long, they were being greeted by Colleen who had put on some makeup and looked fairly glamorous in a flowing pale blue dressing gown and fur-trimmed satin slippers.

"I'm so honored to meet you," Lulu said in the politest voice Molly had ever heard her use.

"Thank you."

"And this is for you." Molly handed her the framed photograph, waiting as Colleen peeled off the tissue paper.

"Hmm?" Colleen wrinkled her nose. "I guess I should say thank you, but it's not easy seeing myself in this condition."

"Someday you might look back on this differently," Molly told her. "Or Geoff might want to see—"

"This will be hidden when Geoff is here." Colleen set it on a side table then eased herself into a chair.

"Have a seat," Colleen said to Lulu. "Molly, why don't you get us something cold to drink? There's some iced tea and lemonade that Mam made for me. She was worried about this August heat." She picked up a magazine to fan herself. "And if I ever have another baby—which is a great big if—I will try to avoid being pregnant in the summer time."

Molly took her time fixing their drinks, using the opportunity to listen to Colleen and Lulu's conversation. Although Colleen was being polite to Lulu, Molly knew her sister was trying to send some not so subtle messages about how important it was to treat people from all walks of life with respect and kindness. "Even when I started to become famous and recognized on the street, I remembered how my parents had trained me. How I'd be working right here in this store and they'd say things like 'the customer is always right.' I try to keep that in mind with my fans. Well, unless they're just plain rude—then I simply ignore them."

"Here you go." Molly set their drinks on the coffee table then sat next to Lulu on the sofa.

"Molly told me about how you lost your fiancé—"

"We weren't engaged," Lulu clarified. "But he was my boyfriend. And I hoped we'd get married one day."

"Well, I'm sorry. I sort of know what that feels like." She took a sip of lemonade.

"I remember when you thought your fiancé was dead, but he was in a Japanese prison camp, which I've heard is almost a fate worse than death."

"Yes, it was pretty grueling. But do you know what helped me to get past it when I thought Geoff was dead? Or at least partly past it—I don't think you ever get completely past something like that. I mean, even now, I'm well aware that Geoff may not make it home. The survival rate of pilots is . . . well, let's just say it's not good." Colleen set her glass down and sighed.

"What helped you get past it?" Lulu asked eagerly.

"Well, Molly could tell you about how I let myself go during that dark era. I just quit caring. I worked at the airplane factory, and I dressed like a man, quit wearing makeup and rarely washed my hair." Colleen seemed to be evaluating Lulu. Molly felt certain her sister was observing the same things she had noticed the first day she'd met Lulu. She didn't care about her appearance.

"That's true," Molly confirmed. "And it really worried us because Colleen had always been so fashionable and chic."

"I discovered that my neglecting myself put others at a distance."

"She didn't smell too nice," Molly added and Colleen laughed.

"I realized that I was just making myself more unhappy, but it was still hard to change. Then, when I did my auditions in Hollywood, I was suddenly forced to attend to my appearance. I suppose it was a turning point for me."

"So you're saying that I'll feel better if I look better?"

"I know it probably sounds shallow, but I think it's true."

Colleen pointed to Molly. "You know how I told you I was feeling low today?"

"Yes." Molly nodded.

"Well, I cleaned myself up." She waved a hand over her gown. "As best as I can for a woman who's about to have a baby." She turned to Lulu. "My due date is less than two weeks away. Anyway, I immediately felt a little bit better." She chuckled. "Oh, I'm still big as a house, but I'm a much prettier house."

Molly and Lulu laughed.

"And you know how you girls could make me even happier?"

"How?" they both asked.

"Well, it's a Friday. I'd like to help you girls fix yourselves up, and then you could go to the USO tonight and dance with the servicemen there." She nodded to Molly. "You're still registered as a junior hostess. And we can both vouch for Lulu."

Molly protested this idea, saying that it would be too much for Colleen. "But I really, really want to do this," Colleen insisted. "It's just what I need to distract myself." Before long they were doing hair and makeup and trying on some of Colleen's beautiful gowns until Colleen was finally bidding them good-bye. She handed Molly the car keys.

"Bring the car back here when you're done," she said. "You can spend the night with me and tell me all about it in the morning."

"I feel like Cinderella," Lulu said as they got into Colleen's car. "Your sister is the sweetest, most generous person I've ever met."

Molly chuckled, remembering a time when no one thought of Colleen quite like that, but she was glad that Lulu could see it now. Hopefully it would make a difference in Lulu's general attitude toward life. Or at least be a start.

Lulu's outlook seemed to get even better as she engaged with the servicemen at the USO, showing that she really knew her way around a dance floor. But Molly nearly fell over when she noticed Lulu dancing with a familiar face in an army uniform.

"Tommy Foster," Molly declared after the dance ended.

"Molly Mulligan!" he exclaimed, warmly hugging her. "It's so good to see you!"

"You know each other?" Lulu asked with arched brows.

"Tommy is an old friend," Molly explained.

"How about a dance?" Tommy asked Molly. "We can catch up."

Molly agreed, but as she and Tommy went out to the dance floor, she noticed Lulu frowning their way. "Say, Tommy, I think Lulu may have taken a fancy to you."

"She's pretty enough." He grinned. "But how are you, Molly? Still in love with that sailor?"

Molly tried to remember what she'd written to him about Patrick. "As a matter of fact, I am." She smiled. "But how about you, Tommy? I thought you and my friend Prudence were corresponding and possibly having a bit of a romance."

"Aw, that kind of fizzled out."

"So what are you doing here?" she asked. "On leave?"

"Yes. Two weeks. It's the first long leave I've had since enlisting."

"Well, good for you." Molly asked him more about where he'd been and what he'd seen, and she couldn't help but notice that he seemed to have grown up a lot. Maybe the army had been good for him. When the dance ended, she nodded to where Lulu stood. "You should ask her to dance again," she whispered to Tommy.

As it turned out, Tommy asked her to dance quite a few more times, and when the dance ended, he asked for her phone number, which Lulu gladly gave to him.

"Tommy seems like a really great guy," Lulu said after they left the USO club. "Do you know him well?"

Molly explained how they'd met at the onset of the war. "We wrote letters a lot for a while, but then I sort of encouraged a friend to write to him. I guess that didn't work out too well."

"Well, I told Tommy I'd like to write to him." Lulu giggled. "And that's when he asked if he could see me during his leave."

"That's wonderful. Tommy really is a sweet guy." Molly told Lulu about how he had been an orphan and missed having a family to connect with while he was overseas.

"Oh, that's so sad. Poor guy."

"And I don't think he knows many people in San Francisco."

"Well, he knows me now," Lulu declared. "And I'll try to help him have a memorable time during his leave."

Molly felt a sense of satisfaction as she got ready for bed that night. She hadn't been exactly thrilled with the idea of going to the USO and dancing with servicemen. She would rather be in Patrick's arms. Just the same, she'd done her best to cheer every fellow she'd encountered, and as she'd danced and smiled and chatted, she'd reminded herself that her purpose was to encourage the soldiers and sailors. Like Lulu had said, she hoped the young men had gotten some pleasant memories of the home front . . . happy thoughts they could carry with them as they headed out to the battlefront. A small thing perhaps, but if it encouraged them and built up morale, she was more than happy to help.

Eleven

Margaret felt stuck—and more so with each passing day. A month had gone by since she'd left Brian, and the gulf between them now felt wider than when he'd been thousands of miles away. The Hammonds hadn't said as much, but she knew they blamed her for their son's marital woes. They probably assumed it was related to Brian's injury, that she was too weak to cope with a one-legged man. Of course, that was ridiculous.

She'd been tempted to tell them the truth more than once but had bitten her tongue. It wasn't her place to reveal Brian's secrets. Instead, she played along with his little charade . . . that it was just easier to live apart for the time being. And, as he'd pointed out, he'd be heading back to college soon, which would put them apart anyway. Perhaps it would part them permanently.

As Margaret walked down to the Hammonds' to pick up Peter on Saturday afternoon, she prepared herself for the usual looks and comments that she knew would be waiting for her. But when she got there, only Mr. Hammond was home. "They went to the park," he crisply told her. "And Brian has asked to keep Peter overnight."

“That’s fine,” she told him.

“He wants to spend as much time as he can with his son before he heads to school.”

“Tell him to let me know when I should get Peter.” Margaret forced a smile, but she felt slightly out of sorts as she headed home. It would’ve been nice if someone had called her earlier with this information. She might’ve remained at the store until closing, or she might’ve stuck around to visit with Colleen. Her sister was a few days beyond her due date and feeling a bit edgy, but at least Molly was with her.

Margaret still felt irked as she went in the house. She’d been careful to make sure Peter had plenty of time with his father. She did it as much for Brian as for her son. But maybe she should’ve scheduled these visits. In the future, when Brian finished law school, she would put these things in writing. Of course, that would probably alarm their families. No one ever spoke of divorce—and the Church forbade it—but sometimes Margaret wondered. What if Brian pushed for it? After all, he’d never been terribly devout when it came to his faith. And if he’d willingly broken his wedding vows in Italy. What difference would it make if his marriage ended in divorce?

Margaret felt inexplicably lonely as she walked through the quiet living room. She wasn’t sure where Dad was right now—probably on his afternoon walk. And Mam was at the store until closing. Margaret was tempted to head back there. She could help Mam lock up then spend the evening with Colleen and Molly. Except that she knew her gloomy spirits were not what Colleen needed today. Better for Molly to cheer her along. She'd moved in with Colleen a week ago and planned to stay until the baby came and as long as needed afterward. Margaret had felt a little jealous but knew that it was the best plan. And Molly had promised to call the minute Colleen went into labor. Margaret prayed it would be soon. A nephew or niece would be most welcome and a happy distraction from Margaret's messed up marriage.

The familiar lump began to build in Margaret's throat, and she knew the tears were not far behind. But instead of holing up in her bedroom like usual, she sank down into Dad's favorite chair and, holding her head in her hands, simply let the tears flow.

"Mary Margaret," Dad exclaimed when he saw her there. "What on God's green earth is the matter? Has someone died?"

"No, no, not at all." Margaret quickly stood, using her damp hanky to blot her eyes. "I didn't hear you come in."

"No, I s'pect you didn't." He frowned as he turned on a table lamp. "What is troubling you, child?"

"Nothing, Dad. I just felt sad."

He sat down, laying the evening paper across his lap but not opening it. "I know that something is wrong, Margaret. I hoped you would tell me about it, but I'm getting weary of waiting."

"I'm sorry."

He pointed to the nearby chair. "Tell me what has happened, sweetheart. I know that something has come between you and Brian. I don't believe your stories about your reasons for moving back home. I want to know the truth."

She sat down in the chair and sighed. "Out of respect for Brian, I haven't wanted to talk about it . . . with anyone."

Dad rubbed his chin. "Is your marriage in trouble, Margaret?"

She looked down to her lap then simply nodded.

"Is it because of Brian's injury?"

She looked up. "No. I know the Hammonds think that I can't cope with his disability, but I can. I was doing just fine with it. That's not why I left."

"Then that leads me down a different trail." He grimly shook his head. "Was Brian unfaithful to you?"

She blinked then tried to conceal her surprise.

"Ah-ha, just as I suspected."

"How did you guess?"

"It's a familiar tale."

"Mam said the same thing." She frowned. "But she assured me it wasn't you."

His pale blue eyes flashed. “That is the truth. I have never been unfaithful to your mother. Never.”

“But someone you know?”

He pursed his lips.

“You don’t have to tell me who it is, Dad. But how did it turn out?”

“You have entrusted me with your secret, Margaret, so I will trust you with mine. It is Brian’s own dad that I’m speaking of. In the previous war, he stepped out on Louise with a young woman in France.”

For some reason, Margaret didn’t feel completely surprised.

“But, to my knowledge, he never told Louise about his infidelity.” Dad’s brow creased. “But Brian told you?”

She just nodded.

“I’m sorry, Margaret.” Dad opened his arms. “Come here, child.”

In the same way she’d done as a little girl, Margaret fell into her dad’s arms, crying as he stroked her head, trying to comfort her. Finally, when her tears subsided, she pulled away and, feeling embarrassed, thanked him. It was a comfort to have him know what was going on.

“I wish I could tell you what to do,” Dad said. “I wish I knew a way to fix this.”

“I’m not sure that Brian wants to fix it.” Margaret sat in the chair across from him. “We haven't really spoken since I moved back home."

"Do you think you can forgive him?"

"I don't know." She shrugged. "And I'm not sure it would make any difference anyway. Brian doesn't seem to care."

"When does he leave for school?"

"Next week. And I honestly don't think we'll patch anything up before he goes."

"Maybe you both need more time." Dad picked up his newspaper, her signal that this conversation was over. It had probably caused him stress.

"You know what they say . . ." She stood. "Time heals all wounds."

"Or wounds all heels."

Margaret leaned down to kiss his cheek. "Thanks, Dad." As she went up to her room, she felt taken aback. That was not the reaction she'd expected from Dad. She'd felt certain he would take Brian's side and remind her of her wedding vows and how she needed to take the high road and perform her wifely duties. But he'd done nothing of the sort—and it had been refreshing.

Molly knew that Colleen did not want to go to Mass on Sunday morning, but she encouraged her just the same. "It'll give you something else to think about," Molly said as she helped Colleen into her shoes. "And just last night I read in your motherhood book—"

"You're reading my motherhood book?" Colleen frowned.

"I happen to like information." Molly stood. "And it said that movement and moderate exercise can help an overdue mother go into labor."

"Really?" Colleen pinned her hat into place. "Then let's get moving. Maybe we should walk to church."

Molly laughed as she pulled on her gloves. "Well, let's not push things. And since we're running late, we'll probably have to park a couple blocks away anyway. That will give you some exercise." Molly went ahead of Colleen as they went down the steep stairs. She knew that Colleen hadn't been out of her apartment for days and the stairs were worrisome. But soon they were in the car.

"I read that our Allied troops are in Paris," Molly told Colleen. "And they'll soon reach the German border. Isn't that great news?"

"Yes. Now if we could just invade Tokyo and end this war once and for all."

"Amen to that."

Mass was already started when Molly and Colleen slipped into an empty pew in back, but Molly knew that Colleen wanted to keep a low—albeit not slender—profile. And she'd made Molly promise that they could leave before Mass ended. "I don't want to give everyone a chance to stare at me like I'm a sideshow act at the circus," she'd whispered at the sacramental, pausing to dip her fingers in the holy water and cross herself.

Molly's plan was to simply humor her sister—and to pray in earnest that the baby would soon arrive. Colleen was almost a week overdue—and not particularly patient. In fact, Molly probably needed the encouragement of Mass even more than Colleen right now. She was just starting to focus in on the gospel acclamation when Colleen grabbed her hand, squeezing it tightly.

Molly turned to Colleen and, seeing her sister's blue eyes opened wide, knew something was up. She mouthed, *What?*

"It's happening," Colleen hissed, pointing to the floor. "My water has broken."

Molly looked down to see a small puddle pooling at Colleen's feet. "Oh my goodness!" she exclaimed. A woman in the pew in front of them turned with a disapproving frown, and Molly nervously smiled. "Excuse me, Mrs. O'Neil," she whispered. "But will you please tell my family that Colleen is about to have her baby?" Mrs. O'Neil blinked then nodded and Molly turned to Colleen. "Come on," she said quietly. "Let's get out of here." Holding Colleen by the elbow, she guided her out of the sanctuary and into the vestibule.

"I'm so embarrassed," Colleen whispered.

"I can't believe that happened in the middle of Mass!"

"I think Mother Mary was simply blessing you." Molly laughed nervously as they hurried outside into the bright sunlight. "Do you think you can walk or should I run and get the car?"

"I'll walk," Colleen insisted. "But let's get going. I don't want anyone else to see me like this."

Molly linked arms with Colleen, leading her down the sidewalk, but they hadn't even gone a block before Colleen doubled over in pain. "Is that a contraction?" Molly asked, bending over to peer into her sister's agonized face.

Colleen clutched her middle and groaned. "I think so!"

"You'll be okay," Molly reassured her. "Just another block to go." But with Colleen hunkered down and moaning, the car suddenly seemed very far away. Fortunately, the labor pain subsided and they were able to slowly make their way to the car. But Molly had barely started to drive when Colleen began to moan again.

"We're going straight to the hospital," Molly declared after Colleen stopped groaning.

"Yes," Colleen agreed breathlessly.

"We should be there in less than ten minutes," Molly assured her. "I'll try to drive fast since there's not much traffic, but I want to be careful." Eight minutes and another contraction made it feel like an hour had passed when Molly finally pulled up to the hospital entrance. An orderly appeared to ease Colleen into a wheelchair. Molly helped her to get registered, and they called her doctor. As Colleen was taken to the maternity ward, Molly parked the car and used the pay telephone to call home. Not surprisingly, no one answered. Although she hadn't spotted them there, she felt certain her family was sitting in their favorite pew in Old Saint Mary's. Hopefully Mrs. O'Neil wouldn't wait until Mass ended to let them know.

As she went to the waiting area, Molly wasn't overly worried about Colleen's wellbeing. She knew her sister was in good hands, but she wished she could be with her. It seemed strange for a woman to be cut off from her loved ones at such a time, but that was how things were done. Molly grew increasingly nervous as she paced back and forth in the smoky waiting room. She wished her family were here with her. More than that, she wished Geoff was here. She had his contact information in her purse and would send him a telegram after the baby came, but it seemed wrong that he should be so far away right now.

He'd written to Colleen about his hopes to get his leave in late August, but he'd also mentioned how things were "really heating up in the South Pacific," making it hard to promise anything. Patrick had hinted at the same thing, but as usual, with no specifics. There hadn't been much about the Pacific battlefront in the news lately, but that was probably because all eyes were on Europe right now. But as troops got closer to German soil, it would probably put even more pressure on the Pacific. Some optimistic news sources were predicting the war could be over by early next year. Molly desperately hoped they were right. But right now only one prayer was on her mind—that Colleen and baby would be just fine.

The last thing Colleen could remember was being in extreme pain while being wheeled into the delivery room. Her doctor had been telling her to take deep breaths, assuring her that it wouldn't be long . . . and then nothing. But as she groggily opened her eyes, she could see she'd been moved again. Now she was in private hospital room and Molly, Margaret, and Mam were looking down on her with sweet expectant smiles.

"Congratulations, dear," Mam said happily. "Your daughter is lovely."

"My daughter?" Colleen reached down to her stomach, disappointed to discover it still quite large. "Are you saying I already had my baby?"

"Yes, silly." Margaret laughed. "Don't you remember any of it?"

"No." Colleen shook her head.

"She's seven pounds and eight ounces," Molly proclaimed. "With a good set of lungs too."

"And she's precious." Margaret set a bouquet of pink roses on the bedside table.

"I sent a wire to Geoff," Molly told her. "And to Bridget and Patrick too."

"Thank you." Colleen still felt confused.

"Is the mother ready to meet her little angel?" a nurse called from the doorway.

"Yes, please," Colleen eagerly answered.

"Then we'll need your visitors to leave for a bit." The nurse waited for the women to exit, explaining that they could get sanitary gowns at the nurses' station if they wanted to come back and hold the baby. Then she wheeled in the bassinette and scooped out a tiny pink bundle. "Here you go, Mommy." She set the baby in Colleen's arms.

Colleen stared at the wrinkly, red, and blotchy face with dumbfounded wonder. Was this really her child? The infant had a few wisps of fuzzy pale hair and clear blue eyes, but she was not nearly as beautiful as Margaret's baby had been. Colleen didn't like to be so superficial, but the truth was she felt slightly disappointed. Shouldn't her baby be prettier than this?

Her sisters and mother, now robed in white gowns, returned to the room and were soon taking turns holding the newborn. They cooed and made the usual positive comments, but Colleen felt increasingly worried. Could they not see how unattractive the baby was? Didn't they feel any concerns? Or were they simply being polite?

"How do I know this is really my baby?" she finally asked Mam. "I never saw her being born—and she doesn't look anything like I expected. What if this is the wrong baby? How would I know?"

Mam just laughed. "Oh, Colleen. You can't be serious."

"I am," Colleen insisted. "How do I know for sure she's mine?"

"Why, she looks just like you did as an infant," Mam declared. "If you like, I'll bring some baby photos the next time I visit to prove it."

"You really think she looks like me?" Colleen frowned.

"Like when you were a newborn," Mam clarified. "Most babies enter this world looking a little worse for wear . . . at first, anyway. My Peter was born with a black eye and crooked nose, but he looked better in a week or so. Your baby won't be red and wrinkly for long. She'll smooth out."

Colleen pointed to her midsection. "I suppose this will smooth out too?"

Margaret smiled. "That's perfectly normal, Colleen. And since you didn't have a caesarian section like I did, you'll probably slim down much more quickly too. Be thankful for that."

"I think your baby is just lovely," Molly told

her. “Look at these delicate fingers and tiny nails. She’s just perfect, Colleen.”

“What are you going to call her?” Margaret asked.

Colleen felt uncertain. “If it was a boy, I wanted to name him after Geoff. And Geoff wanted to call her Maureen if she was a girl. But I wasn’t so sure and Geoff said he’d leave it up to me. But I wanted to see her first.”

Molly brought the baby over to Colleen. “Does she look like a Maureen?”

“To be honest, she looks like a little old man,” Colleen declared. “Maybe I should call her Maurice.” They all laughed.

“Give her time,” Mam said. “In a week, she will be beautiful. Trust me, Colleen.”

“So what is her name?” Margaret pressed.

“I’d been thinking I’d like to name her after our moms,” Colleen told them. *“Mary Ellen.”*

“Oh, that’s nice,” Molly said. “Mary Ellen Conrad. I like it.”

“Will Geoff like it?” Mam asked.

“I’m sure he will.” Colleen slapped her forehead. “And that reminds me—Molly, did you call Geoff’s family?”

“I did, but no one was home.”

“They were probably at church.”

“I’ll go try again. Right now.” Molly handed Colleen her baby then hurried out.

“Mary Ellen,” Colleen tried out the name on

her infant then nodded to Margaret. "The Mary is for you too."

Margaret's face lit up. "Really?"

"Of course, Auntie Mary Margaret."

"I can't wait for Peter to meet his new cousin," Margaret said. "But the hospital doesn't allow children to visit."

"As soon as I get home, you can bring him over." Colleen touched the tiny nose. At least it wasn't bent. "Where is young Peter?"

"With his dad." Margaret sighed. "Brian heads to college next week. He's trying to get in as much daddy time as possible before he goes."

"Speaking of dads, where is ours?" Colleen looked around.

"Dad was feeling a little worn out this morning. I was surprised he wanted to go to Mass," Mam explained. "After Mrs. O'Neil told us your news, we dropped Dad at home, and I told him to take a nap. We'll bring him by later this afternoon to meet his new granddaughter."

Colleen peered down at the baby again. She was still not quite convinced that this wrinkly red face belonged to her, but she was not going to voice it again. Hopefully Mam was right—that the baby would look better in a few days. But Colleen doubted that Mary Ellen would ever be truly pretty. Colleen also doubted that she'd ever get her figure back. As she imagined her Hollywood career going up in smoke, she could feel her eyes misting up then she started to cry.

"Don't worry, Colleen, it's quite normal to feel emotional after giving birth." Margaret passed the box of tissues. "I used to cry all the time."

Mam patted Colleen's shoulder. "I'm sure they're just tears of joy, dear."

Colleen was not so sure, but she didn't intend to admit it.

Twelve

Margaret had mixed emotions as she drove to the train station. "Are you excited to see Daddy get on the big choo-choo train?" she asked Peter. He sat quietly beside her in the passenger seat, looking surprisingly grown up in his little blue suit and matching cap.

"Can I go on choo-choo?" he asked.

"I think so," she told him. "I'll try to take you aboard, if they let us. And we might even get to hear a choo-choo whistle."

"Woo-woo!" He imitated a train whistle. "Daddy?"

"He's with Grandma and Grandpa Hammond at the train station."

"And Grammy and Grandad too?"

"No, they already told Daddy good-bye. Grammy is at the store. And Grandad is home."

"Resting."

"Yes, resting." Margaret felt bad for how often she told Peter this. *Grandad is resting* was the same as saying *be quiet* in her parents' house. She felt sorry for Peter, but there didn't seem any way around it.

Margaret had dressed carefully for this farewell party. She wasn't sure it would make any difference, but Colleen had planned her outfit—a sleek turquoise suit with big black buttons and a black broad-brimmed hat, along with Margaret's slightly worn black pumps and the seams that Molly had meticulously drawn onto the back of Margaret's calves as an imitation of fine silk stockings.

As Margaret and Peter walked out to the train platform, she wondered why she'd even bothered. She couldn't remember the last time Brian had given her a real second look. Perhaps it had been at Colleen's wedding—and that seemed a lifetime ago.

"There's Daddy!" Peter exclaimed, breaking free from her hand and running toward his father. Brian looked handsome in a dark brown suit. Although he had a cane, no one would guess by looking at him that half of his left leg was missing. She felt certain that his time on campus wouldn't be anything like the grim predictions he'd conjured up while making excuses last spring. In fact, he looked so handsome that she suspected he'd be quite sought after by the young college coeds—thanks too to the shortage of men in general. It wouldn't hurt that he was in his final year of law school or an injured vet.

Margaret had never felt more hopeless and worthless as she stood by Brian's parents, watching from the sidelines as Brian took their son aboard the train. Mr. and Mrs. Hammond said little to her, making her feel as if she were the one to blame for their son's problems. A part of her wanted to shout out to them—and the world—that it was Brian's fault and that he'd been the one to betray her and break his wedding vows. Yet she remained silent, stewing, waiting for Brian to return with their son.

Then he delivered Peter back to her, took his briefcase from his father, and said a crisp good-bye. And as he walked back to the train, with just the slightest limp, he looked, for the most part, fine and fit. Margaret no longer felt the slightest twinge of pity for him.

"Wave good-bye to Daddy," she told Peter as the train let out a low whistle and slowly chugged out of the station.

"You wave too, Mommy," he told her.

She barely lifted her hand, fluttering her fingers so slightly as to appear to be swatting a pesky insect, and then she turned away. "Time to go," she chirped to Peter. "How about ice cream?"

Naturally he let out a happy squeal. Without even telling the Hammonds good-bye, she hurried away. Maybe this really was the end of an era. If so, why did she care? And why did she feel like sobbing?

Colleen had only been home from the hospital for a few days and was still struggling with the responsibility of being a new mother. Although

Molly was surprisingly helpful. At the last minute, her younger sister had decided not to take classes for fall term. Colleen hadn't been sure that was the right decision, but Molly insisted. "I'm already younger than my classmates," Molly reminded her. "I could take the whole year off and still be the same age as my peers in my sophomore year. And I'm still learning so much working with Simon Bernard. I don't want to give that up."

But Molly took time off from the photography studio to be with Colleen and the baby for the first week and a half. After that, Margaret and Mam and even Mrs. Bartley were on hand to help out as needed. But Molly still stayed with Colleen at night, and she seemed to enjoy helping with the baby. Molly's experience with Peter must've taught her a lot about caring for infants, because she was a natural. Colleen trusted her little sister and had even taken her advice that, despite the recent trend of bottle-feeding, it was highly beneficial to both mother and child to nurse the baby.

"For at least six weeks," Molly had declared before Mary Ellen was even born. She'd also informed Colleen that, according to the motherhood book which she'd nearly memorized, nursing an infant was surefire wire to lose unwanted baby weight. Well, that alone was motivation for Colleen. She was willing to do most anything to get back into her pre-baby clothes.

Colleen felt embarrassed for her recent return to such shallowness. Although she wouldn't admit it aloud, she blamed her superficiality on nine months of losing her figure. To make matters worse, her desire to return to the screen seemed to have grown along with her waistline. And the whole thing just made her feel guilty. Even her recent letters to Geoff, which she'd always tried to keep scrupulously honest, didn't contain her genuine feelings on the subject. A part of her wanted to be the perfect picture of motherhood, but another part simply wanted to be young and unencumbered again. These were the thoughts she kept to herself.

"A telegram for you," Molly announced as she came into the apartment after working at the photography studio. She attempted a smile, but her eyes betrayed her. No one liked getting telegrams these days.

"Let me have it." As Colleen reached for it, a chill ran through her. Hopefully this was from Geoff. His late-August leave had been cancelled, and she'd been waiting to hear from him. She nervously opened then read the telegram. "He's coming home!" she exclaimed. "He'll be in San Diego by next Sunday, Molly. Can you believe it?"

"That's wonderful." Molly picked up Mary

Ellen from her cradle, cooing to her. "Does he say how long he can stay?"

"He says he's got ten days!" Colleen cried. "Unless something happens. You know how that goes. He could get called back at a moment's notice. He wants to know if I can meet him in San Diego on Sunday morning."

Molly looked concerned. "He wants you to go down to San Diego? That's kind of a long ways to go . . . I mean, so soon and with a newborn baby. Why doesn't he come up here so he could see his parents too."

"Yes, but then we wouldn't have as much time together. And I'll bet he wants to be near the base in case he gets called back. And it would be so sweet to spend time at the beach with him."

"But it's so soon." Molly frowned doubtfully. "Mary Ellen is so young."

"But she'll be three weeks old by then. Surely that's old enough for a short trip like that. Don't you think?"

"Maybe you should ask the doctor."

"She has a well-baby check next Wednesday. I'll ask him then." Colleen peered down at her baby and smiled. "Oh, sweet baby girl, do you want to meet your daddy?"

"I'll bet Geoff can't wait to see this little darling."

"And she has gotten so much better looking,"

Colleen said. “Mam was right. She does look like my baby pictures.”

“She’ll grow up to be a beauty too,” Molly assured her. “But hopefully she’ll have more than just good looks. We want her to have brains and goodness and other strengths, don’t we?” Molly said in a singsong voice as she danced around with the baby in her arms.

“I wish you could come with me to San Diego, Molly.” Colleen sighed wistfully as she sat down. “You’re so good with Mary Ellen. You could play nanny and give Geoff and me some time to—”

“I would love to go with you,” Molly eagerly declared. She handed the baby to Colleen and started to remove her hat and gloves.

“Really?” Colleen was surprised. “What about your job?”

“I actually think Simon could spare me. I’ve been working really hard to catch up on what didn’t get done last week and, with summer weddings behind us, he’s not nearly as busy as before. Just today he said the Christmas rush—families wanting portraits— wouldn’t start until mid-October.” Molly frowned. “But would you really want me there? You and Geoff and the baby may want to be alone, without—”

“But, Molly, if you don’t come, I’d hire a stranger to be the nanny. I’d much rather have you. I would pay you, and I wouldn’t expect you to do everything or watch Mary Ellen all the time."

"Is your beach house big enough?"

"It has a spare room. If you didn't mind, you and Mary Ellen could share it."

"I'd love it." Molly filled a glass with water then sat down. "Being in San Diego would feel almost like a vacation."

"Then it's settled. If you can get off work, you're going with me."

It was Molly's night to write to Patrick and, although she hadn't heard from him for almost a month, she still diligently wrote to him once a week. By now she knew it wasn't unusual to have these long stretches of silence. Just when she started to feel seriously concerned about not hearing from him, a small stack of V-mail would arrive. She would sort them by date and slowly read them—then read them again during the next few weeks while waiting to hear from him. She knew he did the same thing with her letters. They called it "feast or famine," but it was the result of serving under the ocean in a submarine.

Like her past couple letters, Molly wrote a lot about Mary Ellen, telling him of Colleen's invitation to play nanny in San Diego. She also told him about her job and how much she was learning about photography. She even told him about going to some USO dances with her boss's niece and how Lulu had met Tommy and then become a regular at the USO club. She didn't mention how Lulu constantly begged Molly to go there with her. But Molly had successfully used her newborn niece as an excuse to decline, and since Lulu had such high esteem for Colleen, she didn't protest.

As Molly sealed her envelope, she could hear Colleen singing a lullaby in the baby's room, probably putting Mary Ellen to bed. The baby had been nearly sleeping through the night, which Margaret claimed was highly unusual. "Don't expect her to keep doing it," she'd warned. "Peter didn't sleep through the night until he was eighteen months." But one thing that Molly knew about babies and mothers—they were all different. And to her surprise and relief, Colleen was doing a pretty good job of being a mother. Oh, Molly sometimes suspected that her glamorous sister's heart wasn't fully into motherhood and that Colleen probably still dreamed of Hollywood at times, but it seemed she was giving it her best effort. And Molly respected her for it.

"I'm so excited about seeing Geoff," Colleen said as she joined Molly in the living room area. "Except for one thing."

"What's that?" Molly looked up from her letter.

"I won't be able to fit into any of my good clothes." Colleen frowned.

"Oh, you must have something you can squeeze into." Molly studied her. "And you certainly appear to have gotten your figure back." She smiled. "I think you look fabulous."

"Thank you. You're sweet." Colleen struck a model-like pose, holding one arm in the air like a pinup girl. "I'm definitely curvier than before."

"Maybe we can let some things out," Molly suggested. "Or maybe you can do some shopping. I wouldn't think you'd need much. I mean, since you'll be at the beach a lot."

"Well, I've got almost a week to figure it out. And I haven't tried squeezing into a girdle yet." Colleen patted her middle. "I know I probably seem vain, but I do want to look good for Geoff. I'd like to meet him at the pier wearing something stylish and chic."

"Oh, Colleen, you could be wearing a gunny-sack and I'm pretty sure you'd look good to Geoff." She slid her letter into the envelope.

Colleen laughed. "You could be right. Just the same, I want to try on some clothes and estimate the damage. Maybe you can give me a hand with the alterations."

"I'm happy to."

"And anything that's just completely hopeless will go to you, my lucky little sister."

"Now I'm *really* happy to help." Molly sealed her envelope then followed Colleen into her bedroom, where they started pulling garments out of the closet and sorting them into two separate heaps—the *maybe* pile and the *hopeless* pile. To Molly's delight, the hopeless pile was growing faster than the maybe pile. Of course, Molly didn't really have any place special to wear these beautiful things or anyone special here to wear them for, but it was fun to dream. Maybe someday.

Thirteen

Simon Bernard agreed to let Molly have the time off, warning her that she would be busier than ever when she returned in October, but she assured him that was no problem and that she loved being busy. In the meantime, she worked extra hard to get all the latest negatives developed and everything into tiptop shape. Even Lulu was supportive of Molly's plans, promising to do her best to keep things organized for Molly's return. It was amazing how much Lulu had changed in the past few months. Unless Molly was mistaken, Lulu and Tommy would be engaged before too long. She hoped so.

Every evening after the baby went to bed, Molly and Colleen made alterations and adjustments to Colleen's wardrobe. By the end of the week, Colleen was not nearly so worried about her post-pregnancy appearance. And on Friday evening, Colleen invited Margaret over for a farewell dinner of Chinese food. The three sisters enjoyed a festive evening then Margaret stuck around to help them pack.

"I know it seems terribly shallow to be so concerned about making a good impression." Colleen carefully laid a black satin dress in her suitcase. "But my agent informed me that there will be photographers on hand to get publicity photos of me meeting Geoff at the naval base. I plan to wear my pale blue suit for that, and Mary Ellen will be in pink."

"I'm so jealous." Margaret handed Colleen a striped sundress. "I wish I could go too. I absolutely love your beach house. I had such a good time there. You know, when I went with Brian. . . ." Her words dwindled at the end, barely audible.

Molly felt guilty—again. But she'd already asked Colleen if Margaret should go and play nanny. Colleen had instantly nixed the idea, pointing out that would mean Peter would have to come as well. "That's too much for my little beach house," she'd confided. And when Molly had pointed out she could watch Peter here at home, Colleen had soundly put her foot down. "I want *you* with me, Molly Irene. Understand?"

"So, Margaret, are you planning Peter's birthday party?" Molly asked cheerfully, hoping to bolster her spirits.

"Not yet. It's still a ways out."

"Well, don't forget my offer to use my rooms at Mrs. Bartley's. You may need a break from Mam and Dad some evening," Molly reminded Margaret. "I told her I was giving you my key." She handed Colleen an aqua cashmere sweater set. "I wish Peter could stay there too, but I know how noise bothers Mrs. Bartley. And I really don't think she's been feeling too well lately."

"I hope it's not too much for her to work at the store." Margaret tucked a small stack of folded handkerchiefs in a corner of the suitcase.

"She says she loves it, and it's the highlight—" Molly stopped at the sound of the phone ringing. "I'll get it." She ran out to answer, surprised to hear Mrs. Bartley on the other end.

"Molly, I'm sorry to bother you." Her voice sounded slightly stressed.

"Are you okay?"

"Yes, yes. But a telegram was just delivered. For you."

"Oh?" Molly felt her chest tighten.

"And I knew you and Colleen planned to leave early tomorrow morning."

"Please, can you just open it and read it to me," Molly said suddenly.

"Yes, of course. Give me a moment to get my glasses."

Molly's heart pounded as she heard the receiver set down and some rustling sounds. The only one who used Mrs. Bartley's address to communicate with Molly was Patrick. Everyone else wrote to Molly at her parents' address. What was in this telegram?

"I'm back." Mrs. Bartley cleared her throat and proceeded to read. "Dear Molly—stop. Got your letter—stop. I'm in Honolulu—stop. U-boat in for repairs—stop. Have leave—stop. Will arrive San Diego Friday—stop. Meet me there—stop. Love, Patrick—stop."

Molly let out a happy shriek. "Sorry, Mrs. Bartley," she said quickly. "I hope that didn't hurt your ears."

But Mrs. Bartley was laughing. "No, dear, that was music to my ears. Give your young man a big hug for me, Molly. I'm so happy for you."

Molly thanked her and disconnected. Trying not to make too much noise since Mary Ellen was asleep, she hurried in to share the good news with her sisters.

"You'll have to repack your bags," Colleen told her.

"Why?" Margaret asked.

"Because she only packed nanny clothes."

"And beach clothes," Molly clarified. "I'll be fine."

"No, you will not. You didn't pack anything pretty or special," Colleen reminded her. "And Patrick will want to take you out. You'll need an evening dress and perhaps a stylish suit for a daytime date and—"

"You're probably right. My nicest clothes—the ones you gave me—are in my closet at Mrs. Bartley's."

Colleen handed her the car keys. "Go get them right now. And you better stop by the telegraph office first. Be sure to send Patrick the phone number of the beach house."

The drive to San Diego was more taxing than Colleen had expected. Besides being unseasonably warm for September, traveling with a baby came with a whole new set of challenges. Without Molly's help, Colleen would've given up midway through the trip. They took turns driving, diapering, and soothing the baby, but when it came to feeding time, Colleen was on her own. By the time they reached San Diego, the car looked and smelled like a junkyard. And so did Colleen. Besides being a hot, sticky mess, she was exhausted. "I'm glad that's over." She unlocked the door to the beach house.

"Here." Molly handed her the baby. "I'll go unload the car."

"And I'll open this place up." With Mary Ellen cradled in one arm, Colleen went around opening up all the windows, letting the clean sea breeze inside.

"This place is so beautiful!" Molly set their bags inside the door.

"It is nice, isn't it?" Colleen gazed out the window toward the beach.

"I'm surprised you don't want to live here."

"I would love to live here . . . if it was closer to my family." Colleen pushed a damp strand of hair from her forehead, jostling the baby, who was fussing again.

"Sounds like she's hungry," Molly pointed out. "Go ahead and feed her while I unpack your bags."

Colleen sat down in a chair that looked out toward the ocean. Although the view was undeniably gorgeous, she still felt like something the cat had dragged in, and Mary Ellen's diaper needed changing again. What a sight they would be for Geoff right now. She wouldn't blame him if he took off running in the opposite direction. War might be preferable to this.

Colleen was just burping Mary Ellen when Molly emerged from the bedroom. "I hope I can get her back on her eating schedule." Colleen felt something warm soaking into her blouse. "Oh, great. She spit up."

"Let me take her." Molly held out her arms then wrinkled her nose. "Smells like someone needs to freshen up."

"Me or her?" Colleen teased.

"Both of you. I'll clean up the princess. Meanwhile, you go have a bath. I already started it for you. And then I must insist you take a nap."

"But you must be tired too."

Molly held up a hand. "I'm fine. And remember, I'm here to help you. And you need to look pretty and refreshed for Geoff tomorrow." She winked. "And for the photographers too."

"Fine. You'll get no argument from me." Colleen sighed. "Bless you." She went into her bedroom to see that Molly hadn't only unpacked, she'd turned down the bed and put out fresh towels, hung a bathrobe on the bathroom door, and had even put lavender scented bath oil in the tub. As Colleen sank into the warm water, she felt the life coming back into her. This was heavenly.

She felt almost completely refreshed when she emerged from her bath. Wearing her terry bathrobe and her hair wrapped in a towel, she wandered through the house to see that all was quiet and peaceful now. Even the bad smell was gone. Molly's bags and all of Mary Ellen's things had been moved to the spare room, which still looked a little chaotic, but Molly, now wearing shorts and a sleeveless shirt, with Mary Ellen in her arms, was outside strolling down the beach, looking completely at home. That girl was going to make a great mother . . . someday.

Colleen got a glass of water and then, remembering Molly's instructions, decided a little nap was probably a good idea. As she lay down, she couldn't have been more grateful for her little sister. And she intended to show her appreciation to her. When Patrick arrived in San Diego next week, Colleen would encourage Molly to spend as much time with him as she liked.

She just hoped they wouldn't do anything crazy like get married. Although it wouldn't be terribly surprising if they did. It seemed like most servicemen were eager to get married these days. And Colleen remembered when Molly had declared that she'd gladly marry Patrick whenever and wherever he wanted. But Colleen knew that both sets of families would be disappointed to miss out on such a happy occasion. However, Colleen also knew that she wouldn't stand in their way. If they wanted to tie the knot here in San Diego, she would not discourage them. Even if it meant losing her precious nanny.

Molly was relieved to see that Colleen not only looked refreshed the next day, she looked gorgeous and glamorous. "Are you ready?" she asked as Colleen pulled on a pair of short white gloves.

"I feel so nervous, as if this were a first date." Colleen checked her image in the mirror, adjusting her wide brimmed white hat again.

"You look beautiful." Molly handed her Mary Ellen, a small bundle of pink and lace. "You both do."

"You look nice too."

Molly looked down at her gray skirt and jacket, one that she'd inherited from Colleen a couple years ago. "It seemed serviceable nanny-wear." Molly looped a strap of the diaper bag over her shoulder. "How about if I drive?"

"Thanks, that'd be lovely."

Colleen gave Molly directions to the airfield where Geoff had asked her to meet him. "The aircraft carrier is still at sea," she explained. "Geoff is flying in. Apparently to exchange his plane for a new and improved model."

"Do you ever wonder if he could be flying one of the planes you helped build?"

"Well, I was always meticulous at my job, so I'd be glad if his plane had one of my instrument panels in it, but I worked at Lockheed. And Geoff's plane was made by Boeing in Seattle. I assume this next one will be too."

Before long, a naval officer was leading them to the area where Geoff's plane would land. While Molly carried Mary Ellen, the officer chatted pleasantly with Colleen, treating her like royalty. Molly felt pretty certain that not everyone got that kind of attention. Just one of the perks of being a film star—and Colleen appeared to be enjoying it. Meanwhile, Molly was enjoying watching planes taking off and landing and hoping that the noise wasn't too disturbing to the baby.

"The press is already here," the officer informed Colleen. "We asked them to set up over there." He pointed to a nearby cordoned-off area. "They can get their photos without being overly intrusive. We do like good publicity, but we also want to respect your privacy." He nodded to a bench. "Make yourselves comfortable." He checked his watch. “He should arrive in about ten minutes now.”

“I brought my camera too,” Molly told Colleen as they sat down. “It’s in here.” She patted the diaper bag. “If you don’t mind, I’d like to get some pictures to share with Mam and Dad.”

“That’d be great.” Colleen reached for the baby. “I’ll take Mary Ellen now.”

Molly pulled out her camera, getting it all set up for the big moment when Geoff arrived. She wanted to get him coming out of his plane, when he and Colleen embraced, and when he saw his daughter for the first time. By now she knew that the only way to get good action shots was to take plenty of them. And she was ready with a full roll of film. “Smile,” she told Colleen as she snapped a shot of her and Mary Ellen.

“That’s him.” The officer pointed to a plane just starting to descend.

“This is so exciting.” Colleen stood, anxiously watching as he landed.

Molly got a shot of his plane as it taxied toward them and another of him hopping out and sprinting their way. When he got there, he tossed down a duffle bag to hug Colleen and the baby. Then he leaned down to really get a good look at Mary Ellen, shaking his head in wonder. “She’s perfect,” he told Colleen. “Nice work.” He gently kissed them both. Molly’s eyes got a little misty at the tender scene, making it tricky to see clearly through the lens, but she continued snapping shots of the little family's reunion. The press members were busily getting their shots too, and it appeared that one of them was filming with a movie camera. Perhaps it would become a newsreel.

"Molly!" Geoff exclaimed. "I almost didn't recognize you." He hugged her. "You look all grown up."

She laughed as she slid her camera back in the diaper bag. "I'm the nanny." She turned to Colleen with open arms. "How about if I take Mary Ellen now?"

"Yes!" Colleen exclaimed. "Then I can get a real kiss."

Molly watched as the photographers continued snapping shots and rolling film, even stepping past the cordon to get better angles. Of course they wanted to capitalize on what Molly felt should've been a private moment. They were just doing their job, but Molly suddenly felt irritated by it and, wanting to protect Mary Ellen, turned her back to the press. As a fledgling photographer who hoped to someday be a photojournalist, Molly realized she might need to be that bold someday. But she hoped she never became overly intrusive or obnoxious or rude. If that was what it took to succeed at this business, she might have to take her photography in a different direction.

Fourteen

Colleen's next several days with Geoff felt truly magical. "I feel like we're starring in our own movie," she told him as they lay on the beach after a nice midday swim. "I don't want it to ever end."

He rolled over to look into her face. "Interesting that you should mention that, sweetheart."

"What do you mean?"

"You heard the phone ringing, didn't you?" He ran his finger down her cheek. "Just before we came out here and raced to the water—"

"And I let you win," she teased. She sat up, peering curiously at him. "Who was on the phone? I assumed it was Patrick, calling for Molly. He's supposed to get here today."

"It was my CO."

"And . . . ?" Colleen braced herself for bad news.

"I have to report back tomorrow."

"They're cutting your leave short?"

"I don't like it any more than you do, sweetie." He dusted some sand from the tip of her nose. "But the new planes are ready and our carrier is needed and . . ." He sighed. "We have to go back."

She jutted out her lower lip—and he kissed it. "Well, then we'll have to go out tonight," she declared. "We'll dress to the nines and paint the town red. We'll dance all night and—"

"What if we just stayed in?" he suggested.

"Really?" She frowned. "You don't want to go out?"

"I'd much rather have a quiet evening with you and Mary Ellen. And don't forget that Molly will want to go out with Patrick tonight."

"That's right." She tipped her head to one side. "But are you sure you want to stay home, Geoff? On your last night here? I could hire a baby-sitter and—"

"I *want* to stay home, Colleen. More than anything. I just want a relaxing evening with my two favorite girls. I'll make a run to the store. Get some steaks and a bottle of wine. We'll sit and watch the sunset together, and I'll gather some driftwood for a fire in the fireplace."

She nodded. "Sounds great."

He looked out over the ocean. "I love it here. And I want to think of this place as home, Colleen. When I'm out there flying round with Japs on my tail, I want to remember this place. And when the war ends, I want to live here."

"Not in San Francisco? Near our families?"

"Not at first . . . Maybe we'll want to move up there later. But a year or two here, with my sweet girls . . . well, it's something to look forward to.

Would you like to live here? Would it be too hard to be away from your family?"

"You're my family, Geoff. You and Mary Ellen."

He kissed her. "That's my girl."

She pushed back his hair, still damp from their swim, and wondered if this was the moment she'd been waiting for, to bring up something that was troubling her. "And what would you think, Geoff, if we were living down here and I wanted to continue my film career? Would you be okay with that?"

His brow creased and he pursed his lips.

"I'm not saying that's what I want to do, but Georgina has been encouraging me to come back. My last movie was a pretty good success—for a B movie anyway. I could probably get a pretty good contract."

"Is that what you really want to do?" He frowned. "And what about Mary Ellen? Would that be fair to her?"

"I'd get someone to help me," she said quickly. "Like Molly. You've seen how great she is with the baby."

He seemed to consider this. "Well, like I've always said, I want you to be happy, Colleen. You were an independent gal when we met, and I never wanted to change that."

"It's not something I'd want to do right away," she assured him. "And I wouldn't take just any movie. For all I know, it may not even work out." She sighed. "They may decide they don't want me now that I've had a baby. I know I don't look the same and my figure has—"

"You silly girl! Like I keep telling you, Colleen, you've never been more beautiful." He laughed. "Of course they will want you. They'd be fools not to."

"But you'd really be okay with it? Your wife, the mother of your child, back on the big screen? You wouldn't mind?"

His smile was crooked. "I gotta admit that my movie star wife gets me teased at times. But it also gets me a little more respect. And I'd be lying if I said I didn't enjoy bragging you up to the guys."

Colleen hugged him. "Have I told you lately how much I love you, Geoff Conrad?"

Molly couldn't remember when she'd felt this nervous—or excited. Patrick had just called, telling her he'd just gotten into San Diego and planned to pick her up at six. "Is that too soon for you?" he'd asked. Of course, she'd assured him it wasn't, but now it was time to get dressed.

"What do I wear?" she asked Colleen. "Patrick said he made reservations at Giordano's, but I don't even know—"

"That's just the fanciest dinner club in San Diego," Colleen told her. "Geoff and I were there on Wednesday. The food is fabulous and the music is great. You'll have a great time." She opened the spare-room closet and pulled out the turquoise blue satin cocktail dress that she'd recently given to Molly. "You'll wear this. With your pearls. And your tan will look gorgeous with the off-the-shoulder cut. And if Geoff can mind the baby, I'll help you with your hair and makeup."

They grabbed a few things then Colleen led Molly to her bedroom and went to work. Molly wasn't sure what the outcome would be, but too nervous to argue and with no time to spare, she surrendered. "But remember I like a light touch when—"

"I know, I know. Easy on the makeup." Colleen started brushing out Molly's ponytail. "We don't have much time to transform you."

Less than forty minutes later, Colleen was putting the finishing touches on Molly's hair. "This is like a real Cinderella story. You went from a frowzy nanny to a sparkling princess."

"Hey, ladies," Geoff called, "Patrick's here."

"She's almost ready," Colleen called back.

"Should I tell him to send the taxi away? Let him use the car?"

"Yes, of course." Colleen turned Molly toward the mirror. "Voilà."

Molly blinked. "Wow."

"Not too much?"

"It's perfect, Colleen." Molly stared in wonder. Was that really her?

"Your prince is waiting."

Molly took a deep breath then slowly walked out from the bedroom. Patrick was standing tall and handsome in his dress uniform, but it was the expression on his face that took her breath away. *"Molly,"* he said with slow intensity. "You're truly a sight for sore eyes."

She rushed toward him, practically falling into his arms. "So are you, Patrick!"

After a nice embrace, Colleen interrupted them. "You two better get going unless you want to lose your reservation."

"But first, you need to smile for the camera," Geoff said. Molly and Patrick turned to see Geoff, who aimed Molly's camera at them. "Say cheese, kids."

They posed for a couple of shots then hurried out to the car. "I can't believe this," Patrick said as he started the engine. "It's like a dream come true."

"I know." She resisted the urge to pinch herself.

"A few days ago I was under the sea with a bunch of smelly sailors." He chuckled. "Nice guys, but it does get a little rank down there."

"And I was playing nanny," Molly told him. "But here we are."

"It's so good to see you, Molly. Words can't even describe it. I was so shocked to get your letter in Hawaii—finding out we'd be in San Diego at the same time. Like a miracle."

"How long is your leave?"

He frowned. "Unfortunately, it's not very long. I have to go back on Monday."

"Oh." She sighed. "Well, let's just make the most of it while you're here."

"Geoff said his leave got cut short too."

"I hadn't heard that."

"He just got called back. Has to check in tomorrow morning."

Molly felt guilty. "So this is their last night together."

"Geoff said he was really looking forward to a quiet night at home."

"Oh, good." She nodded.

"He encouraged me to stay out late." Patrick chuckled.

Molly wanted to say that was fine with her but wasn't sure that would sound quite right. Instead, she began telling him about their time in San Diego and how much she'd enjoyed helping with the baby. Then she asked him to tell her more about Hawaii, saying how she'd always wanted to go there.

They continued talking and catching up throughout the evening, so comfortable with each other that it almost seemed like they'd never been apart. And when they danced, Molly felt like she was being swept away . . . floating off on a warm and wonderful wave. The restaurant overlooked the ocean, and Patrick led her outside, kissing her in the moonlight. Everything about their evening felt magical, and Molly wished it would never end. But finally, the band announced it was the last number of the evening and Patrick and Molly realized they were the only ones left on the dance floor.

"I guess we closed the place down," Patrick said as he drove along the beach road. "Geoff will be pleased."

"I can't believe it's two A.M." Molly sighed as she leaned back in the passenger seat. "I don't remember ever having such a wonderful evening. Thanks, Patrick. Everything was absolutely perfect. The food, the band . . . but mostly the company."

"I agree. It was perfect."

Neither of them spoke for a while as he drove, but it was a companionable silence. No need to fill up every moment with idle chatter.

"I feel bad for keeping you out so late." He chuckled as he parked in front of the house. "But only because I wanted a full day with you tomorrow."

"That's fine with me."

"So how soon do you think you'll be up?"

She smiled. "Well, Mary Ellen usually wakes up with the sun—and since we're roommates, I do too."

"Geoff told me to keep the car overnight and to come back by eight o'clock to take him back to the base. Think you'll be up by then?"

She assured him she'd be up, and then he walked her to the door. She pointed to an open window then whispered good night, and they exchanged a nice long kiss. Molly felt like she was floating as she tiptoed into the house, silently slipping into the bedroom where Mary Ellen was making quiet sleeping sounds, and it wasn't long before Molly joined her.

Morning came quickly but instead of feeling tired when Mary Ellen let out her first cries, Molly sprang out of bed. She'd just finished changing the baby's diaper when Colleen came in, groggily yawning. "Did you have a good night?" she asked as she picked up the baby. Molly followed her out to the living room, telling her all about it while Colleen fed Mary Ellen.

"Patrick told me that Geoff got called back." Molly frowned. "Sorry to hear that."

"Me too. But we had a really lovely evening." She nodded toward the bedroom. "He's sleeping in."

"Patrick only has until Monday morning, so he wanted me to spend today and tomorrow with him. Do you mind?"

"Not at all. You deserve some time off, Molly." Colleen burped Mary Ellen. "We'll be just fine without you for a couple of days." She sighed.

"Then, with our men gone, I suppose we might as well go home."

"Unless you want to stay down here longer," Molly offered. "I don't mind."

"Great." Colleen nodded eagerly. "Maybe I can use the extra time to check in with Georgina, in Hollywood. I mean, if you don't mind watching the baby for me."

Molly assured her that she was happy to play nanny then went to get dressed. She wasn't sure what Patrick had in mind for today, but for now she decided to keep it casual with clamdiggers, a sleeveless blouse, and sandals.

Patrick, dressed in his casual uniform, arrived with the car at a little before eight, and Colleen decided she wanted to drive Geoff back to the base.

"Would you mind staying with Mary Ellen?" she asked Molly.

"Not at all." Molly took the baby from Colleen then told Geoff good-bye. "I keep you in my prayers."

He thanked her then leaned down to kiss his baby. "Take good care of my girls, Molly." He pecked her on the cheek.

Molly grinned. "Count on it."

Patrick shook Geoff's hand and told him to stay safe, and then Geoff and Colleen were gone. "I keep that guy in my prayers too," Patrick told her. "Flyers have the toughest jobs."

"Your job sounds pretty tough to me."

"I guess it's all pretty tough." He nodded toward the beach. "How about taking that baby out for some morning sunshine."

They walked around in the surf for about an hour, taking turns holding the baby, before Molly noticed Colleen's car pulling up to the house. She knew Colleen would be feeling blue, but she also knew it was nearly feeding time for Mary Ellen. Hopefully the distraction would be good for her sister.

"What would you like to do today?" Molly asked Patrick after she'd handed over the baby.

"I thought we could see the sights, get some lunch, maybe take a swim in the ocean . . . I don't know." He looked down at her. "Mostly I just want to be with you, Molly. I don't really care what we do."

She smiled. "That suits me just fine."

For the next two days they spent every possible minute together. And by Sunday night, when they were walking on the moonlit beach after a perfectly lovely evening and Patrick invited Molly to sit down on a rock with him, she almost expected him to propose to her. Instead, he asked her about his brother. "Brian hasn't answered my letters lately," Patrick told her. "And when I asked Mom about him, she didn't say much. Well, except that Brian decided to finish his law degree down at USC."

"Yes, that's where he is right now. I was a little surprised he didn't choose a San Francisco school. I mean, I realize his loyalty to Gould, but—"

"But it seems like he'd want to be near his wife and child," Patrick finished for her.

She just nodded.

"I've been worried about him." He frowned. "I know something is wrong. I mean, besides the injury. I considered paying him a visit—but when I found out how short my leave was, well, I decided I'd rather spend it with you."

"Now I feel guilty."

"Don't." He leaned over to kiss her. "I've loved every minute."

"But I do understand your concern for Brian. I didn't want to write anything that may trouble you, but I've been worried too."

"What do you think is going on?"

She considered this, wondering how much she should say. But this was Patrick—why should she hold anything back? "I know that he and Margaret are having some troubles," she said slowly. "I'm not sure why . . . Margaret seemed to be trying really hard, at first, to help him. It was hard on her living at your parents' house. She hadn't wanted to give up her apartment over the store, but the stairs were too much for Brian. And then Brian just seemed to get more and more depressed. I'm sure it hasn't been easy for him to adjust to his disability. But then he seemed to perk up. He decided to go back to school. And he was acting more like his old self. We all started feeling like he'd turned a corner. But then something happened."

"What do you think it was?"

"I don't know for sure, but I suspect they got into a fight. Margaret and Peter are back home with our parents. She's been very unhappy too. She's never told me about it, although I suspect she told Colleen. Maybe because it's a marriage sort of thing." Molly felt her cheeks grow warm. She was getting in over her head.

"I'm sure Brian's injury must be a major part of the problem." Patrick rubbed his chin. "But I don't see why it should hurt their relationship. I always thought they really loved each other. That doesn't change just because a man loses part of his leg." He sighed. "At least I hope not."

"I suppose it could be Margaret's fault."

"What do you mean?"

"I'm not sure I should say anything, Patrick. Except that you're his brother and I know you care about them just as much as I do." And so she explained about Margaret's involvement with Howard Moore. "But don't misunderstand," she said quickly. "It wasn't anything more than a friendship. They took walks and shared meals. But it bothered me—it just felt wrong. Margaret and I got into a fight over it. She wouldn't speak to me for a while. But she, uh, she eventually figured things out and stopped seeing Howard."

"Wow." He shook his head. "I never would've expected that of Margaret."

"None of us did."

"Does that mean everyone knows about it?"

"Well, no. Not everyone. Colleen and I knew about it. And Mrs. Bartley."

"Do you think Brian found out?"

"I honestly don't know. But I suspect that could be what they'd fought over."

"I can understand how disturbing it would be to discover something like that. A guy wants to believe his girl is loyal. You hear stories of wives and girlfriends going to dances and running around while their men are risking their lives overseas, but you just don't want to think it'll happen to anyone close to you. Poor Brian. Now I feel sorry for not paying him a visit while I was here."

Molly suddenly felt defensive. She didn't like Patrick thinking so bad of Margaret. And she didn't like being the blame for him not going to visit his brother. But worst of all, there was something in his demeanor that made it feel like he thought *she* might be one of *those girls,* that she might betray him—just like her sister had almost done to his brother. Molly never made a secret of the fact she'd attended an occasional USO dance. She had never felt he minded. But was this how he showed his disapproval? Molly suddenly wished she hadn't confided to him about Margaret.

"It's pretty late," she said quietly. "And I know you're shipping out early tomorrow morning."

"Yes." He stood, reaching for her hand. "You're right."

They walked back to the house without speaking. With the windows opened, Molly could hear the baby crying inside, and Colleen shushing her. Patrick gave Molly one last kiss. But to her dismay, it seemed the magic was gone. It felt as though they'd had an argument, even though they hadn't really disagreed about anything—not in words.

They said an awkward good night then Molly slipped into the house and, grateful that Colleen had moved the baby into her bedroom, tiptoed to the spare room, crawled into bed, and cried herself to sleep.

Fifteen

"You've been awfully quiet," Colleen said to Molly. They were about halfway to San Francisco, and it was Molly's turn to drive.

"I'm sorry." Molly sighed. "I guess I don't have much to say."

"And I probably talked your ear off." Colleen chuckled. "But I'm just so happy. It was fun being back in Hollywood, staying at the Beverly Hills Hotel, having my agents making such a fuss over me, meeting with producers and directors. I know it probably sounds shallow, but I still love that kind of attention. Especially after feeling like my film career was over while I was pregnant. It suddenly feels like I've come back to life and everything is opening up for me."

"I'm really glad it went well for you." Molly wished she could inject more cheer into her tone but it just wasn't there. Maybe she was just tired.

"I wish you'd come with me to Hollywood, Molly. You would've enjoyed the hotel and being pampered. And the food. Oh, my."

"I think I made the right decision to stay at the beach house." Molly hadn't mentioned how difficult it had been the first day. "It was a bit of a challenge to get Mary Ellen adjusted to formula."

Colleen had no idea how much her baby had cried. How much Molly had cried. "I'm sure the guests at the hotel wouldn't have appreciated the noise."

Colleen laughed. "I'm sure you're right. I don't think I would've enjoyed hearing a baby crying either."

"Have you thought much about what you'll do with Mary Ellen if you decide to return to work?"

"I'd obviously need a full-time nanny. Naturally, you'd be my first choice, Molly. You're so good with Mary Ellen. That would be ideal. Please, tell me you'll do it."

Molly felt torn. As much as she loved Colleen and Mary Ellen, she wasn't sure that she wanted to put her life on hold. Already, she missed the darkroom at the photography studio—and even Lulu. And what about going back to school? Not that she'd decided she was ready for that. But one thing Molly knew for absolute certain—she didn't mind being an aunt, but she did not want a career as a nanny, thank you very much.

"There's a possibility that they'll start filming this next project as soon as mid-November, Molly. Did I tell you it's a war film? But they plan to produce it almost entirely in studio, and they hope to wrap it by Christmas. Best of all, I'd have the lead female role."

"That's exciting."

"So, what do you think? Want to go down there with me? We'd get a nice place in Beverly Hills. And I'd pay you well."

"What about Margaret?" Molly said suddenly.

"Should I take that as a 'no'?"

"I love you and Mary Ellen, but I feel like I need to get back to my own life."

"I understand. But do you really think Margaret would be interested?"

"I bet she'd like a change of pace. You've seen how unhappy she's been."

"You could be right."

"And you'll be so busy with the movie, maybe she'd want to keep the kids at the beach house. Wouldn't Peter love it there?"

"I can just imagine him playing in the sand. Plus, that'd save me some money. I could get a little apartment near the studio for during the week. Just a place to sleep. Then I could go to San Diego on weekends or when I get a break from filming. But what about the store, Molly? Wouldn't Margaret be terribly missed?"

"She's only been working part time. And between Mam and Mrs. Bartley, they could probably cover for her. Plus, Mam would have more time if she wasn't minding Peter. Besides that, I could probably help out more if they needed it. I could go over the bookkeeping and bills for them in the evenings, and I could work Saturdays. I'm sure we could figure it out."

"You could have my apartment while I'm gone, if you like."

Molly considered this. "That would make it easier to help out at the store."

"I think this is a great plan. Now if only Margaret will agree."

"I'm sure she will. Margaret has been so miserable lately. And remember how jealous she was about me going to San Diego with you? She'll probably jump at the chance."

"I hope so. It would be so great to have family down there with me, taking care of Mary Ellen. Almost like being home."

"And Margaret would be closer to Brian down there," Molly pointed out. "Maybe he'll want to come visit her and Peter. Maybe they can patch things up."

"I don't know . . . That could be easier said than done."

Molly frowned. "Do you really think their marriage is over?"

"I hope not, but according to Margaret, Brian might be done."

Of course, this reminded Molly about her last conversation with Patrick, and the way he seemed to disapprove of her sister . . . and perhaps of Molly as well. And he would probably disapprove of Colleen pursuing her filming career too. She felt tears building up again but knew this wasn't the time to cry. She needed to focus on the highway. For the sake of Colleen and the baby, Molly would be strong. She could cry later.

Margaret eagerly agreed to become Mary Ellen's nanny. With about a month to get ready for the move to San Diego, she threw herself into getting the store so well organized that Mam and Molly could easily take over the management.

"I'm so excited about getting out of here," she confided to Mrs. Bartley as they prepared to close. "I feel like I'm about to sprout wings and fly."

"I hope it's all you expect and more." Mrs. Bartley put the feather duster beneath the counter.

"I just hope that Mam can handle the store." Margaret pointed to where she was writing in the ledger. "She just needs to remember to write everything down." She turned to Mrs. Bartley. "And it will help if you remind her." Margaret had asked the older woman if she was interested in taking care of this particular responsibility, but Mrs. Bartley had declined.

"Molly told me that she plans go over the ledger every evening. She'll balance out the till and make sure that everything's running smoothly." Mrs. Bartley sighed. "I will miss having her living at my house during that time, but I do understand the convenience of living here. And Colleen certainly did a nice job of making the apartment livable."

"I just hope it's not too much for Molly. You know she'll still be working at the photography studio too."

"You don't need to worry about Molly. That girl's got a very good head on her shoulders. She's old for her age."

"I know." Margaret felt a tinge of jealousy. Running the store used to feel like a real accomplishment to her. She used to derive pride from doing her job well. But more and more it seemed that anyone could do it. She probably wouldn't even be missed. "If Dad's health was better, he could manage the books. But when I tried to teach him the new system—the one that Peter set up before he died—well, Dad just got stressed out and Mam said 'enough.' "

"Your poor father has had a few rough years." Mrs. Bartley began to wipe down the countertop.

"I have a funny story to tell you about him." Margaret chuckled as she closed the ledger. "Last night, after I put Peter to bed, I slipped downstairs to get a cookie—Mam had baked gingersnaps. Anyway, I caught Dad hiding something underneath his newspaper."

"Hiding something?" Mrs. Bartley's brows arched.

"Yes, and looking very sheepish and guilty. I suspected he'd sneaked more cookies—after Mam had told him not to. You know how she worries about his health and his diet. So I made an accusation and Dad lifted up his newspaper." Margaret laughed. "You'll never guess what he was hiding."

"What?" Mrs. Bartley looked slightly alarmed.

"Knitting. He was knitting."

Mrs. Bartley chuckled. "Well, I've heard of men knitting before, but it's hard to imagine your father doing so."

"Mam had taught him, but he made her promise not to tell anyone. He's knitting socks for servicemen."

"I think that's very nice." Mrs. Bartley nodded. "I do that myself. I hear that there's a great need on the European front with winter coming. And everyone knows that a soldier is only as good as his feet."

"Yes, I know. I knit socks for servicemen too. But it was so funny to see Dad hiding his knitting like that. He was so embarrassed." Margaret put the ledger book into the drawer. "Time to go home."

Mrs. Bartley looked tired as she reached for her purse. "Not a moment too soon either."

As Margaret locked up, she wondered if working at the store was too much for Mrs. Bartley. And yet every time she questioned this, the old woman assured her that she enjoyed helping. As they got into the car, Mrs. Bartley told Margaret that Molly was making meatloaf tonight. "That girl is a surprisingly good cook. She'll make someone a good wife someday."

"Someone?" Margaret frowned. "I thought she was going to marry Patrick."

Mrs. Bartley pursed her lips but didn't respond.

"I haven't really talked to Molly since she and Colleen got back. How did her visit with Patrick go?"

"I guess you'd have to ask Molly about that." Mrs. Bartley turned to Margaret. "But tell me, dear, what do you hear from Brian these days? Is he enjoying school? Does he have any trouble getting around on campus?"

"I don't really hear anything from Brian." Margaret gripped the steering wheel tighter.

"Do you write to him?"

"I don't think he cares to hear from me."

"Did you invite him to Peter's birthday party?"

"Well, no."

"Shouldn't you do that?"

"I doubt that Brian would want to come to a birthday party for a toddler."

"But it's *his* toddler, Margaret."

"Yes, but it's a long way to travel."

"But the party is on Saturday. Brian could take a train and make it here in time then take it back on Sunday."

"That's assuming he'd want to come."

"Or that he'd been invited."

Margaret let out a groan. "Fine. I will send him

an invitation tomorrow. But I do not expect him to show up. In fact, I hope he doesn't. If Brian comes, it will just be awkward."

"Peter might appreciate having his daddy there."

Margaret knew Mrs. Bartley was right, but it was irritating just the same. Even though Mrs. Bartley knew about Margaret's situation with Howard, she didn't know about the part Brian had played in the marital troubles. And Margaret wasn't sure that she wanted to tell her. So far only Colleen and her parents were aware of Brian's infidelity, and Margaret planned to keep it that way. At least for the time being.

If ever they did patch things up—which was uncertain—it would be easier on everyone, including her, to keep Brian's secret a secret.

Sixteen

Molly waited a full week before writing a letter to Patrick. And she intentionally kept it short and sweet. But when she dropped it in the mailbox, she felt a wave of sadness sweep over her. She knew the words in the letter were insufficient . . . and somewhat disingenuous. But her reasons were twofold. On one hand, she still felt somewhat hurt by Patrick's insinuations about her loyalty. But on the other hand, and more importantly, she didn't want to write anything that would be disturbing to him.

Molly paid close attention to the news and was aware that war efforts had greatly intensified in the Pacific. About a week ago, US troops successfully landed in the Philippines. While it was big news and a great move for the Allies, it resulted in a steady barrage of kamikaze attacks against US warships in the Leyte Gulf. Japanese forces were pulling out all the stops. Consequently, Patrick and his crew would be in even greater danger.

"Want to go to the USO dance with me tomorrow night?" Lulu asked as they were closing shop on Friday.

"That's great you're going again," Molly told her. "But it's my nephew's birthday."

"Maybe we could go tonight instead," Lulu suggested.

"I'm sorry. I promised to spend the evening with Colleen and the baby. She's getting ready to go down to Hollywood next week, and we're trying to get as much time together as possible." Molly was relieved to have honest excuses for both nights. She'd been tempted to tell Lulu that she probably wouldn't visit the USO again. Not until she straightened things out with Patrick. For now, Molly felt like she was in some sort of limbo. It was possible that Patrick had given up on her altogether—she hoped not. But until she knew for sure, she had no intentions of going to the USO.

As Molly got in line to wait for the trolley, she noticed her old friend from the *Chronicle*. "Mick Blackstone!" she exclaimed happily.

"Molly Mulligan!" He swept her up into a hug. "It's so good to see you."

"How are you doing?"

"I'm great. And I have big news." His eyes lit up. "Come have a cup of coffee with me, and I'll tell you all about it."

She felt a tinge of guilt. What would Patrick say? But then again, this was her old friend and mentor, Mick, and he had big news. "Sure," she agreed. "I'd love to catch up with you."

They were soon seated in a coffee shop, and Mick was telling her about getting an overseas assignment. "I'm going to be a war correspondent."

"How exciting."

He nodded. "You know how I was discouraged about not being fit for the service. I felt pretty useless. But when this opportunity came up I jumped for it."

"Where will you be? When are you going? Who are you working for?"

"Slow down." He grinned. "You sound like a real reporter. I guess I trained you well. So, for starters, I'll be stationed on the European front. I leave in a couple of weeks. I'm still working for the *Chronicle*. Leo Branson's retiring, and I'll be taking his place. Can you believe it?"

"That's wonderful, Mick." She had never seen him this excited and engaged before. "Will this be better than getting a professorship at the university?"

"I guess I'll find out. But I must admit it's given me fresh enthusiasm over journalism. You know how jaded I'd become."

She nodded.

"I ran into Simon a couple weeks ago. He was singing your praises."

"I've learned so much from him. He even lets me do photoshoots outside of the studio. And I'm not half bad, if I do say so myself."

"You know, I'm putting together a small team, Molly. I still haven't found a photographer. No one at the *Chronicle* is interested in going. To be fair, it's pretty rough over there. From what I hear, France is quite depleted and conditions are rustic at best. It's no wonder I'm having a hard time convincing people to join me."

"I would love to be a photojournalist over there," she exclaimed. "Are you serious?"

"You bet." He nodded eagerly. "I know you'd give it your best. Just like everything else you do."

"But would it be a problem—I mean, because I'm a woman." She grimaced.

"This is a modern age. Thanks to the war, you know that women are doing all sorts of jobs that used to be considered male domain."

"Oh, Mick, it would be such a great chance to learn—and to see the war up close."

His face grew grim. "But, Molly, it can be pretty gruesome over there. And you're such a tenderhearted young woman. Maybe it's not such a good—"

"Maybe I just need to toughen up," she told him. "And don't forget that I read everything I can find about the war. I know what's going on over there. Well, sort of. I suppose no one really knows until they get there."

"That's true. And to be fair, the *Chronicle* wants upbeat stories as badly as they want the latest news. You know how that goes."

“So human interest photos, people helping people, servicemen in need of care-packages from home. Tug on people’s heartstrings.” She could already see these shots in her mind’s eye.

“Yes.” He nodded. “I think you could be a real asset to our team.”

Molly really wanted this, but she suddenly imagined how her family would react. Would they think she was too young, too inexperienced . . . and what about her recent commitment to helping with the store? “Well, as badly as I want to do this, I’ll need to talk to my family first.”

“I completely understand,” he assured her. “If it’s the right thing to do, I’m sure it will work out for you.”

“I really want it to be the right thing.”

They talked awhile longer, and Molly promised to let Mick know her answer as soon as possible. And then, remembering that Colleen was expecting her, Molly thanked him for coffee and said good-bye. But as she rode the trolley up the hill to the store, she hoped and prayed that it would all work out. She couldn’t imagine anything more exciting than being a photojournalist with a war correspondent. But as she got off the trolley, she wondered what Patrick would say about it. He’d never been overly enthused about her friendship with Mick, and he’d be scandalized to find out she wanted to travel to war-torn Europe to help Mick with this project.

• • •

Margaret wasn't surprised that Brian didn't show up for his son's birthday party, but she was surprised that she felt disappointed by his absence. The party had been a rather forlorn affair. The Hammonds came but were not in a very jovial mood. She suspected they still blamed her for Brian's troubles. Plus, the Hammonds did not approve of Margaret "carting Peter off to Hollywood." As if she planned to parade him about and put him in a movie. No matter how many times Margaret tried to explain she was simply going down there to care for Mary Ellen and that Peter would be enjoying the sunshine and sandy beaches, it seemed she just couldn't get through to them.

Besides the Hammonds, her parents had been out of sorts. It seemed that Molly had gotten some harebrained idea to become an overseas war correspondent—or photojournalist as she called it. To make matters worse, Mary Ellen was colicky and Mrs. Bartley didn't seem to be feeling well. All in all, it had been a rather dismal evening and Margaret was glad it was over.

"I've changed my mind about the trip," Margaret told Colleen the next day after mass.

"What?" Colleen looked alarmed as she jiggled the baby. "You don't want to be my nanny now?"

"No, no, that's not it. I just decided that I'd

rather drive there with you next week. Instead of coming down later on the train." Margaret bent down to wipe Peter's nose with her hanky.

"But what about Thanksgiving? I thought you wanted to be home."

"I don't care about that anymore."

Colleen looked doubtful. "But I'll need to be busy in Hollywood and—"

"I have it all figured out," Margaret assured her. "You just drop the kids and me in San Diego. We'll get settled in there. Meanwhile, you can take care of whatever it is you need to do in Hollywood before the filming begins. There's really no reason we shouldn't go with you."

"Well, to be honest, I was a little concerned about being so far away from Mary Ellen for that long. It'll be hard enough being away from her while we're making the movie." Colleen smiled. "I think that's a great idea to all go down together. Can you be ready by Thursday? I have an event down there on Friday."

"I could be ready tomorrow if you liked."

"You really want out of here, don't you?"

Margaret nodded. "But let's change the subject." She tipped her head toward the church. "Here come Mam and Molly."

"Poor Molly," Colleen said quietly.

"Why poor Molly?" Margaret frowned. "If you ask me, she was born under a lucky star. Just like you."

Colleen chuckled. "She wants to go to Europe with Mick."

Margaret shook her head. "Well, that is just nonsense. Good grief, she's only eighteen."

"Hello, girls." Mam reached for Mary Ellen. "How's my little girly doing?"

They all visited for a bit then Margaret informed them of her changed plans to go down with Colleen in the car. "It'll save money," Margaret said. "And from what I hear, it's hard to get seats together in the trains these days. Everything is overbooked. And I'd need extra room for the kids."

"But you'll miss Thanksgiving," Mam said with disappointment.

"I'm sorry, Mam, but it seems the best plan."

"I feel like I'm losing all my children." Mam looked close to tears.

"You'll have Molly," Margaret said.

Mam just shook her head. "Maybe . . . maybe not."

"You're not really going to Europe, are you?" Margaret demanded.

"I haven't made up my mind." Molly folded her arms across her front.

"And your poor dad is worried sick about it," Mam told Margaret and Colleen.

"Dad will understand," Molly said quickly. "He's always encouraged me to go after my dreams."

“But to be in the thick of the war and—”

“We wouldn’t actually be in the battle zone,” Molly told her.

“Everyone knows Hitler is a madman. He may drop a bomb on you.”

“Yes, and San Francisco may have another earthquake.” Molly shook her head. “If you’ll all excuse me, I’m going to walk home.” Without another word, she strode off.

“Well, what on earth is the matter with her?” Margaret asked. “I’ve never seen her like this.”

“She’s got her nose out of joint.” Mam sighed. “She told us she won’t go to Europe without our blessing . . . but how can we give it to her? She’s our baby. We don’t want to lose her. Even Mrs. Bartley is concerned.”

“Well, I think you’re being overprotective,” Colleen declared to their mother. “Molly is probably your most mature daughter—well, aside from Bridget. If any one of us girls could handle being in Europe, I would place my money on Molly.”

Now Mam began to cry and both Margaret and Colleen had to comfort her. “Don’t worry,” Margaret reassured her. “Molly will do the right thing. She promised to stay and help with the store, and I’m sure she’ll honor her word. One thing we can always count on with Molly is that she is loyal.”

“Loyal to a fault,” Colleen muttered.

Margaret wanted to disagree about this, but Mam still seemed upset, so she thought better of it. “Let’s go home and spend the day together,” she said with enthusiasm. “I’ll fix supper for everyone. We don’t have a turkey, but we could stuff and roast a chicken and pretend it’s Thanksgiving.”

Seventeen

Molly tried to act happier than she felt as she went into Mick's office at the *Chronicle* after work on Tuesday. Of course, he misread her smile as confirmation that she planned to join his team and go to Europe. "Sorry," she told him. "As much as I'd love to be a war correspondent, my family needs me right now." She explained about Margaret going with Colleen to Hollywood and how Molly had volunteered to help manage the store. "I can continue working with Simon at the studio, but I promised to maintain the store's books in my spare time. I feel like I owe this much to my family."

He nodded somberly. "Family is important, Molly."

"I know."

"As it turns out, Mazzie Proctor expressed interest in being on my team."

"Oh, that's nice. She's a good photographer." Molly felt a wave of jealousy. "But I thought you said you already asked her and she was a definite no."

"She was. But when she heard that you might be going, she reconsidered." He grinned. "I guess she thought if you were tough enough to go over there, she could be too." His mouth twisted to one side. "But with Mazzie in Europe with me, Jim will be short one photographer."

Molly waited, almost afraid to hope.

"Maybe you should apply for her job."

"Do you think?"

"I know Jim likes you, Molly. And you've got some real photography work experience now. It's worth a shot."

"Even if all I did was work in the darkroom or carry camera equipment, I wouldn't complain," she said eagerly. "I wouldn't even expect to be paid much to start with."

"But what about Simon?"

She grimaced. "He won't want me to go, but I know he'll understand."

"Let me confirm with Mazzie that she really wants to go and then get back to you."

Molly thanked him and then, feeling slightly better about losing her chance to go to Europe as a photojournalist, she headed for home. She tried not to feel jealous, but it still bothered her that Mazzie would get the opportunity that Molly had wanted. The idea of traveling around Europe, taking photos, seeing the war effort up close—well, it seemed like a dream. A dream that would never come true for her. As much as Molly loved her family, she sometimes wished she could be free from the "ties that bind." But with Peter gone, Bridget serving overseas with the ANC, and Colleen and Margaret soon to leave for Hollywood, Molly was the only Mulligan child still around to help out. And she knew her parents needed her.

As she went into Mrs. Bartley's house, she felt a different wave of sadness. Mrs. Bartley had been supportive of Molly's decision to move into the apartment over the store, understanding how that would make it easier for Molly to help out there, but she'd been sad to see Molly leave. And tonight, she'd insisted on fixing a special dinner for them. "Something smells good." Molly went into the kitchen to find Mrs. Bartley at the stove.

"I picked up a nice sirloin steak at the store today." Mrs. Bartley smiled. "And I'm making an apple pie."

"You're so sweet to do this." Molly hugged her. "It makes me wish I wasn't moving out."

"Well, you've done most of the cooking since you've been here. I figured it was my turn."

As Molly removed her hat and coat, she told Mrs. Bartley about her possible job opportunity at the newspaper. "I can't say that I'm happy about not going to Europe, but it does take some of the sting away."

Mrs. Bartley smiled as she put a lid on the potatoes that were simmering. "I understand your disappointment, dear, but I suppose I'm a bit relieved." She patted Molly's cheek. "I was nervous about you being in Europe with the war still going. Perhaps you'll get a chance to go over after the fighting is done. Hopefully it won't be long now. Every time I read the news it seems that we're getting closer to putting those Nazis in their places." She went over to the sideboard. "You got a letter."

Molly's spirits lifted to see it was a V-mail. "Patrick?" she said hopefully.

"No, your mother brought it over. She said it's from Bridget. And she asked you to share the news with her when you're done."

"How about if I put down the blackout curtains and then, unless you want me to help you with dinner, I can read it to you."

"Perfect."

Molly hurried about the house putting down the heavy drapes then sat down at the kitchen table, opened the letter, and started to read.

> Dear Molly,
>
> Thank you for your last letter and care package. It was so sweet of you to share some of the items that Colleen had given you. I gave a few things to a fellow nurse when she got married to a B-25 pilot. It was fun to have a wedding here, and Linda looked lovely in a borrowed dress and shoes and with a bouquet of tropical blooms. It has been so hot here that Virginia and I have taken to sitting in

the huge double soapstone laundry sink during our free time. We put our cribbage board on the divider and play until we're cooled off. Or else we soak towels and drape them around ourselves. Our biggest excitement was when a Japanese sniper penetrated our fenced enclosure. Fortunately, he was apprehended by the guard before he got into the building. I do have some less than happy news—Cliff is being transferred to the European front in two weeks. I will miss him terribly. Please pray for his safety. He will be in a unit that is very close to the battlefront.

Love always,
Bridget

"Poor Bridget," Mrs. Bartley said. "I'm sad to hear that her young doctor is leaving."

"It's interesting that she mentioned a wedding. I wonder why she and Doctor Cliff don't get married before his transfer." Molly refolded the letter.

"Didn't she want her wedding in Old Saint Mary's with her family present?"

"That's true. But I think everyone would understand if she changed her mind. After all, these are war times. You never know what might happen next. Besides, we could always have a big reception for them later."

"Did you have similar thoughts when Patrick was here?" Mrs. Bartley's brows arched with interest. "I'd almost expected you to come home with a wedding ring on your finger. Or at the very least, an engagement ring."

Molly hadn't told Mrs. Bartley—or anyone—about her last evening with Patrick. She wasn't sure she even wanted to. The more she thought about it, the more confused she felt. "To be honest, I'm not sure that will ever happen," she said quietly.

Mrs. Bartley sat down at the table. "What went wrong, Molly? I know that something happened in San Diego. I've seen the sadness in your eyes, but I didn't want to interfere. But now I think you should talk about it, dear. What happened?"

Like a soda bottle that had been shaken and opened, Molly suddenly poured out the story of how she'd told Patrick about his brother. "And he just seemed to think the worst of Margaret." She was blinking back tears now. "And of me."

"Oh, dear." She patted Molly's hand. "I can't imagine why he'd think the worst of you."

"He talked about men serving overseas while their women were being unfaithful to them over here, about how girls went to dances and such." She swallowed against the lump in her throat. "And I never made any secret of going to the USO to him. But I've never betrayed him. I never would."

"I'm sure he knows that, Molly. Is it possible you simply misunderstood him? Maybe he was upset about Brian and Margaret and—"

"I think it was more than that." Now she was crying. "I think that Patrick has changed in his feelings toward me. It's almost as if he had me on some sort of pedestal, as if he felt I was perfect—and he suddenly discovered that I wasn't."

Mrs. Bartley smiled sadly. "Well, then it's about time he knew that. You're a dear, sweet girl, Molly. But no one is perfect. Not even you."

"I know that." Molly nodded firmly as she pulled out her hanky. "Probably better than anyone. But I would never do anything to hurt Patrick. I would never do what Margaret did to Brian. And I was so angry with her when she did that. You remember that, don't you?"

"Of course, I do." Mrs. Bartley went to check on the stove. "And Patrick will figure it out too."

Molly wasn't so sure. "I guess I should take Bridget's letter to Mam and Dad." She stood. "I'll be right back." Although she felt a tiny bit better after telling Mrs. Bartley about Patrick, she also felt like it was hopeless. Something between her and Patrick seemed to change on that last night. It was as if Patrick had been disillusioned and disappointed. She'd seen it in his eyes, heard it in his voice. She wouldn't be surprised if his next letter was just as cool and proper as her last one to him had been. Perhaps long-distance relationships were destined for disaster.

It didn't take even two weeks for Margaret to question her decision to go to San Diego. Oh, the beach house was lovely and Peter did like playing in the sand. But each day was painfully the same. Each morning she got up around six to feed the baby and then she fixed breakfast for her and Peter. She changed diapers, did the laundry and housekeeping, fed and cleaned the children, and eventually put them to bed. But with no neighbors close by—the nearest houses were vacation cottages and mostly unoccupied—and only seeing Colleen for a few hours on the weekend, Margaret felt starved for some adult conversation. She was tempted to call home but knew that long distance was expensive. Besides that, what would she say?

Margaret had never realized how much she'd thrived on social interaction while working at the store. So much so that she even loaded the children into the stroller and made the one-mile trek to the nearest Mom and Pop grocery store. She didn't really need anything since Colleen had already brought home all the groceries they needed for the week, but she just wanted to talk to a grown-up. Unfortunately, Mary Ellen had started to fuss as soon as they got there and then Peter knocked down a stack of cereal boxes and

Margaret, feeling embarrassed, had simply left.

By the time Colleen came home on the second Saturday night, Margaret felt like climbing the walls. "I hate to complain," she told Colleen after the children were put to bed, "but it feels awfully isolated here."

"I'm sorry." Colleen frowned. "I suppose it takes some getting used to."

Margaret felt guilty. She could see that Colleen was worn out, and she had blisters on her heels from a long week of shooting in an ill-fitting pair of shoes. She'd brought home several bags of groceries and a small stack of magazines for Margaret.

"Maybe you'd like to take the car somewhere tomorrow," Colleen said. "I can stay and watch the kids."

Margaret considered this. "I don't know where I'd go or what I'd do."

"Maybe it doesn't matter. Just go do something fun. See a movie. Go shopping." Colleen looked out the window to the dusky sunset. "I love it here. I wish I could stay for a whole week and you could take my place in the movie." She laughed. "Do you think they'd notice?"

"Maybe I could don a blond wig." Margaret rolled her eyes. "But I think I will take you up on that offer. I'll go someplace in the car."

"Just be back here by three. I'd like to make it to Hollywood before dark."

"How long does it take to drive to Los Angeles?"

"About two and a half hours."

"I think I'll drive to USC."

Colleen sat up straight. "Are you kidding?"

"Is that a problem? For me to be gone that long?"

Colleen frowned. "Well, I'm pretty tired, Margaret. I hadn't really planned to spend the *whole* day watching Peter."

"I spend every day watching your daughter."

"Yes, of course. But I'm paying you."

"Why are you so tired, Colleen? I thought you loved making movies. Don't they pamper you there? Don't they do your hair and makeup and bring you food?" Margaret tried not to feel envious as she imagined this kind of treatment.

"That's true, but it's also hard work. As you've probably noticed, I'm pretty worn out by the weekend."

Margaret peered more closely at her sister. "Do you think you could be expecting?"

Colleen's eyes opened wide. "No, no . . . I really don't think so."

"But you don't know."

"I'm fairly certain I am not," she declared. "It's just that I'm exhausted, Margaret. I work very long days all week. Do you realize that I go to the studio around six in the morning and sometimes don't get home until nearly eight at night—and then I just fall into bed."

"That's similar to my hours." Margaret sighed. "Although I do sometimes snatch a nap when I can get both kids to sleep at the same time."

"Anyway, why do you want to go to LA?"

"I'm thinking about paying a visit to my husband."

"You're serious?"

Margaret shrugged. "Why not? Maybe it's time."

"Time for what?"

"To forgive him." Margaret sighed. She'd been thinking about this for several days. Perhaps it was the loneliness . . . or maybe it was just time.

"You're ready to do that?" Colleen's brow creased. "You can honestly forgive him. Forget about it and move on?"

"I'm not sure I'll ever forget. Well, unless someone knocks me on the head, and I get amnesia like they do in the movies. But I don't think that happens in real life."

"I think that's great, Margaret. But that's a long day of driving. That's five hours for a round trip."

"And you want to leave here by three." Margaret did the math in her head. "If I leave around six in the morning, I could be at the college before ten. And if I leave the college around one, I could be back here in time for you. That would give me about three hours with Brian." She grimaced. "And if he's not glad to see me, I may be home sooner than expected."

"I'm sure he'll be glad to see you," Colleen assured her. "Especially if you're carrying an olive branch."

"I really feel ready to do this." Margaret stood. "And if all goes well, I thought maybe I could invite him to join us here for Thanksgiving next week. Wouldn't that be fun?"

"That'd be wonderful."

"I'll use my own gas ration coupons tomorrow." Margaret looked down at her frumpy and stained housedress. "I'm going to take a bath and set my hair and get a nice outfit ready to wear. And a good night's sleep."

"Good thinking." Colleen nodded sleepily. "It won't hurt to put your best foot forward."

So Margaret went to work and, feeling strangely energized, she was almost too enthused to fall asleep. But the morning came quickly and before long she was driving into Los Angeles. Since it had been pretty warm these past few days, she'd decided to wear her yellow sundress and a white cardigan. And her hair hadn't looked this good in days. It took a while to locate the campus and then to find someone to give her directions to where Brian was lodging. Apparently it was a dormitory for veterans. But when she stood out in front of the two-story stucco building, she got a sudden case of nerves. Maybe this was a bad idea.

"Hey, beautiful." A man dressed in blue jeans

and a plaid shirt grinned at her as he bounced down the steps. He looked at her like he had no idea she was a mother and nanny. "You new 'round here?"

"I'm looking for Brian Hammond," she told him. "Do you happen to know him?"

"Yeah, sure." He nodded without enthusiasm. "Want me to go get him for you?"

"Would you mind?" She smiled.

"Not for you, doll. But if it doesn't work out with Brian, I'm available." He winked then turned to go back into the building.

Margaret couldn't help but feel amused as she sat down on a shady concrete bench to wait. But she soon began to feel extremely nervous. During the drive here, she had decided that her "olive branch," as Colleen had put it, would be in the form of a confession. She would tell Brian that she understood how he'd gotten enticed since she'd been tempted in a similar way. Although her outcome wasn't nearly as hurtful as his, she could own up to it. Perhaps it would be what they needed to put this all behind them. Because Margaret was tired of being lonely. And Peter needed a daddy.

Eighteen

Margaret felt her heart in her throat as Brian emerged from the building, agilely descending the stairs with his cane. He looked surprisingly youthful and handsome in brown cords and a casual pullover sweater. Very collegiate. She could tell he hadn't observed her sitting in the shadows. But suddenly excited about this meeting with him, she stood and waved, calling out his name.

Seeing her, Brian's brow furrowed and his expression turned grim. He seemed disappointed . . . or perhaps he'd been expecting someone else out here.

She took in a quick breath as she approached him. "I didn't mean to take you by surprise."

"Is something wrong?" He frowned. "Where's Peter? Is he okay—"

"Peter's perfectly fine. He's with Colleen."

"What are you doing here?" It sounded more like an accusation than a question.

She nervously explained about staying in San Diego, Colleen's film, caring for Mary Ellen. "Colleen gave me the day off." She forced a smile. "I thought I'd pay you a little visit. I hope you don't mind."

"Why?" he demanded. "Why did you want to pay me a visit?"

"We need to talk."

He glanced over his shoulder as if worried someone might be listening then nodded toward a grassy area nearby. "Over there." He led her over to a wooden bench beneath a tree and they both sat down. "You're right," he said gruffly, "we do need to talk."

She was preparing to say her rehearsed speech, but before she could begin, he jumped in ahead of her. "Patrick told me about you and Howard."

Margaret blinked. "What?"

"I don't know his last name. Just Howard. But I know about your involvement with him, Margaret. And I must say that I'm—"

"That's why I'm here," she interrupted. "I planned to tell you all about it."

"Well, don't bother. Patrick filled me in. He said you were seeing Howard while I was overseas. Apparently a lot of the family knew about it too." He slugged a fist into his palm. "And when I think of how you carried on about Vittoria, acting so self-righteous, playing the poor wounded wife—all the while knowing what you'd been up to with Howard. And right here in our own town, with a baby—"

"I came here to confess and to say that—"

"Save your words." He scowled. "I know what you did, Margaret. I may seem an invalid to you, but I'm not a child. I know what goes on in an affair. I don't need you to describe the sordid details."

Margaret was taken aback. "What exactly did Patrick tell you?"

"He told me enough."

"And how did he know? Who told him?"

"What difference does it make?"

"Well, it does make a difference to me. I'm not sure you got the true story, Brian. And since I drove more than a hundred miles to talk to you, I demand the right to be heard."

"Fine. Say your piece. But you may as well know that I'm drafting divorce documents."

A chill ran through her and she was tempted to simply walk away—except that she was getting angry. How dare he treat her like this? "I don't know what Patrick told you, Brian. Or why he felt he had the right to interfere, but I—"

"He's my brother, which gives him the right to 'interfere' as you put it. And apparently he's the only member of my family willing to tell me the truth about you."

"I will tell you the truth about me, if you can shut up and listen." She gripped the handle of her purse so tightly that her fingernails dug into her palms. Now she explained about how Howard had befriended her, how they were both lonely, and how they took a few walks and met for coffee. "And finally, we shared a couple of meals together."

She locked eyes with him. "But that was all there was to it. That was as far as it ever went. If you don't believe me, you can ask Colleen or Molly. They knew all about it and warned me that being friends with Howard was a mistake. And they were with me when I cut things off with him. And the only reason I got involved in the first place was because I was so lonely. I missed you so much. And I was having a hard time being a new mother. And—" She couldn't talk because her tears were flowing now. She opened her purse to extract a handkerchief, wiping her eyes and waiting for Brian to make some sort of response. But he just sat there.

"I don't know what Patrick wrote to you, but if he said it was more than that, he was lying."

"Patrick wouldn't lie." His eyes flashed. "You should know him better than that."

"Then he was misinformed." Margaret stood. None of this had gone the way she'd planned. But when did anything? "I came here to confess about Howard to you, Brian. And to tell you that I'm sorry. I wanted to ask you to forgive me. And I planned to offer my forgiveness to you. But seeing you like this—well, I can see it's pointless." She looped her purse handle over her wrist and stood straighter. "Please, send me a copy of your divorce documents as soon as they're finished."

Brian stood with a slightly perplexed expression, but saying nothing, simply clutched his cane with both hands.

She glanced around to see students walking about in the sunshine, laughing and joking as if they had no problems whatsoever, as if they lived on a completely different planet. A happy looking couple strolled past them, hand in hand . . . and Margaret remembered the young man who'd flirted with her. "You seemed to be expecting someone else when you came out of your dormitory," she said crisply. "Perhaps you already have a girlfriend waiting in the wings." She stared intently at him. "And, really, why would that surprise me?"

She remembered the card she'd slipped into her purse last night, when she'd been feeling so hopeful. It had the beach house address on it, something she'd planned to give to Brian in case he decided to visit them for Thanksgiving. "Here!" She shoved it at him. "In case you get those divorce papers ready to send."

Then she turned on her heel and stormed away. A part of her wished that he would follow and beg her forgiveness—but another part of her was finished with him. Something inside her had snapped the moment she'd mentioned the word *girlfriend.* Unless she'd imagined it, Brian had flinched, as if she'd guessed right. That would certainly explain his eagerness to draft divorce papers. Well, just let him. She was done!

Molly had never known a more miserable Thanksgiving. It was bad enough having all her siblings away, but at the last minute the Hammonds had excused themselves from the festivities, which left Mam and Dad bewildered. Not only that, but Mrs. Bartley had begged out as well. Although her excuse was legitimate because she had a cold or maybe the flu. She planned to spend the day in bed.

After Molly and her parents were done eating, and there was no more small talk to be made, she offered to clean up. And while in the kitchen, she put some of the plentiful leftovers together to make a pot of turkey soup. Then she told her parents thank you and good-bye and took the soup over to Mrs. Bartley.

"You didn't miss much," Molly reassured her as she set a tray with soup and tea onto the old woman's lap. "We were a pitiful little group today. Just Mam and Dad and me."

"What happened with the Hammonds?"

"I think they're not too happy with the Mulligans right now."

"Whatever for?" Mrs. Bartley spooned into the soup.

"I'm afraid—whether it's due to Margaret or me—their sons are offended."

Mrs. Bartley made a tsk-tsk sound as she dipped her spoon again.

"For Mam and Dad's sake, I hope the Hammonds get over it soon. It's pretty bleak over there right now." She glumly shook her head. "They're both knitting socks . . . and listening to *Little Orphan Annie* on the radio."

Mrs. Bartley chuckled. "And what of Colleen and Margaret and the children? What were they doing to celebrate today?"

"Colleen called this morning. She had an invitation to go to a big fancy party at her agents' house today, but she declined it." Molly sat down in a chair by the bed. "She said Margaret is feeling pretty low."

"What is troubling her?"

"It sounds as if Brian wants a divorce." Molly frowned. "But I probably shouldn't have shared that. Colleen said not to tell anyone."

"You can trust me, dear. But that is sad to hear."

"And I'm terribly worried that I'm partly to blame."

"How is that possible?"

"Remember I told you about my trouble with Patrick? How I told him about Margaret? Well, it seems he wrote to Brian. And Patrick must've misunderstood me—or else Brian misunderstood him, I don't know for sure which it is. But Brian was under the impression that Margaret had an affair with Howard Moore."

"Oh my word." Mrs. Bartley dropped her spoon into the bowl with a clang. "That's not good."

"I guess Margaret straightened him out. But Colleen said she is none too pleased with me. And you know how Margaret can be when she's mad at someone."

"Surely she knows you wouldn't intentionally mislead anyone." She picked up her spoon again. "By the way, this soup is very good, Molly."

"Thanks. But I never should've told Patrick about Margaret. I feel as if I broke some sort of sisterly code. I don't blame Margaret for being angry."

"Oh, she'll get over it, dear."

"I'm sure she will . . . in time. I'm not so sure about Patrick."

"If Patrick is the man we believe him to be, he will get over it. If he's not that man, then I don't believe he's worthy of you." She smiled. "And, as I'm sure you've heard before, there are many fish in the sea."

Molly sighed. "The only fish I want is *under* the sea . . . down in a submarine."

"You've had a hard time of it lately." Mrs. Bartley sipped her tea. "But I do believe it's the difficulties in life that make us strong."

"You and Father McMurphey." Molly smiled. "He told me that at confession the other day." She peered over to see that Mrs. Bartley had nearly finished her soup. "I brought you a piece of pumpkin pie. Do you feel up to—"

"No, I think not. I'll save it for my breakfast." She sipped her tea. "But I do thank you for this. I believe it's just what the doctor ordered."

"If you want, I can stay the night."

"No, no. I'm feeling much better. You run along before it gets dark."

"Let me do the blackout curtains before I go."

"You're a darling."

"And I told Mam not to expect you in to work at the store for a while. So don't even think about it. I'll be working there tomorrow and Saturday." She pulled the blackout drape over the bedroom window. "I start my job at the newspaper on Monday. I'm so excited about it."

"Well, that's good to hear. Are you still feeling blue about not going to Europe?"

"I try not to think about it."

"I was giving it some thought . . . and I'm sure my opinion isn't terribly significant, but I hope that you get to go over there someday."

"You do?"

"I think it would be good for you. And if you get another chance to go over as a photojournalist, I hope you'll take it."

"Well, thank you for saying that." Molly smiled as she picked up the tray. "Although I suspect that good is going to come out of me not going. I hear there might be a budding romance between Mazzie and Mick."

"Really?" Her pale brows arched. "And didn't Mick used to fancy you?"

Molly shrugged. "He's a good friend. But wouldn't it be romantic if they fell in love and got married in Paris?"

"Similar to that last movie Colleen was in?" Mrs. Bartley seemed amused but weary. "Yes, I suppose that would be romantic."

"You take care." Molly kissed her cheek. "And call me if you need anything or if you want something from the store. I can easily come back here to stay if you'd need any help."

"I'll be fine, Molly. I know you've got a busy couple of days ahead. And, really, I feel much better. Your turkey soup was just the ticket. Thank you."

Molly told her there was more soup in the icebox then said good-bye. Mrs. Bartley's illness probably wasn't serious, but it was strange to see her bedridden like that. It made her seem old and frail. Of course, she was old, but she didn't normally seem so weak. However, she had seemed better—more like her old self. Perhaps she was on the mend.

Nineteen

Margaret felt like a machine as she mechanically went through the paces of each day in the weeks following her disappointing conversation with Brian. It didn't help that the weather had turned and they were now getting torrents of rain. Of course, Peter didn't understand. He would stand and beat on the sliding glass door, begging to go out to play in the sand. She wanted to beat on the door too, begging to leave this place.

She'd been in San Diego for more than four weeks now and wasn't even sure she could make it through one more day when Colleen informed her that the movie wasn't going to wrap in six weeks as planned.

"What do you mean?" Margaret demanded on Sunday as Colleen was getting ready to leave for Hollywood.

"I mean it's not going as quickly as they hoped. No one expected to get weather like this." Colleen peered out the window to where rain was coming down in sheets. "And they claim it never rains down here." She shook her head then kissed Mary Ellen on the cheek. "I'm going to miss you, baby girl. But you be good for Auntie Margaret."

Margaret wanted to stomp her feet and throw a fit. Instead she reached for the baby. "Be safe while you're driving in that rain," she said quietly.

"Thanks." Colleen kissed Margaret on the cheek too. "And thank you again for taking such good care of my little angel."

"Well, do everything you can to get that movie finished up," Margaret told her. "Because, whether or not you're done, I am going home for Christmas."

"Oh, I'm sure we'll be done by then. And if by chance we're not, we will still go home, Margaret. Even if I have to fly us home. Don't worry."

Margaret forced a smile, but as soon as Colleen was gone, she set Mary Ellen in the playpen then sank into the couch, fighting back the urge to sob.

"Mommy, play?" Peter held a building block in each hand with a chubby cheeked smile. "Make house."

Knowing she couldn't refuse him, she got the bucket of building blocks and got down on her knees. They began to build, which mostly meant she would stack the blocks and he would knock them down. But eventually, he seemed to realize that it was fun to stack them too.

"I wish we could build a real house," she murmured as she put a triangular block on top. "A place for you and me."

"And Daddy?"

Margaret pursed her lips, trying to think of a good distraction. "Want graham crackers and milk?" Of course this worked. Soon they were in the kitchen, and Peter was happily dipping and re-dipping soggy crackers into his milk. She knew that someday she'd have to think of a good explanation about his daddy and why they were not getting back together. But she would procrastinate for as long as possible.

Molly tried not to obsess about not hearing from Patrick. After all, it wasn't unusual to experience large gaps in their correspondence. And then, just when she wanted to wire a query to the war office, she would suddenly get a small stack of V-mail letters. Of course, that might not happen this time. It was possible that their relationship really was over.

Anyway, she was determined not to worry about it. And fortunately she had her new job at the *Chronicle* to keep her busy and focused, as well as the store business in the evenings. But when she flipped through the store's pile of mail, which was mostly vendor bills that she needed to pay, she felt hopeful when she spotted a V-mail in the mix. But it was from Bridget. Molly opened it, dismayed to discover it was very brief. Just a few sentences. But as she read them, she knew there was a lot to be read between the lines.

It said, in essence, that Bridget and Cliff had cancelled their engagement with no future plans to marry. Cliff was in Europe and Bridget's unit was being moved.

Molly could feel the sadness in the brevity and immediately called Colleen at her Hollywood apartment. "Are you terribly busy?" she asked.

"No, I just got home. What's wrong?"

Molly spilled out the bad news. "I just needed to talk to someone."

"Poor Bridget."

"I know. And she didn't say what happened or why they called things off. She just sounded so terribly sad to me."

"That's just rotten. Do you think Doctor Cliff found himself another nurse?"

"I honestly don't know. But I do recall Bridget's concerns that he had a number of them chasing after him."

"Poor Bridget," Colleen said again. "I wish we could send her a great big hug."

"I do too. I was just putting together a Christmas package. I'll make sure it's extra good."

"Put some things in from me too. I'll reimburse you."

"Well, I probably shouldn't talk long. This is long distance."

"But how are you?" Colleen asked. "Last time we talked, you sounded a little blue. Any word from Patrick?"

"No . . . not yet." Molly told Colleen a bit about her new job and inquired about Margaret and the kids.

"The kids are fine. But Margaret is still pretty down. I promised her we'd be home for Christmas. I think that helped. Anyway, please send our love to Bridget. I'll try to write to her too. And you take care, Molly."

After they hung up, Molly walked around the apartment just shaking her head. Why was life so hard on everyone? Was it all because of this horrible war? She remembered shortly after the war started and how badly she'd wanted to grow up so that she could play a part in the war effort. But now that she'd seen three long years of it, she wished she could turn back the clock and just be a kid again. She went over to the box she'd been packing for Bridget and wondered what else she could stuff into it that would make her sister's Christmas a bit merrier. Colleen had left a few things in the apartment, things she didn't need down there.

Molly poked around, finding a small and mostly full bottle of *Evening in Paris* perfume, which she wrapped in plastic. Then she found a pair of real silk stockings—Colleen was probably saving them for something very special. She also got some chocolates from the store and a silky blue scarf that Colleen had given Molly for her eighteenth birthday. She knew these items wouldn't fix a broken heart, but hopefully they would remind Bridget that she was loved. And Molly would mail it out tomorrow.

In the meantime, Molly planned to pay a visit to Mrs. Bartley. She'd been going over there every evening after work the past few days. Mrs. Bartley had insisted on Molly using her car, which made it much easier to get back and forth. But unless Mrs. Bartley's condition had improved, Molly planned to spend the night at her house. She'd go home to gather a few things as well as some groceries to take to her.

The house was still dark when Molly went inside. The blackout curtains were drawn, suggesting that Mrs. Bartley had never opened them. Not a good sign. "Hello?" Molly called quietly, tiptoeing through the house. She heard a coughing sound from Mrs. Bartley's bedroom. "How are you doing?" she asked with concern.

"This cold." Mrs. Bartley's voice was hoarse. "Just can't seem to shake it."

"I'll make you some tea," Molly said. "And I have soup to heat up for you and some applesauce."

"I'm not hungry. But tea would be nice." She coughed again.

As the water for tea heated, Molly put groceries away and arranged tea things on the tray, as well as a small dish of applesauce. Maybe she could tempt Mrs. Bartley to eat a little something. She was getting quite concerned. But every time she mentioned the doctor, Mrs. Bartley simply waved her hand, saying her doctor couldn't do a thing for her. "They brag about modern medicine but don't know how to cure a common cold."

"Here you go." Molly set the tray down. "Have you eaten anything today?"

"I had something earlier."

Molly wanted to challenge this. She'd seen no sign of anything having been disturbed in the kitchen, no dirty dishes in the sink. But at least the water pitcher she'd left by the bedside was nearly empty. She took it and the glass to wash and refill. And then, feeling quite worried, she called Mam, explaining her concern. "And her cough seems to be worse."

"I don't know what else you can do, Molly. If she refuses to see a doctor."

"Isn't there anything else you know of that can help?"

"Just the things I already told you to push on her. Tea and honey, chicken soup, applesauce."

"But she says she's not hungry."

"Then there's not much you can do. Just let it run its course. She'll probably be better in a day or two. It takes elderly people longer to get well."

"You're probably right. I have a letter from Bridget that I'll bring over later."

"Want me to save some supper for you? It's Irish stew."

"Sure, that sounds good." Molly considered telling Mam about the contents of Bridget's letter, but knew that would only prolong the conversation—and Mam would probably break into tears. Best to take care of Mrs. Bartley first and let Mam read the letter for herself later. Molly heated some broth, hoping she might get her neighbor to eat just a few spoonsful. Especially if Molly sat and chatted with her while she ate. That had worked before.

Molly took the broth in with a smile. "If you'll eat a bit, I'll tell you about what happened at work today." She set the bowl on the tray.

"You're bribing me?" Mrs. Bartley looked slightly amused then coughed again.

"Just a few spoonsful," Molly urged as she sat down.

"I'll do my best for you. Go on and tell me your stories."

So Molly told her about the photos she developed of some B-29 bombers. "I don't know that they weren't the actual planes that bombed the Nakajima aircraft factory in Tokyo, but they could've been. Twenty-four bombers successfully launched that attack a few days ago. It was quite a victory." She continued to chatter, making the workplace incidents seem much more interesting than they actually were, but it seemed to work. Mrs. Bartley managed to get down about half of her broth and applesauce.

"That's the best I can do, dear." She pushed the tray away.

"That was very good."

"And now I am tired."

"Rest well." Molly picked up the tray. "And call me if you need anything." She held up a finger. "I've got a better idea. We had a little bell for Dad to ring when he was sick. I need to take a letter over to Mam. I'll bring the bell back for you."

"Yes . . . thank you." She closed her eyes.

Molly took the tray to the kitchen and washed up the few dishes. Then she took Bridget's V-mail as well as the package to send to her over to her parents' house. While Molly sat down to a bowl of stew, Mam read the brief letter.

"Oh, dear!" Mam reached for her hanky. "Poor, poor Bridget. She must be heartbroken."

"I know," Molly said sadly.

"She doesn't even say why they cancelled." Mam waved the letter. "What are we to think?"

"Colleen thinks another army nurse caught him."

"Goodness, I hope not."

"Maybe it's just the war . . . and the distance between them," Molly suggested.

"Maybe so." Mam blew her nose. "I'm just so sorry for our Bridget. So sorry."

Molly pointed to the Christmas package. "I put that together for her. It's from all of us. I want to send it tomorrow, but I go to work before the post office opens."

"I'm happy to post it for you." Mam picked up the box, giving it a shake. "It's so good of you to do this for your sister . . . and for us."

"Well, I heard that it needs to be mailed this week if it's to get there on time."

Mam kissed Molly's cheek. "You are our most thoughtful and kindhearted child."

Molly shrugged. "I'd say that award should go to Bridget. She's over there sacrificing everything to help the wounded."

Mam nodded thoughtfully. "You're right. You are both thoughtful and kindhearted. And I'm grateful for the both of you. I'm especially grateful that you didn't run off to take photographs of the war, Molly. Thank you."

"I told Mrs. Bartley I'd borrow the little brass bell that Dad used to ring for us when he was bedridden."

"That's a good idea. I'll get it for you."

Mam returned with the bell as well as a bottle of camphor oil. "You could try putting some of this on a rag and setting it on her neck. It may help with her cough."

"Thanks." Molly finished off the stew and picked up a roll. "Will you tell Dad about Bridget?"

Mam nodded sadly as she picked up the empty bowl. "A sorry task that will be."

"I guess there's no hurry." Molly took a roll. "I better get back to Mrs. Bartley's. I'll be spending the night there until she starts to improve."

"Be sure to tell her to call me during the day, either here or at the store, if she needs anything."

"I'll do that." Molly thanked her for the stew then headed next door. Mrs. Bartley was sleeping when Molly checked on her. She set the bell by her bedside then poured a bit of the oil on a washcloth, laying it on Mrs. Bartley's chest and hoping not to disturb her, then tiptoed out of the room.

She took her time tidying up and setting things in the icebox so that Mrs. Bartley could easily find them if she got hungry tomorrow. But as she went upstairs, Molly felt uneasy. Perhaps she should insist that Mrs. Bartley see her doctor. The problem was that Mrs. Bartley was a strong woman, set in her ways. Even in her weakened state, Molly didn't think she could strong arm her to do anything she didn't want to do.

The next morning, Molly heard movement on the first floor and went down to find Mrs. Bartley sitting at the kitchen table in her dressing gown, eating a bowl of applesauce. "Are you better?" Molly asked hopefully.

"I believe I am." She pointed to the tea kettle that was starting to steam. "Would you mind making me a cup of tea?"

"I'm happy to."

"That camphor oil you put on my chest seems to have helped. Thank you."

"It was Mam's idea." Molly dropped loose tea into the pot then added hot water. She put a spoonful of honey into a teacup and was soon handing the aromatic brew to Mrs. Bartley. "I was starting to get worried about you." She poured herself a cup. "I was going to try to talk you into calling your doctor today."

Mrs. Bartley waved her hand. "No need for that. I think I'm on the mend. Thank you for your help, dear."

"Well, I'll come by again right after work," Molly assured her. "Maybe you'll feel like something heartier for dinner tonight. Mam made Irish stew yesterday. Quite a big pot too. We could beg some of that from her. It's always better on the second day."

"That does sound rather good."

"Most of the vegetables in it are from our own victory garden."

"That makes it sound even better." She smiled and sipped her tea. "Thank you."

Molly felt relieved as she drove to work. It seemed that Mrs. Bartley really was on the mend. Perhaps another night or two with her and Molly could return to the apartment above the store and her duties there. She was surprised that she actually sort of missed the little apartment. Of course, she'd have to relinquish it when Colleen and Margaret returned at Christmastime. But it would be nice to be back with Mrs. Bartley again too. She sensed that the older woman needed her. And it was rather nice to be needed by someone.

Twenty

Early December 1944

When the director informed the cast and crew that filming would not wrap until the end of the month, hopefully before the new year, Colleen felt bone tired. Of course, she had to pretend this news was no problem, that she was a trouper. Already she'd been questioned a few times, both by press and crew members, whether it was difficult to continue her acting career "as a new mother." Naturally, she'd brushed their questions off, claiming that her nanny had everything under perfect control. She would simply smile with confidence, feigning energy, strength, and happiness. After all, she was an actress—that was what she did. But underneath it all, she felt like crying.

And as she drove from Hollywood to San Diego on Friday night, after a long week of twelve-hour workdays, she felt like all she wanted was to sleep undisturbed until Sunday afternoon. Although she knew that wasn't going to happen. Margaret, as usual, would probably be fed up with her week. She would talk nonstop as soon as Colleen stepped into the house. And she would expect Colleen to manage all the care for Mary Ellen and she might even ask her to watch Peter too so that she could have a break. It would've been so much easier to have had Molly down here.

The only highlight to Colleen's worn-out weekends was spending time with Mary Ellen. It seemed like she'd changed a little each week. Not only was she getting cuter by the day, not to mention less colicky, she was starting to smile and babble and she could even grasp and shake a rattle. Last weekend she'd even been trying to roll over. Colleen was surprised at how much she enjoyed watching her daughter's development. And it made her sad to think she could possibly miss some of these milestones.

She'd written Geoff about these little things, talking more about the baby than she did about her current film project. She wanted to reassure him that her career wasn't going to overshadow her role as a mother. But the truth was she had second thoughts. Perhaps it wasn't possible to "have it all."

She'd recently had a nice chat with Jane Wyman in the studio commissary. Jane and Ron Reagan had a daughter about the same age as Peter. And based on Jane's publicity, this young mother was handling everything with grace and style, filming one picture after the next. Plus, Jane's husband was an actor as well. That came with its own challenges. However, Colleen suspected that Jane's life wasn't as smooth on the inside as it appeared on the outside, and she even confided over coffee that it was just plain hard work. Still, Jane seemed perfectly happy about motherhood and hoped to have more children.

Colleen wasn't sure she would ever want more children. Oh, this wasn't something she was comfortable admitting to anyone. Certainly not to Geoff, although she knew he'd like to have a son . . . someday. But the last time they'd discussed this, they'd both agreed it would be wise to wait until after the war. And although she felt more exhausted than ever, Colleen was relieved to know that she was not pregnant. Margaret would probably be relieved to hear it as well.

As Colleen parked in front of the beach house, she felt herself relaxing. Whether it was the ocean air or the pretty little house or knowing she was about to peek in on her sweetly sleeping baby, it felt good to be home. She just hoped that Margaret wouldn't be all keyed up and ready to talk all night.

"Welcome home," Margaret said cheerfully as Colleen went inside.

"Thank you." Colleen looked curiously at her sister as she kicked off her shoes. She seemed in much better spirits than usual.

"I made meatloaf and mashed potatoes tonight, and there are lots of leftovers if you're hungry."

"Thanks. I wouldn't mind a slice of meatloaf." She removed her hat. "But first I want to check on the baby."

"I'll heat it up for you."

"Cold is fine, with a little ketchup." As Colleen went to her bedroom to check on Mary Ellen, she was curious about Margaret. Why was she being so nice? Hopefully she wasn't about to ask Colleen to watch Peter all day tomorrow. If so, Colleen would have to decline. Politely. By the nightlight, Colleen could see her baby sleeping with her fist in her mouth. Chubby and sweet and smelling like baby powder. Colleen kissed her fingertips then touched them to Mary Ellen's head. She would have time with her tomorrow.

"Here you go." Margaret set a plate on the kitchen table. "How about some orange juice?"

"That would be lovely. Thanks." Colleen sat down, watching as Margaret hummed to herself, filling a glass. "Why are you so happy?" She forked into the generous slice of meatloaf.

Margaret set the glass down with a smile. "I was just waiting for you to ask." She sat across from her with eager eyes. "At first I was rather upset. A letter was delivered here this morning—to me from Brian. I felt certain it was some kind of legal notice regarding our divorce. But to my surprise, it was just a letter." She pulled a white envelope from her cardigan pocket and waved it in the air.

"A good letter?"

"Yes, I think so. Do you want to hear it?"

"Naturally." Colleen took another bite. "Good meatloaf."

"Thanks." Margaret unfolded the letter. "It's just one page. Here it goes."

Dear Margaret,

I have given our recent conversation careful consideration and now feel that I owe you an apology. I reread my letter from Patrick and realize that I misunderstood his communication. He never said that you'd participated in an extramarital affair with Howard but simply that he was aware that you'd been involved with him. His purpose in writing to me was to express his concern and to encourage me to continue corresponding with him, which I have done. All this to say that I am sorry for reacting so strongly against you.

In retrospect, I can see that you came here hoping for restoration and I, unfortunately, behaved badly. Please forgive me. If you would like to meet and discuss the future of our relationship, I will make myself available to you. Christmas break is about two weeks away and, if you are still in San Diego, perhaps we can arrange

to meet at your convenience. I would like
to see my son.

Sincerely,
Brian Hammond

"Well, that sounds as if it was written by a lawyer." Colleen chuckled as she polished off the last bite of meatloaf. "But it is an improvement from the last time you two talked."

"I'll admit his words sounded rather crisp and chilly the first time I read them, but then I read it a few more times, and I actually think he is trying to reopen the door with me. At least I hope so."

Colleen nodded, although she wasn't so sure. It was possible that Brian simply wanted to maintain a civilized relationship while pursuing a divorce. And, of course, he wouldn't want to burn any bridges when it came to involvement with his son.

"If you don't mind, I'd like to invite him to come visit me here during his Christmas vacation time."

"I think that's a fine idea." Colleen was relieved that Margaret didn't plan to drive over to Los Angeles again. That had been a very long day for both of them. "Speaking of Christmastime . . ." She sighed then quickly shared the news she'd just heard.

Margaret let out a low groan. "Not until New Year?"

"But what if you and Brian start to patch things up?" Colleen said with enthusiasm. "Maybe you should be down here so you two could get together. Maybe Brian would want to spend time here. You two could be together as much as you like. After all, you're still married." She chuckled. "Maybe you'll want to have a second honeymoon."

Margaret's brows arched. "Oh, I don't know . . . it's been a long time."

"Well, just see what he's thinking and take it from there."

"What if Brian doesn't want to get back together?" Margaret picked up the dishes with a creased brow. "What if he just wants to meet to go over divorce details?"

"That's possible."

"In that case, I would want to go home in time for Christmas." Margaret set the dishes in the sink.

"What do you mean?"

"I've been thinking about this all week. And hearing that your movie won't wrap for almost a whole month . . . well, I've made up my mind, Colleen. I want to take the kids home."

"Take the kids home?" Colleen felt confused.

"I have it all figured out. You'll put us on a plane to San Francisco. Molly will pick us up. I'll take Mary Ellen and Peter to the apartment over the store, and we would live there together until you're done with your movie and back home."

"But taking Mary Ellen?" Colleen frowned. "I will miss her so much."

"It's only for a short while, Colleen. And your weekend times with her are pretty limited anyway. Plus, you know how tired you've been. If we were gone, you could stay in your Hollywood apartment and sleep all weekend if you like. No more driving back and forth."

"I'm too tired to think about this right now." Colleen stood. "And just so you know, I am not pregnant. But I am exhausted. Let me sleep on this idea and we can talk about it tomorrow. Okay?" She forced a smile. "And I am glad to hear that Brian is talking to you again."

"And if he does want to get back together, well, maybe I wouldn't want to take the kids back to San Francisco after all."

"Yes," Colleen said eagerly. "Hopefully, he wants to repair things with you." And for more than just Margaret and Brian and Peter, Colleen prayed that her brother-in-law was finally coming to his senses. She would ask Molly to pray too. But first she was going to bed.

It hadn't escaped Molly's notice that today was December 7—the third anniversary of the attack on Pearl Harbor and her brother's death. Naturally, the *Chronicle* was running stories related to this historical milestone as well as encouraging reports of victories on both fronts. The general consensus of the editorial department was that by the fourth anniversary of Pearl Harbor, this war would be behind them. She hoped so. But she couldn't forget the news stories and photographs the newspaper had chosen not to print today. As usual, there was a responsibility to uplift morale on the home front. But sometimes Molly wondered whether that was such a good thing. Maybe people needed to be made aware of how dark the world out there really was—man's inhumanity to man.

As Molly drove to Mrs. Bartley's house, she tried not to dwell on sad things. After all, her plan tonight was to cheer up her old friend and hopefully lighten her own spirits as well. Molly had been surprised to discover that she hadn't felt quite as sad over the loss of her brother—much better than previous years. Maybe time did heal all wounds . . . eventually. And maybe in time her heart would stop aching over Patrick too. He still hadn't written to her, and she knew he'd had ample opportunity to get something out by now. Submarines could only stay down for so long. They had to return to port to refuel and get supplies . . . and to pick up and send mail. He was simply ignoring her.

Just the same she'd gone ahead and written him another letter last week. Her excuse was to send some recent photos, including some from their reunion in San Diego. She'd also told him that she was sorry that they'd parted on a somewhat sour note, and then she'd reassured him that he would always be in her prayers and that she would always love him. Of course, she'd added a disclaimer to this by saying she would always love him "as a brother."

She parked the car in front of Mrs. Bartley's house then hurried up to the porch, quickly checking the mailbox, just in case. There was an electric bill and nothing else. Apparently Mrs. Bartley hadn't been out here today. Although she'd assured Molly that she'd been improving these last few days, Mam had expressed her concerns this morning. She felt Mrs. Bartley was going downhill. As a result, Molly had decided to pay her a visit. She planned to fix them both a light dinner and spend the night. And before she left tomorrow morning, she would strongly encourage her old friend to go see her physician. Mam had even offered to drive her there.

The house was dark and the blackout curtains pulled closed, but that wasn't so unusual. Molly set her bag of groceries on the counter and called out a greeting as she headed for Mrs. Bartley's bedroom. As expected, she was in bed, but something about the room felt odd—too quiet, too still, and slightly cool. "Hello?" Molly spoke softly as she turned on the bedside lamp. Then seeing Mrs. Bartley's pale, expressionless face, Molly felt her chest tighten. "Mrs. Bartley?" she whispered as she approached the motionless figure in the bed. She reached out to touch the old wrinkled hand, finding it strangely cold.

Mrs. Bartley was dead.

Molly sank into the nearby chair and, holding her head in her hands, she just sobbed and sobbed, crying out like a wounded animal. After a while, she questioned whether these tears were only for Mrs. Bartley. Although her friend's death had triggered the outburst, she knew it was something more, something bigger, something darker.

As Molly sobbed and cried and even ranted at God, she knew she was crying for her brother and all the other servicemen and women who had lost their lives over these past three years. She was crying for all the pain in the world at large. For the captives suffering and being killed in Nazi internment camps and the POWs in cruel Japanese camps. And she was crying for every single sailor and soldier and marine and for Bridget's broken heart and for all those who were risking life and limb on a daily basis on the battlefield. Molly had never felt such heavy sadness, such total darkness . . .

Twenty-One

For the next few days, Molly tried to hide the sadness that seemed to hang on her like a heavy black cloak. She threw herself into her work at the newspaper, doing whatever was asked or needed—from making coffee and emptying the trash to developing film and occasionally going out on a human-interest photoshoot and even writing a short article to go with it. She knew she was paying her dues and that others took advantage of her youth and inexperience, but she appreciated being busy. In the evenings, she kept herself busy with the store. Making up for the several days she'd neglected the books, she soon got everything into apple-pie order. Hopefully Margaret would be pleased when she got home, although it now sounded like it might not be until after Christmas.

Molly and Mam were dismayed at the low attendance at Mrs. Bartley's funeral. Just a few of her husband's side of the family and few members of her church. The short, simple service had been preplanned by Mrs. Bartley, including her eulogy, but it was so brief that Molly felt bad for her old friend. And so, although she hadn't intended to say anything, Molly stood up and spoke on her behalf.

"Mrs. Bartley and I had only been friends for these past three years," she began nervously, "but I considered her to be one of the finest people and a very good friend. She was wise and witty and one of the best listeners I've ever known. And she gave really sound advice. I could take problems to her and she would quietly listen and then she would think for a bit and finally she would make a very good suggestion. Even though she was old in years, I feel that she was young at heart. But she'd had some hardships in her life. She lost her son in the previous war and her husband later. And I know that she must be happy to meet up with them again." Molly said a few more things, but then feeling too choked up to continue, returned to her seat.

Mam clasped her hand, giving it a comforting squeeze. "Nicely done, dear."

After the service, Molly and Mam drove to the cemetery for the internment, but they were the only ones, besides the funeral director, to show up. Molly laid a single pink rose on the casket, said a prayer, and then they left.

"I knew Mrs. Bartley was a lonely sort of person." Molly parked the car behind her parents' house. "But I never realized she had so few friends."

"Well, remember how she was rather cantankerous." Mam reached for her purse. "You kids used to be afraid of her and called her Mrs. Sourpuss."

"I never called her that." Molly opened the gate leading into the victory garden, which was looking rather sad and dead in the December fog.

"Your siblings did. I was always reprimanding them for it. But I didn't blame them. I remember how she'd yell at them for knocking a ball or toy into her yard and stepping on her precious roses." Mam pointed to the other side of the small backyard.

"Then she let me remove a lot of those rose bushes to expand this garden."

"You helped change her, Molly." Mam headed up the steps to the back porch.

"She was just lonely . . . needed a friend." Molly sighed as Mam opened the door. "I'm going to miss her."

"I will too." Mam nodded. "I enjoyed working with her at the store. And when I called Margaret with the news, she actually cried."

"She did? Really?"

"Mrs. Bartley had become a good friend to her, Molly."

"How was the service?" Dad asked as they came into the kitchen.

"Small," Molly told him.

"You got an official looking letter in the mail." Dad handed her a legal sized envelope.

Molly read the return address. "It's from an attorney." She hurried to open it, skimmed the brief letter, and sank into a kitchen chair.

"What is it?" Mam demanded.

"Are you in some sort of legal trouble?" Dad leaned over her shoulder to peer down at the paper in her hand.

"It's from Mrs. Bartley's attorney," Molly said slowly, "asking me to arrange to meet with him to settle Mrs. Bartley's estate."

"To settle her estate?" Mam sat down too.

"It seems that she's appointed me as her heir."

"Her heir?" Now Dad sat down. "What does that mean?"

"I'm not even sure." Molly reread the brief letter then frowned.

"I met some of Mrs. Bartley's husband's relatives at the funeral today," Mam said. "Wouldn't they be heirs too?"

"I would think so."

"Maybe she's left you another piece of jewelry." Mam stood, putting on the tea kettle. "Remember how shocked we were when she gave you that beautiful aquamarine necklace for your birthday?"

Molly did remember. "I still love that necklace." Maybe not as much as she loved the pearls from Patrick, but it would be even more special to her now.

"Call the lawyer," Dad said suddenly. "Find out what this is about."

"Right now?"

"Yes." Dad tugged her hand. "Do you want Mam and me to suffer from dire curiosity?"

So Molly called the number on the letter. The attorney invited her to come by his office later in the afternoon, and since she'd asked for the whole day off, she agreed to go in. Her parents offered to go with her, but knowing that Mam was expected at the store and Dad looked tired, she assured them she could deal with whatever this was on her own. When she went in, she was shocked to learn that she was the sole heir of Mrs. Bartley's estate—and that her estate included her house and everything in it, her belongings, and her bank accounts.

With the bulky envelope that contained titles and bankbooks and keys under her arm, Molly slowly walked toward home. She didn't even know what to think. Although it was a kind and generous gesture on Mrs. Bartley's part, Molly felt unworthy. She wasn't even nineteen and yet she now owned a house and a car and had a fair amount of money in the bank. It almost made her head hurt to think about it. What would her family think?

Of course, she wanted to use this unexpected landfall to help her family. She could even just hand it over to her parents and had said as much to the attorney. But he had reminded her of the letter that Mrs. Bartley had recently written to

Molly, which was included in the inheritance package. “Don’t forget that she expects you to handle your inheritance with good sensibility. She believed in you and was convinced you had a good head on your shoulders. She trusts your judgment to manage this, Molly. Don’t let her down by handing it off to someone else.”

That seemed a big responsibility, but Molly was determined to do her best. And right now, she felt the need to check on Mrs. Bartley’s house—to make certain that all was in order. She hadn’t been there since the night she’d found Mrs. Bartley deceased and felt a little uneasy about being there now, but as she went inside, she reminded herself that Mrs. Bartley was her dear friend. She would be pleased to see that Molly cared enough to check on things, to empty the icebox and take out the trash, turn out the lights, and make sure that all was well. Then Molly would tell her parents about the meeting with the lawyer and later she would return to the apartment above the store, because she wasn’t really ready to stay in Mrs. Bartley’s house alone.

December 16, 1944

“Did you hear the news?” Colleen asked Margaret when she came home on Saturday.

"You mean about Mrs. Bartley?" Margaret asked.

"No, I already know about her death. That was last week." Colleen set down her purse then removed her hat and gloves. "I mean the news about Glenn Miller. I just heard it on the radio as I was driving here. His plane went down in Europe."

"Oh, dear." Margaret handed Mary Ellen over to her.

"His plane went down in the English Channel yesterday. He was getting ready to relocate his band to France."

"Was it shot down?"

"They didn't say. They're calling it missing in action." Colleen grimaced. "He's got a wife and two small children."

"Oh, I do hope he's okay. I love his music. I'd hate to think . . ." Margaret sighed to a halt.

Colleen kissed Mary Ellen's cheeks. "I missed you so much," she cooed at her. "I would've come last night, but it was so late." She glanced at Margaret. "I left as soon as I woke up this morning. I hope you don't mind."

"It's okay." Margaret picked up a stray block from the floor. "But I meant did you hear about Mrs. Bartley and what she left to Molly?"

"What she left?"

"Mam called a couple days ago. It seems that Mrs. Bartley has left everything—her lovely house, her car, and all her money—to our baby sister."

Colleen smiled. "Well, good for her. And good for Molly."

Margaret frowned. "Molly is only eighteen—"

"She'll soon be nineteen."

"Even so. She isn't married, doesn't have children, and now she has her own house and car and, from what I hear, a pretty nice bank account."

"Molly has been the best friend ever to Mrs. Bartley." Colleen sat down on the sofa with the baby, tickling her tummy to make her smile. "I suppose that means Mrs. Bartley didn't have any family to leave it to."

"Well, if I were her family, I'd probably contest that will."

"Oh, Margaret. Really?" Colleen just shook her head. "Are you having a particularly bad week or something?"

Margaret shrugged. "I haven't heard back from Brian."

"Is it his finals week?"

"Maybe. But he'd sounded so eager to talk to me and every day I go check the mail—and nothing."

"I'm sure he's busy." Colleen kicked off her shoes. "But it's probably his Christmas vacation now. Maybe he'll come through."

"It just makes me think that he really has no

interest in reuniting." Margaret flopped into a chair with a loud sigh and Peter ran over, climbing into her lap. "And I'd think he'd want to see his son."

"He said as much, Margaret. Just give him time." Colleen nodded toward Peter. "And don't forget about what Mam and Dad used to say. 'Little pitchers have big ears.' "

"I don't get that. What does it mean anyway?"

"I asked Dad once and he told me it was because a small pitcher had a big handle—that was like the ear. And obviously it means that a small child can—"

"I know what that part means." Margaret frowned.

"Well, I just think when you speak of certain parties who are specifically related to little pitchers, you should watch your tone and use your words carefully, Margaret. If you get my drift."

"What do you think Molly is going to do with her inheritance?" Margaret asked.

"I have no idea. But knowing Molly, she will do the right thing." Colleen carried Mary Ellen into the kitchen. "I didn't have any breakfast. Anything good to eat around here?" As she poked around in the icebox, she heard the phone jangling and Margaret answering.

"Brian?" she said eagerly. "I was just thinking about you."

Colleen felt rude for eavesdropping, but it wasn't as if she could help it. Holding Mary Ellen, she hovered in the kitchen while her sister talked to her estranged husband.

"I'd love for you to come visit us, Brian. Do you have a way to get here?" She paused and then told him that "any day would work." So much for playing hard-to-get. Colleen chuckled as she poured a glass of orange juice. Well, at least he'd called. The conversation wrapped up quickly, and suddenly Margaret, with Peter in her arms, was dancing around the living room. "Daddy is coming," she sang to Peter, and he cheerfully repeated her mantra as they danced into the kitchen. "Did you hear that?"

"I couldn't help but hear it." Colleen smiled. "Sounded like good news."

"He's coming for the day on Monday," she said. "He can get a ride with a classmate who's going home for Christmas vacation."

"And then what?"

Margaret's mouth twisted to one side. "Then what?"

"Will he go home to San Francisco? Or back to USC? Or what?"

"What if I invite him to stay here?" Margaret said quietly. "Remember you said you wouldn't mind."

Colleen considered this. "I suppose if you two are patching things up . . ." She shrugged.

"Sure, why not. Just let me know how it goes, okay? And if you need more time—without me crashing in on you—I suppose I could spend the next weekend in Hollywood. In fact, the director hinted that if things don't pick up, we might have to film straight through for the next two weekends. Although I was really hoping that wouldn't happen. But the weather has slowed some scenes down, and the movie has to wrap by the end of the month or someone will be looking for a job."

"You?" Margaret looked alarmed.

"No, not me. But some of the crew might be in hot water. And I suppose the studio could try to sue the weatherman." She laughed.

"What about Christmas? Surely you won't have to work then."

"The director told everyone to only expect two days off for the holidays."

"So you probably won't want to go home then."

"I don't see how I can." Colleen sighed. "But I suppose *you* could . . . if you want to. Like you suggested before."

Margaret seemed to consider this. "I'm guessing that Brian will want to be home with his family since he's been gone so much. If we patch things up, maybe he and I could go together." She pointed to Mary Ellen. "If you wouldn't mind me taking her up there without you. And if you're going to be working that much, you probably wouldn't be back here to see her anyway."

Colleen knew she was right, but she didn't like the idea of being separated from Mary Ellen on her first Christmas. Especially after hearing that news about Glenn Miller. It just felt wrong. And it didn't help matters that Geoff had already sent word that he wouldn't have another leave for at least two months.

"Do you use your car very much when you're in Hollywood?" Margaret asked suddenly. "Didn't you say that your apartment is walking distance to the studio?"

"Yes, it's on the studio lot."

"So what if Brian and I borrowed your car to take the kids home for Christmas, rather than me flying like I'd suggested before? Wouldn't Mam and Dad love it? And it would cheer up Molly too. Mam said she's been awfully blue since Mrs. Bartley died. Then when your movie wraps, we could drive the car back down here. Or else you could just fly home."

Colleen really did not like the sound of this but suspected it was just plain selfishness on her part. "Maybe we're getting the cart ahead of the horse," she told Margaret. "Let's see how it goes with Brian on Monday before we make any definite plans."

Margaret looked slightly dismayed but nodded. "I'll call at your apartment when I know where this is going with him. You're usually in by eight, right?"

"Usually. But sometimes we go later." Suddenly Colleen felt completely drained and somewhat overwhelmed. "Say, little girl," she said pleasantly to Mary Ellen. "I'll bet you haven't had your midmorning nap yet."

"She hasn't."

"Great. I'll feed her a bottle and maybe the two of us can get a little shut-eye together." As Colleen got them both ready for a nap, she felt more than just weary—she felt downright discouraged. The idea of working so hard, such long days without weekends off, and only getting two days for Christmas—which she might end up spending by herself in the little studio apartment—well, it was just plain depressing. So much for the glamorous lifestyle of a famous Hollywood film star. If only people knew the truth . . . perhaps Hollywood wouldn't be crawling with so many hopeful lovely faces.

Twenty-Two

December felt dark to Molly. She knew it was partly over losing Mrs. Bartley, but there was a lot more to it than that. Glenn Miller's plane had recently gone down in the English Channel with no remains or survivors recovered. The day after that, the Nazis launched what was now being called the Battle of the Bulge. The attack began in the dense forests of the Ardennes region, catching the Allied forces completely off guard, which was resulting in thousands of casualties and deaths. Although these statistics were, as usual, played down by the press, Molly had read some actual reports . . . and the numbers were staggering. And even though winter had soundly set in and weather conditions deteriorated daily, the battle wasn't even close to being over. All Molly could do was to pray for the troops caught in the thick of it. And just when everyone had thought that war on the European front was slowing down. . . .

It wasn't only the battlefront that seemed dark and dismal, but the home front as well. Mam was feeling down and Dad seemed more lethargic than usual. He wasn't even knitting. Everything had seemed fine just a few days ago. Margaret had called, happy and excited, announcing plans to drive home with Brian and Peter and even Mary Ellen in time for Christmas. Apparently she and Brian were repairing their marriage, ready to make a fresh start. The plan had been for the Hammonds and Mulligans to celebrate together—just like they used to do.

Naturally, Mam had been thrilled over the news. She'd immediately set out with festive holiday preparations. And Molly had thoroughly cleaned Mrs. Bartley's house with the intention of inviting Margaret, Brian, and Peter to stay there. She'd even put up some Christmas decorations to make the old house cheerier. And Mam had offered to care for Mary Ellen with the hopes that Colleen might be able to catch a flight to San Francisco, even if only for two days. Family was expected to arrive on the Saturday before Christmas. Dad had even knit a dark green scarf for Brian.

They'd all been happy and busy, and then, just this morning when they'd been expecting their loved ones to arrive, Margaret had pulled the plug. Since it was the last Saturday before Christmas, Molly had been helping at the store, busily ringing up a customer when the telephone jangled. Mam answered, but it didn't take long for Molly to figure things out. Then Mam hung up the phone, rushed to the back room, and burst into tears. She was too upset to say exactly what had happened, except to assure Molly that no one had died.

It wasn't until that evening, long after Molly had sent Mam home and after the last customer was gone and Molly had locked up the store, that she was finally able to call Colleen's beach house in San Diego to find out what had happened. To her relief, it was Colleen who answered. At least she'd probably get a more accurate account of the details now.

"Oh, I'm glad it's you," Colleen said in a weary tone. "I got home about an hour ago. My agent hired a car to bring me here. Anyway, I just heard the whole story, and I was afraid that was Mam calling. I was worried I'd need to put a happier spin on things."

"Just give it to me straight." Molly carried the phone over to a chair and sat down. "And I can fill Mam and Dad in later."

"I'll start at the beginning. Brian came to see Margaret on Monday. And he actually stayed here all week long and—" Molly could hear Margaret yelling in the background. "Yes, yes," Colleen said with impatience. "*Excuse me,* Margaret wants everyone to know they stayed in *separate* rooms."

"Fine, I get that. But what happened?"

"Well, they seemed to be getting along just fine when I spoke to Margaret in the middle of the week. I'd left my car here for them, and they were planning to leave for San Francisco this morning."

"Yes, I knew about all that. Mam and Dad were over the moon about seeing the grandkids and planning for the Hammonds to join us."

"So . . . according to Margaret, as they were packing the car, Brian mentioned that he'd be returning to Los Angeles right after Christmas. Well, that didn't set well with Margaret, and she questioned him about it. He informed her of his plan to return to school. Although his degree is finished, there are a few beneficial classes that he wants to take while he still has his veteran's benefits to cover tuition. Well, our dear Margaret wasn't happy to hear—" Margaret was yelling in the background again, and Colleen relinquished the phone.

"I want to tell my own story," Margaret declared. "I told Brian that if we planned to remain together as a married couple, it was time to live under the same roof. If he wants to return to USC, he needs to take Peter and me with him. We can locate some family housing and make do until he's done there. And if he doesn't want to do that, I told him he needs to return to San Francisco. While he takes his bar exam and gets his license, I'll find us a place to live, and he can start practicing law and supporting his family. Well, he threw such a fit, you'd think I'd asked him to cut off his other leg." Margaret broke into sobs, and Colleen was back on the other end again.

"So they got into a big horrible fight, and apparently they both said some very regrettable things, and Brian stormed off with his suitcase. Margaret thinks he hitched a ride or caught a bus or something, but he's definitely gone. And she asked for you to let us know if he shows up at his parents' house later today or tomorrow."

"I'm sorry to hear that." Molly sighed. "That's too bad. Tell Margaret I feel bad for her." Molly also felt bad that Margaret felt the need to give Brian such an ultimatum. She could just imagine her sister getting up on her high horse. Really, it wasn't that surprising that Brian had reacted so strongly.

"It's an unfortunate mess." Colleen sighed.

"So you're really not coming home for Christmas?"

"I cancelled my flight, and I honestly don't think we're up for a road trip right now. And I have to be back to work on the twenty-sixth. To complicate matters, Peter's been throwing some ferocious temper tantrums, and it looks like Mary Ellen's got a cold. It just seems best to stay down here."

"I understand."

"Tell Mam and Dad that I'll call them tomorrow night for Christmas Eve."

Molly promised to do so and, after expressing

her love to her sisters and niece and nephew, she hung up. Now to convey this information to her parents. Colleen was right—this story could use a happier spin. Not so different than the way much of the press was covering the war.

She really would've preferred to wait until tomorrow, but she knew her parents were in a bad way. And so she went over to attempt to cheer them up. She couldn't be dishonest, but she could leave out certain pieces. And so she told them about Mary Ellen having a cold and how, although Brian and Margaret had been working on reuniting, it was premature for them to spend Christmas together, and how Colleen was worn out and needed to be back to work the day after Christmas. "So you see, it's probably for the best."

"Maybe so," Dad grumbled, "but it's too bad to get people's hopes up and then dash them like that." He nodded to Mam. "She's been working like a dog to get everything ready here." He pointed to the Christmas tree. "She even put that up all by herself."

"Well, it's perfectly lovely," Molly said cheerfully. "And I will certainly enjoy it. I'll take photos of it. And of you two in front of it. I can send prints to everyone. And if you don't mind, I'd like to sleep in my old room for the next couple of days." She reached for the chessboard. "And now I think it's about time I beat you in a game, Dad."

While Molly set up the pieces, Mam started for the kitchen then called over her shoulder, "Oh, Molly, I nearly forgot. You have mail. I've been checking Mrs. Bartley's mailbox like you asked, and you got what looks like a Christmas card and a V-mail too."

Molly jumped up, rushing to where they always set the daily mail. She recognized Patrick's handwriting on the Christmas card but was dismayed to see that it simply said *Holiday Greetings from the South Pacific*. She almost would've preferred he'd sent nothing. Although, on the brighter side, at least he was still alive. That was something.

The V-mail from Bridget was equally dismal. She was obviously blue and discouraged, and although she'd gotten the letter telling her it was coming, she still hadn't received Molly's Christmas package.

"What's the news?" Dad asked as she rejoined him at the chessboard. Mam stuck her head out of the kitchen, waiting to hear. Molly knew it was time to put out another spin.

"The Christmas card was from Patrick," she said cheerfully, holding the card up so they could see the bright tropical picture. "It sounds as if he's doing well."

"Oh, that's nice," Mam said. "I haven't heard much about him lately."

"And the V-mail was from Bridget. She

sounded okay, but she still hadn't gotten my package. Although she wrote the letter more than a week ago, so I'm sure it's there by now. I wonder what it's like celebrating Christmas in a place that's so hot and muggy. Do you remember what she wrote about sitting in the laundry sinks, playing cribbage with Virginia?" Molly laughed. "I can still see that image in my mind's eye." She continued to chatter at them throughout the evening, trying to make light of their dismal holiday prospects, but by the time she went to bed, she felt completely drained and slightly irritated at Margaret. Why had she gotten everyone's hopes up like that?

Margaret was miserable. Christmas had been a disaster, both in San Diego and at home. And she felt it was mostly her fault. The day after her fight with Brian, which their son witnessed, she'd gotten into a fight with Colleen—and that was on Christmas Eve. Fortunately, it didn't happen until the kids were in bed. But as a result, their Christmas Day had been rather somber. Oh, Margaret had apologized—a couple of times—but she could tell that Colleen was holding it against her that they hadn't gone home. But, according to Molly, things hadn't gone too well at home either. Brian had not gone home and, when the Hammonds got wind of what happened in San Diego, they blamed Margaret for their spoiled holidays. Consequently, they didn't even go to her parents as planned. It was just Mam and Dad and Molly.

Margaret was glad that Colleen was back at work in Hollywood now. She'd even encouraged her to stay over if she wanted to attend any New Year's Eve celebrations there. Margaret knew her generosity was partly motivated by guilt and partly because, if she was going to be this miserable, she'd rather not have another adult around to witness it. However, when Colleen called on Thursday night to inform Margaret that she wanted to take her up on the offer, Margaret instantly regretted it—but she tried to conceal her emotions.

"You're sure you'll be okay?" Colleen asked with concern.

"Of course, we'll be fine." Margaret bit her lip.

"It's just that the producer is hosting this big New Year's Eve bash to celebrate wrapping the movie, and it would be considered quite rude for me not to attend."

"Yes, I understand. Really, we'll be fine."

"How's Mary Ellen's cold?"

"I think it's completely gone. She's back to her happy little self."

"Oh, good."

"What are you going to wear to the party?" Margaret tried to inject cheer into her voice.

"That is exactly what I wondered." Colleen

chuckled. "You know how I packed pretty light since I hadn't planned on doing much more than just working? But my agent had a gown delivered to me on set this morning. It's a gorgeous creation of metallic gold satin, with a draped bodice and very low back and sweeping skirt. Very glamorous. Of course, it needs some minor alterations, but the wardrobe girls are on it."

"Sounds beautiful. You'll be the belle of the ball."

"Well, I doubt that I'll stay late. And I'll be home on New Year's Day, hopefully before noon," Colleen promised. "And then we can head for San Francisco whenever we both feel like it."

"I'm not in any particular hurry now," Margaret said glumly.

"Well, maybe we'll want to enjoy some relaxation before we go home. I know I could use downtime. We can take turns watching the kids, and we'll eat fattening food and take some nice long walks on the beach." Colleen let out a long loud sigh.

"That sounds good to me."

"Give Mary Ellen a big kiss from me. And one for Peter too."

"I will."

"I love you, Margaret."

Margaret blinked back tears. "I love you too, Colleen. I hope you have a really great time at your party. You deserve it." They said good-bye and Margaret hung up the phone and burst into tears. She was glad for Colleen's sake, but the thought of spending New Year's Eve—her third wedding anniversary—alone with the kids, well, it was just terribly sad.

As Margaret got ready for bed, she knew this whole debacle with Brian was partly her fault. In fact, if she were being completely honest, it might be mostly her fault. Well, except for the part about Vittoria—Brian got to own all of that. But Margaret had been ready to forgive him. She had, in fact, believed she'd already forgiven him. But then during his week here at the beach house, the subject had come up. And, to be fair, it had been Margaret's doing.

After spending several fairly peaceful and pleasant days together, they'd been getting things ready to depart for San Francisco the following morning. But Margaret had an idea for how to spend their last evening in the beach house. She'd asked Brian to stay with the children while she drove to the store "for more formula," but she'd come home with more than formula. She had gathered seafood, a crusty loaf of bread, and a bottle of Bordeaux. After the kids were in bed and their romantic candlelit dinner was finished, they had sat by the fire, enjoying a last glass of wine.

Although this hadn't been part of her plan, Margaret asked Brian to tell her more about

Vittoria. Initially he refused, but when she pressed him harder, he eventually caved. It was possible that the wine had contributed to their conversation, making them both a little too relaxed. But Margaret had feigned nonchalance while listening to him recount the one-night encounter. And, really, it hadn't even sounded terribly romantic. Just two lonely people in a desperate situation. She almost understood.

And it had almost made her feel sorry for Brian—or else it was the wine—but she'd wrapped her arms around his neck then given him the most passionate kiss ever. As a result, they wound up in the same bedroom that night.

Margaret had felt like a new woman the next morning, full of great hope and high expectations. She'd believed this was the real turning point for them. She couldn't wait to go home and celebrate a truly happy Christmas with both their families. And naturally, she assumed this meant they'd live together as man and wife now. So when Brian informed her of his plans to return to USC—without her and Peter—she'd been deeply hurt. She'd felt used and betrayed, and the fight that resulted was not pretty.

In retrospect, Margaret could see that none of that ever would've happened if she hadn't pushed things. Her little plan to create a romantic evening had backfired on her. And her pressing questions about Vittoria had not helped matters.

Brian had probably felt just as used and betrayed as she had. But she had no idea of how to remedy this. Perhaps she should tell him she was sorry. Maybe it would be clearer in the light of day. She hoped so.

Twenty-Three

If December felt dark, Molly thought that January was even darker. The Battle of the Bulge raged on, casualties and deaths continued to accumulate, and the general spirits on the home front were low. This war was wearing and worrisome, and deprivations and rationing seemed to be taking their toll on everyone. Including the customers at the store. Poor Mam had suffered the impatience of several rude patrons when the items they wanted were unavailable. The usual excuse of, "These are war times," seemed to be wearing thin on many.

It hadn't helped that Colleen and Margaret decided to remain in San Diego for a couple of weeks. Molly had been looking forward to their return—and to their help. But Colleen had said they needed a break. Well, who didn't? Colleen hadn't said as much, but Molly suspected she was worried from not having heard from Geoff since before Christmas. "I like being down near the naval base," she'd admitted. "It makes me feel closer to him."

Molly also knew that Margaret and Brian were still at odds. Their third anniversary had passed with them remaining stubbornly apart. Brian was back in school, and Margaret felt certain that he was preparing divorce papers. As badly as Molly felt for them and young Peter, she was more concerned about Bridget. She could tell that her sister was more than just blue. Based on her last letter, it sounded as if Bridget might actually be ill. She'd lost weight, wasn't sleeping well, and felt homesick.

Molly knew that Bridget was in a region where tropical diseases ran rampant, but being that she was a trained nurse and part of a medical unit, it seemed that the staff would be aware of that potential. Molly even wrote her concerns to Bridget, asking if it was possible she was seriously ill—did she need to have a complete physical examination? She'd even quoted the old adage about how the shoemaker's children go barefoot. Was it possible that medical people were ignoring their own maladies?

The only bright spot in January was hearing that Lulu and Tommy had gotten engaged. Molly was truly happy for them. "And I want you for my maid of honor," Lulu told her. "We want to be married on Tommy's next leave . . . although that may not be for a while." Molly offered her congratulations, assuring Lulu that she'd be pleased to stand by them. And it would be her third time to participate in a wedding party. Perhaps this was her destiny. *Always a bridesmaid but never a bride.*

• • •

Colleen hadn't told anyone about the new role she'd been offered at the director's New Year's Eve party. Well, besides her agents, but she'd even asked them for a couple of weeks to consider her answer. Naturally, Georgina had called a few times, encouraging her to take it before someone else did. There was no denying it was a great role but Colleen was uncertain. She did, however, know one thing—if she took the role, she was taking Mary Ellen with her. Her hairdresser had suggested the idea of hiring a nanny and having her right there in the studio with her so that she could spend time with her during her breaks.

"And with this next contract, you could afford to buy a house in Hollywood or Beverly Hills," Georgina had pointed out. "Get something with a pool and room for a child to grow up and play. A place for Geoff to come home to."

While it was all enticing, she still wasn't sure. The last movie had been so hard on her. But she knew that was partly due to being away from Mary Ellen all week and then the commute on weekends. But it also had to do with Geoff. She hadn't heard a word from him for almost a month. She'd even checked with the Department of the Navy last week but had been assured that he was still listed in active service. "Our fighter pilots are extremely busy," the woman had explained with a tinge of impatience. "And the South West

Pacific Theater is extremely busy. Sometimes the V-mail gets delayed for various reasons. But I'll send a communication about your query, and I'm sure you'll hear from him soon."

It was the end of the week and Colleen and Margaret were cleaning the beach house and packing things up for the trip home. Colleen was just sweeping sand into a dustpan when she heard a knock on the front door. Startled by the sound, since no one ever came here to visit, she dropped the broom and hurried to answer it. To her stunned amazement, it was Geoff. Dressed in his casual uniform and holding a bouquet of roses, he swept her into his arms. "Surprise!"

She burst into tears, clinging to him. "I can't believe it! You're really here." She pulled herself back, staring up into his tanned face, and then he kissed her. It had been months since she'd felt this happy. "What are you doing here?" She wiped her damp face with the hem of her shirt—actually, one of his old shirts. "Are you on leave?"

"Liberty. We're in port for seventy-two hours."

"Why didn't you tell me you were coming?" Colleen touched her hair. "I would've fixed myself up for you."

"You look gorgeous to me." He glanced over her shoulder. "Hey, Margaret. How's stuff?"

Margaret greeted him, and while he plucked Mary Ellen out of her bassinette, Colleen took

Margaret to the kitchen to explain the change in plans. "I can't go home now. Geoff's got three days and—"

"I told Mam we'd be home in time for dinner tonight." Margaret frowned. "They're really looking forward to it."

"Well, I'm obviously not going anywhere." Colleen folded her arms across her front. "If you want to take my car and drive you and Peter home, that's fine. I guess Mary Ellen and I can catch a flight sometime next week."

Margaret simply nodded. "Okay, that's what we'll do."

Colleen blinked in surprise. "Really?"

"I just can't stand to disappoint the family again." Margaret tossed a sponge into the kitchen sink. "If you really don't mind, we'll go."

Colleen considered this. "You're right. And come to think of it, I think it's a good plan. You'll make better time without Mary Ellen and me slowing you down. Think of it—no diaper changes or extra feeding stops."

"Okay." Margaret checked her watch. "Do you mind if we take off now? I've got all our stuff packed, and Peter is eager to go."

"Not at all. Tell Mam and Dad and Molly I'm sorry not to be there tonight. I think they'll understand. And I'll let them know when I get a flight home." As Colleen hugged her, she tried to conceal how happy she felt about this sudden change of plans. Not only did she get to have Geoff for three whole days, she got to have him all to herself. Of course, she would share him with Mary Ellen. But she would not have to share him, or this compact house, with Margaret and Peter.

Molly was disappointed to discover that Colleen and Mary Ellen hadn't come home with Margaret, but she was happy to hear that Geoff was okay and that they were getting a few precious days together. "I'm glad you and Peter decided to come home today anyway." She carried two of their bags, leading Margaret and Peter over to Mrs. Bartley's house, which she'd offered to share with them. She unlocked the back door, letting them in through the kitchen. She'd already turned on the lights and the heat and pulled the blackout drapes.

"It looks like you've made some changes around here." Margaret looked around with curiosity.

"I've been trying to thin it out some. Mrs. Bartley lived here for decades, plenty of time to fill the house with years of living. I've been packing a lot of it up, stashing the boxes in the attic for now." She led them to the main downstairs bedroom, which she'd completely cleared out then set up like a guest room with a pair of twin beds that used to be upstairs. "I thought you and Peter may like it down here. I wasn't sure how well he'd handle the stairs. Besides, the larger bathroom is down here."

Margaret set a suitcase by the door, and Peter bounded over to a bed, scrambling onto it and bouncing up and down on his knees. "I'm happy for you," she told Molly. "I mean, that you've inherited all this. I'll admit I was a little jealous at first. But I can understand why Mrs. Bartley wanted this to be yours. You were such a good friend to her."

Molly set the luggage on a bench at the end of the other bed. "And I'm happy there are no hard feelings between us, Margaret, in regards to that letter Patrick wrote to Brian." They'd already gone over this on the phone, and Margaret had reassured Molly that all was forgiven.

"What do you hear from Patrick these days?" Margaret unpinned her hat.

"Not much." Molly shrugged.

"What do you mean?" Margaret tugged Peter from the bed.

"I guess we're sort of, well, we're not exactly together like before."

"What happened?"

"I don't really know. Maybe it's just not meant to be." Molly really didn't want to talk about it. "But, as it turns out, it's a good thing." She smiled. "I haven't told Mam and Dad yet, but I've been invited to go to Europe again."

"With that newspaper guy—Mike?" Margaret frowned.

"*Mick* Blackstone. He's the war correspondent with UPI, representing the *Chronicle* and head of the news team. Right now their office is in Paris, but they want to expand."

"But isn't it terribly dangerous, Molly? The war's still going, and I hear it's a mess over there with bombed out buildings and criminals around every corner. And if you're near the battlefront, you could get seriously hurt . . . or even killed."

"We'll have the protection of our armed forces, but I'll probably spend most of my time in the peace zones anyway. It's been my dream to do this, Margaret. I want to be a real photojournalist, and I really regretted not taking the opportunity before. I can't let it go now." She sighed. "Mazzie—the woman who went over with the first team—was injured—"

"Exactly my point. Don't you see what could happen to—"

"She tripped and broke her ankle."

"Well, I'm sure there's plenty of rubble to stumble on over there."

"Oh, Margaret." Molly rolled her eyes. "I could trip getting onto the trolley right here in town. Anyway, Mick wired today, asking me to replace her. And not just to take photographs but to report as well. Do you realize how big this is for me?"

"You seriously want to go over there?"

"More than anything, Margaret. I really, really do."

Margaret just shook her head. "Well, I can't imagine wanting to do something that crazy, but I guess if that's what you really want, well, I'll do my best to support your decision."

Molly hugged her. "Thanks! Please, don't mention it to Mam and Dad yet. I want to tell them myself. But I know how they'll react, and I didn't want anything to spoil their evening. Especially seeing that Colleen and Mary Ellen won't be here." She looked at the alarm clock by the bed. "Speaking of that, I'll bet Mam's got dinner on the table by now." Molly swept up Peter. "Let's go, young man." As they walked back, she told Margaret the rest of her plan. "While I'm in Europe, I'd like you and Peter to use this house as your own."

"Oh, Molly, that's so generous. Thank you."

"I think Mrs. Bartley would like the idea of her house being put to good use."

"Someday you'll have to stop calling it Mrs. Bartley's house, Molly. It's your house now."

Molly chuckled as they went into Mam's aromatic kitchen. "I don't feel like I'm old enough to own a big house like that."

Mam nodded as she pulled a roast from the oven. "I agree. It seems like just yesterday I was nagging at you to clean your room, Molly Irene."

They all laughed and, for a sweet change, Molly enjoyed the feeling of family all around her. Sure, it was only a small portion of the Mulligan family, but it was better than what they'd had at Christmas. And Molly knew she needed to relish these moments while she had them. Because she planned to wire Mick of her acceptance tomorrow morning. And if Mrs. Stern at the newspaper had managed to arrange for Molly's transport as promised, Molly could be leaving as soon as Monday. She hoped so!

Although Mam and Dad were disappointed that Colleen and Mary Ellen were still in San Diego, they were happy her sister was with Geoff. "We will just have to do this again next week," Mam said as Molly and Margaret started clearing the table after dinner. "It's hard to complain, knowing how I'll have three of my girls nearby—and my two grandchildren. I'm very thankful."

"Have you moved into Mrs. Bartley's house?" Dad asked Molly as she refilled his teacup. "Although I suppose there's no big rush, but I assume Colleen will want the apartment back."

"She may but I also plan to offer her the second floor of Mrs. Bartley's house. It's roomier and may be more comfortable."

"I would love to have them there with us," Margaret said.

"But we'll leave it to Colleen to decide." Molly almost told them it made no difference to her—since she'd soon be a few thousand miles away—but decided to wait.

"I've never liked the idea of you young mothers carrying your children up and down those steep stairs," Dad told Margaret. "They were only built for access to the attic, and if I were in better shape, I'd tear that thing down and put in a real staircase."

"Colleen considered that," Molly told him. "But her builder made it sound very expensive."

"Well, I do hope Colleen and Mary Ellen decide to stay next door." Mam set a cherry pie on the table. "And Molly can remain in the apartment. I'm sure you'd like that too, Molly. You wouldn't have to move all of your things."

Instead of making what would be an insincere response, Molly pointed to the pie. "That looks scrumptious, Mam."

"Well, it's just canned cherries. And I used up my sugar rations for Christmas, so it's honey and cornstarch for the syrup. And with no lard, the crust is made with bacon fat. It may look pretty, but the proof of the pudding is in the eating. I hope it's not too much of a disappointment."

Molly had to bite her tongue. She wanted to declare that compared to the deprivations she'd been reading about in war-torn Europe, this pie seemed practically decadent. Would she be regretting her decision in a week or two? Would she be craving western food and the comforts of home? She honestly didn't think so.

For two days Colleen and Geoff and Mary Ellen were like a normal little family, but by the third day, knowing their time together was dwindling, they both tried to make the most of it. Fortunately, the sun was out and while the baby was napping, they sat outside the back door, looking out onto the beach. "There's something I need to ask you about," Colleen began.

He turned to look at her with a furrowed brow. "Sounds serious."

She smiled. "Not terribly serious." She explained about the new movie offer, Georgina's suggestion that Colleen get a house in Hollywood or Beverly Hills, and the idea of having a nanny with her at the studio. "That way I could spend more time with Mary Ellen . . . and you'd have a full-sized house to come home to." She explained about how having Margaret with her had been less than ideal. "Molly would be great though."

"Yes," he agreed. "You should get Molly."

"So are you saying I should accept the movie offer?"

He shrugged. "I guess, if you want to. When is it supposed to start? And how long?"

"It's scheduled to begin in March, and they're giving it eight weeks, so it should wrap in May."

"Well, don't tell anyone I said so, but I doubt the war will wrap by then." He glumly shook his head. "Sometimes it feels like two steps forward and three steps back."

She reached over to touch his cheek. "I was so worried about you, Geoff. When I didn't hear from you for so long, I didn't know what to think. I'm so glad you're okay."

"There was a glitch with some V-mail." He frowned. "A ship carrying a lot of letters went down. I'm guess I had a couple on it."

She sighed. "I'm sorry about the ship . . . and the crew . . . but I'm glad to hear you'd written to me, even if your letters are at the bottom of the ocean." She chuckled. "Anyway, it's a good excuse."

"It's true." He grinned. "Anyway, back to your movie deal. It sounds good. And I like the idea of you being in a house near the studio. I worried about you being tired and driving back and forth."

"And as much as I love this little house, it's not really ideal for a full-time residence."

"Much better for a little love nest getaway," he teased, kissing her again. And she had to agree, it was a great place for a romantic rendezvous. Even one that was completely unplanned and unexpected. Hopefully they would be able to have many more.

Twenty-Four

Early February 1945

Colleen had been home a couple of weeks and was just feeling settled into the apartment over the store. She'd been disappointed to miss seeing Molly before she left on the train, but at least they'd talked on the phone. And Molly had left her a sweet "welcome home" note in the apartment. Colleen felt quite comfortable in the compact space. It really wasn't that much smaller than the beach house, but thanks to the renovations, it was more modern. Although it did make her look forward to having a larger home. Georgina had a real estate agent on that task, and already he'd sent her several photographs and detailed descriptions of available properties. Shopping for a home from a distance wasn't ideal, but Colleen felt fairly certain she'd like any of the beautiful properties.

In the meantime, Colleen was trying to spend time with her family and helping out at the store. Margaret eventually got over Colleen's choice not to live at Mrs. Bartley's house. It wasn't that she didn't love Margaret and Peter—although Peter's terrible twos phase did try her patience—

she just didn't want to live with them. Plus, she didn't want her family getting too comfortable having her here. She suspected they all assumed she was in San Francisco for good now.

It was probably her fault since, in a state of severe exhaustion in the midst of her last film, she'd told Margaret that she never wanted to make another film—ever! Naturally, Margaret had repeated that to everyone. Even customers at the store expressed their regrets that her "stint in motion pictures was over." Colleen simply had to bite her tongue and, being an actress, play along with them for the time being.

Her plan had been to announce her new movie contract as soon as she got home, but everyone was still in a dither over Molly, off on her journey to become a European photojournalist. In fact, Molly was the only family member, besides Geoff, who was aware of Colleen's new movie contract. They'd had a long phone conversation the night before Molly left. But Molly had promised to tell no one Colleen's plans, and then she'd asked for suggestions on what to take to Europe. "I have to pack light—only as much as I can carry without assistance."

Although Colleen didn't consider herself an expert on foreign correspondent fashion, she knew a thing or two about packing, wardrobe, and style. "Well, you'll probably be wearing a serviceable traveling suit. And you'll want to pack another sturdy suit, one that wears well and cleans easily, and several washable blouses. Besides that, I'd think a pair of good trousers would be handy, and a warm cardigan, some sturdy shoes—"

"Wait," Molly had interrupted. "I want to write this down. How do you know all these things, Colleen?"

She had laughed, admitting that she was pulling some of this from the war movie she'd been in last year. "Now, besides those serviceable items, you'll want a few pretty things. A couple of scarves, some simple pieces of jewelry—nothing valuable, although I'm sure you'll want your pearls since you almost always wear them anyway. But you should also take that black cocktail dress I gave you. Just in case."

Molly had argued this suggestion, but Colleen had remained firm. "You never know. And don't forget to pack plenty of stockings. I left several pairs in my bureau, so help yourself. I left a few pair of shoes behind too—ones that were too tight after the baby. They'll fit you perfectly. Take some with you. I've heard there's a terrible shortage of shoes in Europe. And now for your cosmetic bag. I know you, Molly—you'll probably think you don't need this, but be sure to take plenty of toiletries with you. I'm sure they'll be hard to find over there. And after you've been there awhile, if you find you need anything else, just wire me care of the studio and I'll have one of the assistants send you a package."

They'd chatted for a while longer and, when Colleen finally hung up, she was painfully aware of how much she'd miss her little sister. But she would keep her promise to pray for Molly every day.

And now, two weeks later, it was time to tell the rest of her family about her plans. Especially since Georgina had just called to inform her that the latest issue of *Hollywood Stars* was in the newsstands, with a nice piece about *Maureen Mulligan's new movie contract.* It was time for Colleen to let this cat out of its bag, and to that purpose, she'd offered to bring Chinese takeout food to her parents' tonight. With Mary Ellen in her car bed in the backseat and half a dozen white cartons in the front, she drove to their house. It wasn't that she was particularly worried over their reaction. She just wanted to soften the blow.

Just this morning, she'd overheard Mam telling a customer about how she'd been overjoyed at the thought of having three daughters home at the same time, but then it had never happened. Not only that, but Mam was overly concerned about Bridget right now. It seemed that Molly had raised a flag over Bridget's health and had even written to her questioning whether she was receiving good medical care. Unfortunately,

Bridget hadn't written back yet. And Mam seemed to grow increasingly worried.

Colleen parked in front and was just getting out of the car when Margaret appeared and offered to help. "You get the baby, and I'll get the food," she told Colleen. As they went up to the house, Margaret warned Colleen that Mam was a little out of sorts. "She got a short letter from Bridget this afternoon. Actually written to Molly but naturally Mam opened it. It seems that Bridget had confided to Molly that she actually was having some health problems, but she asked Molly not to mention it to Mam and Dad."

"And Mam read it?"

"Yes." Margaret set some cartons down in order to reach for the doorknob.

"Did she say what kind of health problems?"

"Malaria."

"Oh, dear."

"Mam isn't going to tell Dad, but I can see that it's eating her alive."

"Should I say anything to her about it?"

"Probably not. I just thought you should know."

Consequently, dinner felt somewhat stilted. Colleen and Margaret did their best to lift Mam's spirits and eventually the antics of the grand-children seemed to win out. Peter impressed his grandparents with his increased vocabulary, and Mary Ellen awed them by sitting up unassisted. When they gathered in the living room, Mary

Ellen provided more entertainment with her attempts to crawl, which were actually quite hilarious. But it was her giggles when Colleen played peek-a-boo that really lit up the evening.

Before long, Mam was smiling and laughing and seemed back to her old self. Colleen knew this was her big moment. If she didn't tell her family about her next film project, there was a good chance that one of the store's customers would mention it tomorrow. Possibly the young fans that sometimes popped in after school in the hopes of getting a glimpse of a "real movie star."

"I have a happy announcement," Colleen said just as Peter began to show signs of a temper tantrum coming on. He sometimes resented sharing the limelight with his young cousin.

"Oh, darling, are you expecting?" Mam's eyes lit up.

Colleen laughed. "Thank goodness, no. Geoff and I don't want to have more children until *after* the war."

"Then tell us," Margaret insisted. "We need some good news."

So Colleen quickly explained about the big movie contract she'd accepted and how it would allow her to purchase a house in Hollywood. "Just a few minutes from the studio. It'll be a nice place for Mary Ellen and me to feel at home in, and I'll hire a full-time nanny to help with her. And we'll get a complete nursery all set up in the studio, so I can visit her whenever I have a break between scenes. Sometimes it can be for hours."

"But Margaret said you were finished with movie making." Dad's brow creased.

"We thought you were home for good." Mam looked sadly at Mary Ellen now nestled in her lap. "You're taking my darling baby girl away again?"

"The movie will wrap in May," Colleen said meekly. "We can come back for a while then."

"For a while?" Mam looked close to tears. "Will Hollywood become your permanent home?"

Colleen held up her hands. "I don't know about that. When the war ends and Geoff comes safely home, I may be ready to give up acting for good. But in the meantime, Geoff felt it was a good idea. He seemed genuinely pleased for me—for us."

"But you were so exhausted after your last picture," Margaret said. "Are you sure you really can do this?"

"This time will be different." She explained her plan in more detail but could tell they weren't pleased. All they could see was that, once again, she was putting a lot of miles between them. "Someday this war is going to end," she declared. "Bridget will come home. Molly will come home. It's very likely that Geoff and I will come back here to live too. His family hopes so." She looked from Mam to Dad. "You'll suddenly be surrounded by children and grandchildren. There'll be so many and we'll be so noisy that you'll probably get sick of us."

Mam sadly shook her head. "I don't think that could ever happen."

"And I'm starting to feel like this war is never going to end." Margaret bent down to pick up Peter from where he was lying down and kicking his legs, his warning that the tantrum was about to start. "It's late. I think someone is ready for bed. Let's call it a night."

"Good idea." Colleen felt guilty for extracting Mary Ellen from Mam's arms. Not for taking the baby but for ending the evening on a slightly gloomy note. Still, it seemed better than allowing them to hear her news from a stranger or gossip magazine. But as she drove Mary Ellen through town, headed for their little apartment above the store, she felt a familiar wave of loneliness. This wasn't the life she'd wanted for herself or for her child or for Geoff. But what could she do? It wouldn't be easy being away from her family, working on a film, trying to be a good mother, praying that Geoff's plane didn't get shot down. It was a lot to expect of a person.

She just hoped she hadn't made the wrong decision.

Mid-February 1945

Molly loved Paris. Oh, she knew that the beautiful City of Lights wasn't enjoying her finest moment. Some of the old buildings were bombed-out and crumbling, some were pockmarked with bullet holes, but the splendor shone through. And, so far, Molly had no regrets about accepting this position. She'd kept a journal from the very start of her trip, writing about traveling across the United States by trains filled with troops—some on their way to the front and others, mostly the wounded, on their way home. Then she flew from the East Coast across the Atlantic Ocean in a military cargo plane that landed in an airfield in rural England. From there she was transported by a US Navy cruiser from Dover to Calais.

She would never forget the chill she'd experienced as the naval ship crossed the English Channel, and it wasn't just the damp winter weather either. She was well aware that thousands and thousands of brave young men had given their lives in this very stretch of sea. From the British servicemen in the Battle of Dunkirk, back when she was still in high school, to the Allied forces on D-Day last June during the Invasion of Normandy. She had felt extremely humbled to even be there on the same water.

From Calais she had traveled by army jeep to Paris, arriving just as the sun was setting on the magnificent old city. Everything had been bathed in golden light, and it had been love at first sight for her. Even the apartment she shared with Mazzie, who was laid up with a cast, was surprisingly nice.

For the next couple days, Mick had encouraged her to settle in and explore some of her surroundings. But when she told him about walking mile after mile, using her own camera to take photos of the Louvre and Eiffel Tower and Arc de Triomphe and Champs-Élysées and Notre Dame and Sacré Cœur, getting almost everywhere on foot, he was astonished.

"You're a real trouper," he told her. "I better put you to work before you walk your legs off—or break one like Mazzie." So the next day, she went to work in the press office. Her responsibilities varied from the darkroom, where she spent most of her time, to transcribing stories, to just mundane office work. She knew that, being a woman, she wasn't only a minority but an oddity. Mazzie had warned her not to expect much respect from her press peers. "And even if you get a good photo or write a good story, the guys will take the credit for it."

"Even Mick?" Molly had asked.

"You're part of his team," Mazzie explained. "He's responsible for all you do."

Molly had just shrugged it off. Did it really matter who got the credit? The important thing was that she was here. And even if she never got out of the press office, she was still seeing and experiencing things she would never have seen before. Her only complaint, if she were to make one, was that the food really was a challenge. Besides beets, beans, and cabbages, the markets were very limited. Other than an occasional soup bone, meat seemed nonexistent, and luxuries like cheese, butter, coffee, or cream were only available on the black market. But Molly had expected as much, and after her first week, she discovered the best times and days to go foraging. Even her two years of French in high school were paying off. She was improving each day.

She'd been there nearly a month before Mick invited her to go on location with his team. He wanted her to get some photos of the Allied troops still stationed near Luxembourg, where the Battle of the Bulge had recently ended. And although the Allied forces had successfully driven the Germans out and claimed the victory, making Paris even safer, Mick reminded her that this war was not over.

They left at daybreak, wedged in with some soldiers and other press agents, and rode in the back of a military transport truck. Molly was the only woman and, even though she was dressed in trousers, a heavy jacket, and a wool beret she'd borrowed from Mazzie, she got more attention than she liked. But still enthused over her first "assignment," she took their flirtations in stride. As it turned out, it actually came in handy for getting what she hoped were some pretty good shots. It seemed everyone was eager to help her. And by noon, she was nearly out of film.

"If I knew you'd be this popular, I would've brought you on location weeks ago," Mick teased Molly. Some of the soldiers had given Molly K-rations, and she'd invited Mick's team to a "picnic lunch" in a nearby abandoned barnyard.

Sitting on an old chopping block, Molly removed her coat and hat and shook her hair out in the spring sunshine. "What a gorgeous day," she proclaimed as she opened her box of K-rations. "And thank you, Lord, for this fine meal, and bless the hands that shared it. Amen." The rest of her team echoed with an "amen," and before long, some of the other press groups came over to join them. Some just wanted a cigarette break, some were making a meal with what little food they'd managed to purchase from a local farmer, but everyone seemed to be in pretty good spirits.

A young cameraman from a government film crew came over to sit on a stump next to Molly, peering curiously at her. "Has anyone ever told you that you look just like Maureen Mulligan?"

She just grinned, chewing a mouthful of sardines.

"Did you see her in that movie with Darlene Devon and Robert Miller?" he asked.

"Aw, Louie, quit flirting with the kid." An older press agent smacked him on the top of his head.

"I mean it," Louie persisted. "Maureen played the little sister." He pointed at Molly. "And you look just like her."

"That's because I *am* a little sister." Molly winked at Mick.

"That's right," he said. "She *is* a little sister."

"Don't you think she looks just like Maureen Mulligan?" Louie asked Mick.

Mick turned to Molly with a grin. "Miss Molly Mulligan, I'd like to introduce you to Louie Marzini. Louie, meet Molly."

"Molly *Mulligan?*" Louie's brow creased. "Oh, so you really are the little sister?" He chuckled. "I think that's what I'll call you. Little Sister."

She nodded, chewing a piece of hardtack, and suddenly the other press agents were pestering her with questions. Knowing that Colleen was probably already shooting her next movie, she politely answered, satisfying their curiosity about the goings on in Hollywood these days. Then as their lunch break wound down, Mick waved to the commanding officer nearby. "I want to go talk to him," he told Molly. "You can get more shots if you want or just wait here until it's time to return to Paris."

Molly picked up her camera bag, checking to

see how much film was left in the camera and trying to decide if it was worth using it now or wondering if she might get some good shots on the way back to Paris. Meanwhile, Louie watched on with a curious expression.

"So, Little Sister." He grinned down at her, casually cleaning his camera lens. "Why aren't you a motion picture star like your big sister?"

She laughed as she stood, holding up her camera. "Because I would rather be behind the camera than in front of it."

He chuckled as he moved away from her and then, holding up his movie camera, focused it toward her. "Would you mind if I got some footage of you in action?"

She shrugged. "I guess not."

"How about we go over by the troops and you can just pretend to be taking photos," he suggested.

"Or maybe I'll take some real shots," she said lightly.

She attempted to ignore him as she went around the camp, getting a couple of random shots and then just chatting with various soldiers, all who seemed happy to engage with her. Some offered her cigarettes, which she politely refused, but one soldier insisted on giving her a chocolate bar, and she took his photo.

"And that was my last shot," she announced with a bright smile. She waved to the soldiers and headed back to the barnyard to wait for Mick.

Louie continued to trail her. His camera was down now, but he continued to chat with her, asking about her age and how it was she'd gotten assigned to a press team.

"Is this an interview?" she asked him as she sat down on the stump again.

"Sort of." He grinned. "You gotta admit it makes a pretty fun human interest story."

She shrugged, peeling open her chocolate bar, which was already getting soft from the warmth of the sun. "Want some?" She held out half of the bar.

His eyes lit up and he set down his camera. "Sure, thanks." He sat on the stump near her and proceeded to eat the chocolate.

"Is it hard to run one of those things?" She pointed to his movie camera.

"Not at all. It's not that much different from your camera."

"Do you think I could ever learn to use one?"

"Sure." And now he let her hold his camera and gave her some tips on how to use it. "Do you ever get a day off?"

"Of course." She handed the heavy camera back. "I don't usually work on weekends."

"Maybe you'd like to come on a shoot with my team sometime. I could bring along a spare camera and show you how to use it."

"Really? That'd be super."

"So it's a date."

She frowned.

"I mean it's a deal." His grin was slightly sheepish. "We're getting ready to go over to the Rhine—"

"The Rhine? Isn't that an active battlefield?"

"Not exactly. Not yet anyway. The troops are assembling there now." He nodded toward the nearby camp. "Even these guys are about to move over there. The prediction is that they'll cross over the Rhine by the end of March—and maybe even end this war for good. But I'd like to get a reel of the troops by the river in the next week or two. Just to have it ready to release when the action starts."

"And I could go with you?"

He nodded. "Sure, if you want."

Molly wasn't completely sure that Mick would approve—mostly because he tended to act like a protective big brother. But he had told her that her free time was her own—to do as she pleased. "I'd love to go."

Mick was approaching now, waving toward her as a supply truck slowed down behind him. "Come on, Molly. We got a ride back to Paris," he yelled.

As she grabbed her things, she told Louie how he could reach her when he was ready to go to the Rhine. Then running to catch up with Mick, she called "good-bye."

"See you later, Little Sister," Louie shouted as she climbed into the back of the truck with Mick and the rest of the crew.

"We were lucky to get this ride," Mick told her. "We'll be back in Paris a little before dark. The rest of the press guys will probably be stuck there overnight."

As the bumped along in the back of the truck, Molly cheerfully chatted about how much she'd enjoyed her first "on location" photoshoot. And then she rambled on about how much she loved Paris and hoped she would be able to stay there for a long time. "Maybe even after the war ends."

"You're still in the honeymoon stage," Mick teased her after they were dropped off in Paris. "You'll get over it soon enough. We all do in time. The deprivations eventually get to you." He'd insisted on seeing her home since it was quickly getting dark.

"I'll agree that the food shortages are a challenge here," she admitted as they walked along the Seine. "But I can't complain about my accommodations." She was actually looking forward to returning to the apartment this evening. "Much better than the camp we saw today. Although, despite their hardships, the troops seem to be in good spirits."

"I suspect some of them were so pleased to see a pretty American woman that it lifted their spirits." Mick paused to light a cigarette.

She laughed as they turned toward her neighborhood.

"I'd wager that every single one of those men, every soldier you saw today, has suffered a loss. Sure, they're still whole and alive and may seem to be in good spirits, but they've lost some of their buddies. Some are permanently gone, some are missing. Many are in hospitals, getting patched up in order to return to the battlefield, and others are on their way back to the United States, hoping to put all their broken pieces back together."

She nodded somberly as they strolled past a building that had been gutted by bombs. "Yes, I'm sure you're right."

"The numbers for the Battle of the Bulge are staggering, Molly. Have you heard the latest count?"

"No." She shook her head.

"I don't want to be too grim, but I just wired an article home—not that the numbers will make print. Not on the front page anyway. But our American troops suffered more than 100,000 casualties total. Close to 20,000 of those are dead, more than 60,000 are wounded, and close to 25,000 are missing or captured. All in less than one month."

"Oh, my." Molly couldn't even imagine such numbers.

"War is hell, Molly." He paused in front of her

building and, dropping his cigarette stub, ground it out with his heel. “Tell Mazzie hello for me.”

Maybe Mick was right, Molly thought as she went up the stone steps and into the lobby of the building. Maybe her honeymoon here would come to its end. Certainly it was hard to feel happy after hearing those awful statistics. And she knew that the numbers were mounting on the other side of the world too. She tried not to obsess over the telex messages that constantly came into the press office, but she knew the war in the Pacific was hotter than ever right now. Casualties and deaths were mounting there too. And she felt farther away from Patrick than ever over here, but she tried not to dwell on it too much. All she could do about Patrick these days was to pray . . . and she did plenty of that, especially in the middle of the night when the tears sneaked in on her.

Twenty-Five

Late March 1945

Bridget felt defeated and weary as she waited in the lobby for Mam to pick her up at the military hospital in San Francisco. She'd only been at Letterman for three days and had told no one in her family that she'd been shipped back to the mainland. Partly because she didn't want to trouble them and partly because she hadn't been certain the doctor planned to let her go home. And maybe it was foolish pride, but she couldn't bear the thought of having her family coming here to visit her. It was humiliating. She felt like a failure.

"I'll discharge you, Lieutenant Mulligan," the elderly physician had sternly agreed this morning. "But only as long as you promise to continue your treatment—and that means plenty of bed rest. I've treated too many army nurses of late, and it greatly concerns me that these ailing young women have taken better care of their patients than they have of themselves. How can you help someone else if you can't help yourself?" He peered over his spectacles into her eyes. "And, believe me, a good army nurse is worth her weight in gold right now."

She'd apologized to him and promised to do better. But knowing she was taking up limited space and medical attention, she had begged him to let her go home and was relieved he'd conceded and relieved to get back into her uniform. Although, not wanting to be confused as a Letterman nurse and asked to help with something, she'd pulled on her cape then hurried down to the main lobby to call the store. Naturally, Mam was surprised to hear her voice, but Bridget refused to give any details and simply asked for a ride home.

As she'd sat there, waiting for Mam to drive over from the store, Bridget passed her time by reading a newspaper. The latest and biggest story was that the Battle of Iwo Jima had ended in victory for the US and Allied forces. That horrible fight had dragged on for more than a month. Bridget was glad to hear it was over, but not being able to care for the wounded felt more sickening to her than having malaria. Thousands of injured servicemen were pouring out of there. Many of them were arriving right here at Letterman, transported by the dozens throughout the day. So for her to occupy precious bed space for a stupid case of malaria wasn't only wasteful, it was stupid. Especially since her malaria symptoms were, for the most part, similar to a troublesome case of flu. Although sometimes, when it got really bad, she wished she were dead.

Seeing her parents' car pulling up to the portico, Bridget gathered her duffle bag and purse and hurried out to meet her mother. The wind and rain blew through the covered area like a small tornado, whipping her cape all around her. Chilled to the bone and slightly breathless, she climbed into the car, thanking Mam for coming out in this weather.

"Oh, darling." Mam leaned over to hug her tightly. "I would've driven through a blizzard to get you. Are you okay? What are you doing here? Is it a leave? Or are you sick? And why didn't you tell us sooner?"

"I'm fine." Bridget couldn't stop from shivering. "Just need some rest."

Mam grasped her hand, clasping it tightly. "You're cold as ice!"

"I'm not acclimated yet." Bridget wrapped her cape more tightly around her. "It was so warm when I left. And so cold here."

Mam turned the heat to high then reached around to get the wool blanket from the backseat, handing it to Bridget. "Is it the malaria?" Mam asked with concern as she started to drive.

"Who told you that?"

Mam explained that Molly had left to be a photojournalist in Europe more than a month ago. "So I opened her mail. I didn't know what else to do. I hope you don't mind."

"Molly is in Europe?" Bridget tried to absorb this strange information. "That must be why I haven't heard from her."

"Yes, she's been very busy. We just got a short note yesterday. She said she's enjoying herself and that her press friends took her to see the Rhine River and that she celebrated her birthday in Paris. She said it was the first good meal she'd had since leaving home. Poor thing." Mam sighed. "This doggoned war is so hard on everyone."

Bridget wondered if Mam even knew the half of it. Thankfully, Mam didn't understand the significance of Molly visiting the Rhine River. Did she not understand that the Rhine was Hitler's backyard? Or that Molly must've been there around the same time that McArthur had successfully driven troops across the river, forcing the Nazis to retreat and resulting in the surrender of thousands of German soldiers? According to the press, the Nazi troops were demoralized by this attack, and this was the beginning of the end for Hitler and his evil forces. And to think that Molly was there right now . . . well, it was almost too much to absorb.

Early April 1945

Colleen loved her new house. Well, it wasn't really *new* since it had been built in the late

1920s—before the depression—and, according to the real estate agent, had been briefly occupied by Charlie Chaplin and one of his wives. The Spanish-style home wasn't overly large and was handily located in Hollywood, just minutes from her studio. The curving wrought-iron staircase and colorful tiled floors made for an elegant entrance, and the arched windows and doors looked out over a gorgeous backyard patio, complete with a small jewel of a pool. It was perfect.

Because the director had allotted for more time to shoot this film, the cast and crew had been granted more time off, which Colleen was thoroughly enjoying. Hopefully, with the weather cooperating and if all continued to go well, their relatively relaxed filming schedule would continue. Of course, the days they filmed were always long ones, averaging about twelve hours or more. But at least she had Mary Ellen nearby. Unfortunately, Colleen wasn't terribly pleased with the nanny she'd hired. Greta Holstein had come with a good recommendation, but the older woman, with her numerous rules and regimentations, seemed a bit stern. So much so that Colleen's hairdresser had started calling her Nazi Nanny.

But when Colleen caught Greta swatting eight-month-old Mary Ellen on the bottom, she promptly dismissed her, telling her to evacuate her home immediately. "And do not ask me for a recommendation," she declared hotly as she tried to comfort her crying child, walking her back and forth in the sweet little nursery that she'd set up before the movie went into production. "Well, well, well," she cooed to Mary Ellen. "We got rid of the wicked witch, but now we need the good fairy to come and care for you." Not for the first time, Colleen wished that Molly was nearby. But her sister was having a good time in Europe—at least, her letters made it seem that way. And she'd been befriended by a cameraman named Louie from New York, who was teaching her to film motion pictures. Colleen suspected he wanted to be more than a friend to her pretty little sister, but Molly claimed otherwise.

Since it was Saturday, Colleen wasn't sure who to call in order to secure a new nanny—and how to find one who was not so stern. And thinking of Molly made her suddenly miss her family. So she called the store's number, hoping to hear Mam's comforting voice. And perhaps, if Bridget was feeling better, she could see about enticing her to come care for Mary Ellen for the next month, until the movie wrapped.

But it was Margaret who answered. "Colleen," she declared. "I was just thinking about you. How are you?"

Relieved to hear a warm friendly voice, Colleen poured out her troubles and how she was glad to be rid of Nazi Nanny. "But I shouldn't take up your time," she finally said. "It's a Saturday and you're probably busy with customers and—"

"I'm just balancing books in the office," Margaret said glumly.

"How are *you* doing?"

"Oh . . . I don't know. I'm okay, I guess."

Colleen didn't think she sounded okay but decided to leave it at that. Everyone knew that Margaret could sometimes complain about the smallest things. "How's Peter?" she asked cheerfully.

"He's doing just fine. I put him in nursery school a few weeks ago, after I was certain that he was completely potty-trained. And he just loves it. No more tantrums."

"That's wonderful. And how is Bridget?"

"She's better. Still a little weak but not nearly as skinny as she was when she got home. Mam's main goal in life seems to be fattening her up."

"I'm sure she needed it." Colleen sighed. "And I suppose she's not well enough to come down and help me with Mary Ellen."

"Is that why you called?"

"Not exactly. I just wanted to hear a friendly voice. And then I thought Bridget might like spending time with her niece and—"

"Why can't I come down there?" Margaret said suddenly.

"Would you want to? What about Peter's new

school? And aren't you needed at the store? And—"

"I'm sure there are preschools down there," Margaret said quickly. "And Bridget recently asked if she could help with the store. She thought it would help her get stronger if she had something to do. She even asked about living in the apartment. I think she wants a bit of independence from Mam and Dad."

Colleen set Mary Ellen back down in her playpen. "Would you really want—"

"How soon do you need me?"

"Right now wouldn't be too soon."

"That's fine with me," Margaret said. "But I doubt I can get us on a train. I've heard they're filled to capacity with servicemen on the move. Molly left me the keys to Mrs. Bartley's car . . . I suppose I could drive down."

"Oh, Margaret, would you?"

"Do you think Molly would mind?"

Colleen assured her that their generous little sister would probably be completely supportive of this plan, and they soon agreed that Margaret and Peter could leave Sunday morning and arrive in Hollywood by midafternoon. As Colleen hung up, she hoped that this would be good for both of them. As she picked up Mary Ellen, walking her through the roomy house, she thought this setup was highly preferable to the tiny San Diego house. Plus it sounded as if Peter had grown up some. "Auntie Margaret and Cousin Peter are coming to visit," she cheerfully told Mary Ellen as they went out onto the patio. "Won't we have fun?" And it would be fun to show her house to a family member. She just hoped that Margaret wouldn't feel too envious.

Bridget was truly pleased to hear that Margaret actually needed her help at the store. She immediately went to work packing her bags in order to move into the apartment on Saturday evening. Working at the store had provided her with the perfect excuse to move out of Mam and Dad's house. It wasn't that she didn't love them, but Mam had practically been smothering her with attention. As a result, Bridget had grown worried that Dad was being neglected. And she knew his health was more perilous than her own. But it was impossible to convince Mam of this fact without putting her into a worse state of worry.

"I'm really glad to do this," Bridget told Margaret as they carried her bags up the stairs to the apartment above the store. She hadn't been up here since Colleen's renovations, but as Margaret opened the door, Bridget released a happy sigh. "Oh, my." She walked around the clean modern space, taking it all in. "It's beautiful. Do I really get to live here?"

"Of course." Margaret set her bags in the main

bedroom. "Colleen is responsible for all this. Being a rich movie star has its perks."

"I'll say." Bridget poked her head in the bathroom. "So modern and nice. Everything is perfectly lovely."

"I'll tell Colleen you like it."

"It'll be so nice for her to have you and Peter down there."

Margaret led her over to the little kitchenette, opening the icebox. "I stocked you up on some essentials, but if you need more, you know where to get them. Just be sure and write them down in the 'family business expenses' section I showed you on the ledger."

"I will do that." She nodded happily. "And don't worry, Margaret, as a nurse, I'm used to making careful notations about everything, and your bookkeeping system makes a lot of sense to me. I doubt I'll have any problems with it."

"Just call me if you do." Margaret heaved a tired sigh. "I'm really grateful for you doing this, Bridget."

"Are you okay?" Bridget peered curiously into Margaret's face. "You look a little pale to me. And you've seemed so tired lately."

Margaret made what seemed a forced smile. "I'm fine."

Bridget cocked her head to one side. "Are you sure about that?"

"Oh, Bridget." Margaret started to cry.

"What is it?" Bridget hugged her. "What on earth is wrong?"

"Oh, Bridget, please promise not to tell anyone—but I'm . . . I'm afraid that I'm expecting."

Bridget slowly released her, staring at her with concern. "Are you certain?"

She nodded. "I just heard back from the doctor a couple of days ago."

"But you and Brian . . . you aren't even together—"

Margaret hurriedly explained about a one-night encounter they'd had in San Diego. "But no one else knows and I don't want them to know."

"But eventually . . . they'll have to know."

Now Margaret confided about how she'd lost a baby. "I wasn't quite this far along, but I felt there was a chance I could lose this one."

"Do you want to lose it?" Bridget tried not to look alarmed.

"No, of course not. But I thought, well, in case that happened . . . perhaps it was better to wait to tell them." She sighed. "Not to mention it will be awkward to say the least."

"Brian doesn't know?"

"We haven't talked since December. I thought he may come up here from college a few weeks ago, for spring vacation . . . and to see his son. I thought I'd tell him about my suspicion, but he didn't show up."

"Oh, Margaret." Bridget sadly shook her head. "I'm so sorry."

"So, you see why I'm eager to get away. It'll give me time to figure things out. I just can't bear for Mam and Dad to know about it yet. Or the Hammonds. Please, I'm trusting you not to tell a living soul."

Bridget pressed a forefinger to her mouth. "Loose lips sink ships."

"And it already feels like this ship is going down."

"No, it's not," Bridget proclaimed. "A baby is something to celebrate. And even if Brian doesn't come through for you, your family will. When is the baby due?"

"The doctor said the third week of September. Peter will be almost three by then."

"And he'll make a sweet big brother. Just like our Peter was to me."

Margaret sighed. "Thanks, Bridget. You've given me hope." She hugged her again. "Keep getting better, sis. We need you around here."

"I am getting better." Bridget tried to sound more confident than she felt. As much as she wanted to get well, she sometimes felt hopeless. She wasn't sure if it was because of the malaria and just the general weariness of war . . . or perhaps it was because of her broken heart. The truth was she just didn't have the same kind of energy she'd once had—and she wasn't sure that she'd ever have it again. Sometimes she envisioned herself as a weak invalid, quietly subsisting in her childhood bedroom and wasting away for whatever time was left in her life.

Twenty-Six

Thanks to a late start and waylays on the road, Margaret didn't get to Hollywood until nearly dusk. And then it took another twenty minutes just to find Colleen's house, but only because she drove right past it several times. "I just couldn't believe this was really your house," she told Colleen after she finally parked in the circular driveway. "You really played it down on the phone. It's so gorgeous." She stared in wonder at the graceful stucco structure as they carried bags inside. "Just like a real movie star's house."

Colleen laughed. "Well, Charlie Chaplin did live here."

"That's interesting." Margaret took in the beautiful entryway, colorful tiles, and wrought-iron staircase. "Everything is so pretty, Colleen. You must feel like a princess living here."

Colleen pointed over to where the playpen was set up in the middle of a spacious living room and Mary Ellen was beating on the rails with a wooden rattle, making loud baby noises. "That little princess keeps me rooted in reality." She set Margaret's bags down and went to the playpen. "I kept her up past her bedtime so you could see her," she told Margaret as she picked up Mary

Ellen. "Say hello to Auntie Margaret and Peter."

Colleen gave them a quick tour of the house. "I hope you and Peter don't mind being on the second floor." She opened the door to a pretty yellow and white room. "If you're concerned about the stairs, we could get one of those baby gates to—"

"Peter has gotten quite good at stairs," Margaret told her. "We'll be just fine."

"The nanny stayed in the maid's room in back," Colleen explained. "But I didn't want you stuck in there."

"Thank you." Margaret looked around the attractive guest room. "This is lovely—and big too."

"There's another room up here, in case you and Peter want separate—"

"We will happily share a room," Margaret told her.

Mary Ellen was starting to fuss and Colleen said she'd go feed her while Margaret and Peter got settled. "There's milk and a few things in the icebox. Help yourself to anything. Then we'll get the kids to bed and sit down and catch up."

Margaret hated feeling envious as she made herself at home in her sister's luxurious house. The kitchen, like everything else, was spacious and beautiful. Even Colleen's dishes and glasses were pretty. It was all like a fairy tale, making Margaret's life seem more like a tragedy. Still, as she tucked a very tired Peter into the big bed they would share, she was determined not to be jealous. Colleen had worked hard to get to this place, and she'd always been generous with her family. Really, Margaret knew she should be nothing but grateful—so why did she feel like crying?

Margaret went back to the kitchen, pouring herself a glass of orange juice and sitting down at the pretty breakfast nook that she suspected looked out over the beautiful yard that she'd barely seen when they'd arrived. It would probably be quite pleasant in the morning sun. And Colleen even had a swimming pool. Although that might prove a challenge with Peter since he didn't know how to swim. But Margaret would be careful about that.

"There you are." Colleen joined her, pouring herself a glass of orange juice too. "Peter all settled in?"

"He was half asleep when I got him into his jammies."

Colleen smiled. "I'm so glad you could come."

"Me too." Margaret nodded, still feeling on the verge of tears. "Your home is so beautiful, Colleen. Far better than I expected."

"Well, this is Hollywood, after all. Everything has to be over the top." Colleen peered curiously at her. "Are you okay, Margaret? You seem sad. Are you sorry you came?"

"No, I'm glad I came." Margaret bit her lip.

"Are you sad about Brian? Does being down here make it harder . . . I mean, knowing he's nearby?"

"I don't know . . . not exactly." Margaret started to cry. Not a loud blubbering cry, but just silent tears streaming down her cheeks.

"Oh, honey." Colleen handed her a box of tissues. "What is it?"

"I'm pregnant." And now she cried harder.

Colleen was clearly shocked, but Margaret quickly explained how it happened and when she was due. "I feel like such a fool." She blew her nose. "Something like this could only happen to someone as stupid as me."

"You're not stupid."

"I sure feel stupid."

"Does Brian know?"

"Of course not."

"Does anyone know?"

"Just Bridget—and I made her swear secrecy."

"How are you feeling? Do you think you're really up for taking care of Peter and Mary Ellen?"

"I feel perfectly fine." She sniffed. "I had wondered if I may, well, you know . . . if what happened before . . . not that I want to lose a baby . . . but it could happen. But I haven't had morning sickness or anything. I felt so normal that I didn't even suspect I was pregnant at first.

Then just finding out that I was, well, that's when I started to feel bad. Not physically. Just sad at heart. I can't imagine raising two children by myself."

"You'll never be by yourself, Margaret. You have our family."

She nodded. "Yes, that's what Bridget said too. But you know what I mean. It's one thing to be alone while your husband is in the service, but you hope for the day when you'll all be together."

"Now that I know you're pregnant, we may want to reconsider having you and the kids at the studio all day. I'm afraid it will wear you out."

"I thought about that too." Margaret explained her idea of driving herself and the kids to the studio later in the morning. "We could stay until it's time for afternoon naps, then come back here."

"That sounds just fine." Colleen explained some details concerning the house and what days the weekly housekeeper and yard man came. "And the neighborhood pool guy comes every few days, usually in the morning." And, of course, there was the daily diaper service and dairy delivery. "I wrote all this down." She pointed to a paper taped by the telephone. "As well as any phone numbers you may need."

"It seems you've thought of everything." Margaret sighed. Who knew that her flibbertigibbet sister would grow up to be the responsible one? Margaret's life, compared to Colleen's, was just a big fat mess.

April 12, 1945

Bridget was working late. Holed up in the store office, she was balancing the books with the radio tuned to a music program for company. She set down her pencil and listened when the music stopped for an "important announcement."

> We interrupt this program to bring you a special news bulletin. A press association has just announced that President Franklin D. Roosevelt is dead. He passed away late this afternoon in Warm Springs, Georgia from a cerebral hemorrhage.

Bridget felt a lump in her throat for the loss of her hero . . . now gone. And before he could see the conclusion of this war that he'd given his all to support. Everyone knew that the president had health issues, but it was also widely believed that he had for the most part conquered them. As a nurse, however, Bridget understood better than most how the president's health had been impacted by a sudden illness back in 1921. It was something she'd studied in school, something that even the medical professionals seemed baffled by. Had his paralysis been the result of poliomyelitis or something else?

Whatever the cause, she felt certain that his death by "cerebral hemorrhage" was related to his previous illness. And it grieved her deeply to hear that he was dead.

Bridget closed the books and turned out the light, trudged wearily up the stairs to the apartment, and turned on the radio up there to listen for updates. As she put the tea kettle on to heat she remembered when she was twelve and FDR was campaigning for the presidency. She'd been an avid supporter, debating in sixth grade over why he was the best candidate to lead their nation. Later on, when she was sixteen, she'd actually volunteered to campaign for his reelection, zealously handing out flyers and attending rallies.

Even when she was twenty and busy with nursing school—and still not old enough to vote—she'd taken time to hang campaign posters on campus and encourage classmates of voting age to support him. And finally, in the last election year, while serving overseas with the ANC, she'd been able to cast her first presidential vote for him. Bridget sat down with her cup of tea, listening as the newscaster on the radio quoted from FDR's speech following the attack on Pearl Harbor: *"This is a date which will live in infamy . . .*" He went on to remind listeners of how quickly their president declared war, how fully he supported the troops. "And although our beloved leader will not get to celebrate this long-awaited victory here on earth, we will honor his memory as we press onward toward it."

Tears came as Bridget listened to various broadcasters commemorating the life and service of FDR. But she knew her tears weren't only for the deceased president. She remembered stories of how bravely he'd fought to beat his disease, pushing through severe pain and disability, dismissing discouraging diagnoses and prognoses, with a sole focus on getting better. He managed to convince the public at large that he was not suffering, even though medical professionals knew otherwise. He was so persuasive that he managed to win the office of president for a fourth time—even though he was confined to a wheelchair. FDR had been a real trouper.

Suddenly, Bridget knew that if FDR could press through his many challenges, she could too. She would follow his example and get stronger and fitter. Before long she would be back at doing what she loved most—nursing. Even if the war ended before she could be reassigned overseas, she knew they would still need nurses on the home front. Letterman was shorthanded right now. Somehow, Bridget was determined—she would be working there by summer.

April 30, 1945

It was the end of the workday when Molly read the surprising message just coming through the telex machine. She couldn't miss the ironic timing of this occurrence—while America was still grieving the loss of their beloved FDR, one of the most despicable leaders of all times, Adolph Hitler, had just killed himself.

Molly called out to the other clerks and female assistants who, like her, were stuck in the UPI office while their male counterparts covered the Battle of Berlin. "Hitler is dead!" she announced loudly. "The war must be nearly over!" And suddenly everyone in the press office was shouting and dancing, holding an impromptu celebration.

"Listen to how he did it," a UPI secretary named Clara called out from where she was reading the telex machine as it continued to print. "It says he took his new bride Eva Braun into the bunker with him where he reportedly shot himself and she bit into a cyanide pill. They committed suicide together."

"What a coward," Mazzie said. "Afraid to face our Allies and afraid to die alone."

"And listen to this," Clara continued. "He and Eva Braun had only been married for *forty hours.*"

"Less than two days?" Mazzie echoed. "And

she was willing to take her own life for him?"

"Isn't it equally amazing she was willing to marry him?" Molly mused.

"Maybe he forced her," Mazzie suggested.

"What a monster!" Clara pulled a bottle of champagne out of her desk. "Let's all drink to his demise."

"Here, here!" Mazzie ran to get some paper cups, waiting as Clara popped it open and began to fill their cups.

Mazzie held up her cup. "Here's to him rotting in hell!"

"And his bride too," someone else yelled.

As Molly sipped her champagne, she remembered a source that Mick had told her about a few days ago, right before he'd left with the others to cover Berlin. He'd met someone in Paris who was acquainted with Hitler's girlfriend. "May make for a good side story," Mick had told her. Molly pulled her notebook from her purse. The source's name was Hans Muller and since the address wasn't too far away, she decided to check it out.

As she walked down the avenue, she hoped that this fellow spoke something besides German—otherwise, she'd need a translator.

The address turned out to be a small clock shop that was just closing. When she asked the man locking the door about Hans Muller, he tapped his chest and said, in perfect French, that was him. In less than perfect French, she explained that she was an American reporter, inquiring as to his willingness to be interviewed.

"You vant interview me?" He smiled as he switched from French to slightly stilted English. "Vat for?"

"It's in regard to Eva Braun," she said tentatively. "I was told you knew her."

His smile faded. "Eva Anna Braun?"

"Do you know her?"

"Yah, I know her . . . *before,* I know her."

"Do you have time to talk?"

He studied her with interest. "Talk to pretty girl like you? Yah, I make time." He nodded inside to the shop. "You come inside?"

Although she wasn't eager to be alone with this man, who appeared to be in his thirties, she didn't think Mick would've recommended him if he was untrustworthy. So she went inside, explaining that her boss Mick Blackstone had told her about him.

"Oh, yah, yah. Mick ees goot man. He bring watch to me. I fix it goot." He led her to the back room and to a small work table covered with various tools and pieces of watches and clocks. He pointed to one of the two wooden chairs, waiting for her to sit and then sitting across from her with a somber expression. "What ees you vant know about Anna Braun?"

"Did you know her well?"

"Ve vere kinder in Berchtesgaden. Goot freunds . . . family freunds." He glumly shook his head. "Anna, she change. She change because Heinrich Hoffman."

"Who is Heinrich Hoffman?"

"Heinrich photograph for Nazi party. He hire Anna to vork for him. She siebzehn."

"Siebzehn?"

He held up his hands, flashing his fingers as if numbering them.

"Seventeen?" Molly asked. "Do you mean she was seventeen years old?"

"Yah. Siebzehn—seventeen. Anna assist Heinrich in photograph studio. She model for photograph. She vork darkroom."

Molly made quick notes.

"Anna vork for Heinrich. Anna, she photograph." He used his hands to pantomime a camera.

"Do you mean Anna was a *photographer* too?"

"Yah, yah. She ees photographer."

Molly nodded as she made more notes. How strange that this Anna had been on a similar path at a similar age . . . so much like Molly. It was downright creepy.

"Yah. Eva Anna Braun ees vell known photographer."

Molly frowned, suddenly realizing he probably didn't know that his old family friend was dead. "Have you heard the news? Is it on the radio?"

"News? Radio?" His brow creased.

Molly explained how Eva Anna Braun had married Hitler two days ago and how they committed suicide together. "About two hours ago—in Hitler's bunker in Berlin."

Hans didn't seem too surprised. "Yah, ees goot that Satan ees gone. Very goot. He ruin Deutschland."

"Yes." She nodded.

He pursed his lips. "Anna verstorbene?"

"Verstorbene?"

He closed his eyes, tilted his head, as if pantomiming death.

"Yes, yes—Anna is dead too."

"Anna—she versuchen—she try before . . . to end life." He held up two fingers.

"Two times?"

"Yah." He sadly shook his head as she wrote this down.

"How did Anna get involved with Hitler? Do you know?"

"Anna's sister Margarete. She also vork for Heinrich Hoffman. She—"

"Margarete . . . her sister?" Molly couldn't help but notice another commonality with Anna. A real shiver went down her spine, and she almost wished she hadn't come here today.

"Yah. Margarete. Also call Gretl. Drei Braun sisters." He held up three fingers. "Anna, Margarete, and Ilse. Margarete ees introduction Anna to Herr Wolff and—"

"Herr Wolff?"

"Hitler."

"Oh." She made quick note of this name, listening intently as Hans used words and pantomime to recount Eva's off-and-on-again relationship with Hitler, starting at the age of nineteen. He said that Eva's sister Ilse had confided to his family that Anna had been pulled into Hitler's world, suggesting that she was too young and got in too deep, and that perhaps it was why she'd tried to kill herself those other times. Or else Eva had felt trapped in a relationship of which her family disapproved and which she was forced to keep secret. Molly suspected that Hans Muller had liked Anna a lot, when they were young. They were the same age—thirty-three now. But they had parted ways when she got involved with the Nazi party. He was clearly not a Nazi sympathizer. He said that Hitler had had another wife, but Anna became part of Hitler's household in his Bavarian home. She was his secret mistress. He believed she'd been brainwashed by the Nazi party in her early twenties, saying she was never the same after that. "Hitler ruined her."

When he asked how she'd died, Molly explained that although Hitler died of a self-inflicted gunshot wound, it was suspected that Eva had taken a cyanide capsule.

He simply nodded. "Ve know no goot vill come

of Anna and *Herr Wolff.* Goot it ees uber und done." And then he buried his head in his hands and wept.

Molly didn't know what to say or do, so she just sat there, waiting.

Finally, he looked up. "Is goot Herr Wolff is verstorbene—dead." He shook a fist. "Brenn in der Holle!"

Molly had heard that German phrase before. *Burn in hell.*

Hans slowly stood, going over to unlock the door.

She followed him. "Thank you for telling me about Eva Anna." She reached out to shake his hand. "I am sure if Herr Wolff hadn't ruined Anna, she would've been a good person with a good life."

"Yah." He sadly nodded. "Herr Wolff ruin many goot people."

Molly felt overwhelmed as she walked to her apartment building. Hitler's girlfriend and wife of forty hours had once been a young girl not so different than Molly. It made her feel slightly sick to imagine this. And for the first time since coming to Europe, she wanted to go home.

Twenty-Seven

Early May 1945

Colleen's movie finished filming on the eighth of May, but at the wrap party later that evening, the cast and crew celebrated more than just the completion of the film—they also celebrated that the war in Europe was finally over. Germany had officially surrendered to the Allies yesterday and, as a result, the eighth had been proclaimed VE Day in honor of the Victory in Europe.

Colleen stayed at the party for what she felt was a polite amount of time then, excusing herself to go home to her daughter, she made her exit. Because of Margaret's condition, Colleen had agreed it was best for her to care for Mary Ellen and Peter at home. But that had meant less time for Colleen to be with her baby, and she'd been missing her. Of course, the kids had already been put to bed by the time she got home, but she and Margaret had a little celebration of their own, indulging in a fancy box of chocolates that had been given to Colleen by the director, along with glasses of milk.

"Do you think this means the war in the Pacific

will soon be done too?" Margaret asked as she bit into a cream-filled chocolate.

"I sure hope so, but from what I've been reading, the Japanese are being very stubborn."

"Too bad the Japanese emperor didn't follow Hitler's lead and kill himself."

"Maybe he will." Colleen held up her milk glass up like a toast. "Here's to Hirohito committing hari kari."

"Here, here." Margaret held up her glass too.

Colleen took a sip of milk. "I can't imagine how the Japanese can hold out much longer. For my own selfish sake, I hope it ends soon. I miss Geoff."

Margaret sighed. "I miss Brian too."

"Really?" Colleen peered curiously at her. This was the first time she'd mentioned Brian since coming down here. "He's only about a half hour away, Margaret. You have a car. What about paying him another visit?"

Margaret firmly shook her head. "I just can't. I tried it once, Colleen. He doesn't want to see me."

"But what about—"

"No." Margaret stood. "I mean it. I have no intention of running to him now. I can't bear the idea of telling him that I'm . . . I'm pregnant . . . and having him feel sorry for me. If Brian comes back to me, I want it to be because he loves me."

Colleen nodded. “Okay. I understand.” She let out a tired yawn. “It will be so nice not to hear that alarm going off at five-thirty. I plan on sleeping in tomorrow morning—that is, if Mary Ellen will cooperate and sleep in too.”

“Don’t worry, I’ll slip in and get her when she wakes. It’s usually around seven, and Peter is always up by then anyway.”

“That would be fabulous.” Colleen hugged her. “You’re an angel.” She told Margaret good night then tiptoed into the nursery, just like she did every night, to gaze upon her little cherub by the soft glow of the nightlight, kissing her fingertips and gently touching Mary Ellen’s head. And then she went to bed.

The next morning, it was nearly nine when she finally got up. Margaret and the kids were in the living room, Peter playing with a toy truck and Mary Ellen in her playpen. “Oh, there you are.” Margaret stood up from the sofa. “I didn’t want to wake you, but this came—”

“What?” Colleen rushed over to take the telegram from her.

“It’s not from the War Department.”

“Oh, thank God.” Colleen let out a relieved sigh. “I had a bad dream about Geoff last night.” She slit open the envelope and quickly read it. “My goodness!”

“What is it?”

“I’ve been invited to participate in a USO tour.

It's with Bob Hope. In the South Pacific. And they leave in just ten days."

"Are you serious?" Margaret peered down at the telegram. "Wow, that must mean you're really famous."

Colleen laughed. "Too bad I can't go."

"Why not?"

"Oh, I can't imagine dragging Mary Ellen on a—"

"You'll leave her with me."

"Oh, Margaret, how can I do that to you?"

"How can you say no to the USO? And Bob Hope? And if you're in the South Pacific, you may get to see Geoff."

"Geoff . . ." Colleen considered how wonderful it would be to see him. "But it's for *three weeks,* Margaret. How can I leave you for that—"

"We'll be just fine, Colleen. Honestly, I think you should go." She pointed to the phone number at the bottom of the telegram. "Call them. Say yes."

And so without really giving it any more careful thought, Colleen did call them . . . and she said yes.

"Oh, that's wonderful, Miss Mulligan. We apologize for the short notice. Lana Turner was scheduled to go on this tour, but she had to cancel yesterday. I heard her little girl got sick. Anyway, we spoke to your agency, and they suggested you may be available." Now the woman explained that Colleen would need a passport, a medical examination, some immunizations, and a few other things. Colleen agreed to get on it, and the woman said that a contract with instructions would be delivered to her by courier before noon.

"Well, I guess it's settled," Colleen told Margaret. "I'm replacing Lana Turner."

"My, my, my . . ." Margaret's brows arched. "Aren't you something."

Colleen grimaced. "I just hope the servicemen aren't disappointed. I've heard that Lana Turner is one of the most popular pinup girls."

"I guess she's about to have some competition." Margaret headed for the kitchen. "How about some coffee to celebrate?"

As Margaret made coffee, Colleen made a list. "There's a lot to get done." She set down her pencil. "And, if you don't mind, I'd like for you and Peter to move into my room when I go. So you'll be closer to Mary Ellen."

Although Colleen was busy for the next few days, she also got to spend a lot of time with Mary Ellen. She even babysat Peter so Margaret could enjoy some downtime. And although they'd gated off the swimming pool for safety's sake, Colleen started taking Peter in each afternoon while Mary Ellen and Margaret were napping, in order to have swimming lessons, which Peter loved. And on the day before she was to leave for the USO tour, they invited Margaret to the pool to see Peter's progress. With Colleen's supervision, he plunged into the pool then held his breath and floated on his tummy, energetically kicking his legs behind him.

"I can't believe it." Margaret clapped her hands. "He's a regular Johnny Weissmuller!"

Peter performed a few more tricks, and then Colleen lifted him out of the water and onto the pool's deck. "I wish this pool had steps to make it easier for everyone to get out." As she climbed out, she reminded Margaret to keep the gate securely locked. "Now that he likes the water, we need to be extra watchful."

"Don't worry, I'm very careful." Margaret toweled Peter dry.

"And we'll continue our lessons when I get back." Colleen tousled his damp hair. "Right now I need to pack for my big trip." Fortunately, she didn't have to pack much. The USO had hired wardrobe experts to organize gowns for her, most of them donated from the studios. All she needed to pack was the clothing she would need for when not performing, and, according to the list she'd been sent, she wouldn't need much. Just comfortable, cool, "wash and wear" clothing that was suitable for the humid tropic zone. And, she'd been told, "expect rain."

Although Colleen was sad to part with Mary Ellen for three long weeks, she was really looking forward to this trip. For starters, she was thrilled to meet Bob Hope, but besides that she was eager to encourage the troops. Perhaps most of all, she was excited over the prospect of seeing Geoff. Although she'd sent him a telegram nearly a week ago, informing him of the tour's schedule, she hadn't heard back from him by the time the hired car picked her up to take her to San Diego. All she could do was hope for the best.

"The agency told me that the reason I picked you up this early is because you have an errand to run," the driver said as he pulled away from her house.

"That's right." Colleen hadn't told Margaret of her plans. "I need you to drive me to USC. I don't plan to be there more than an hour. Maybe not even that long. Then we can head down to San Diego."

"You got it."

Colleen gave him the address that she'd copied from Margaret's address book the other day. Brian had no idea that his sister-in-law was about to pay him a visit, but because it was Saturday and fairly early in the morning, she expected him to be in his dorm. And she had her little speech all ready to deliver to him.

"Here you go." The driver parked in front of a large stucco building then got out to open her door. "It's not a parking zone, but I'll wait here. If anyone gives me a hard time, I'll just circle around and come back."

"Thank you." Colleen smoothed her cream-colored jacket and adjusted her hat then started up the steps. Before she could knock on the door, a couple of young men—with wide eyes—stopped to ask if she was Maureen Mulligan.

She flashed her wide Hollywood smile and explained why she was there.

"You're Brian Hammond's sister-in-law?" the taller one said. "Who knew?"

"Would you mind getting him for me?" she asked pleasantly.

"Not at all." The tall guy nudged the other guy. "Go get him, Fletch."

"If you get her autograph for me," Fletch said.

While she waited for him to get Brian, she signed two autographs for both of them. When Brian appeared with a bewildered expression, she waved to the two fans and led him away to a nearby grassy area where she'd spotted a bench that appeared relatively private.

"What are you doing here?" Brian asked. "Is something wrong? Is it Peter? Or Margaret? What—"

"It's *you,* Brian." She sat down and waited for him to sit. "You are what is wrong. You are being completely unfair to Margaret. I realize that she hurt you by her brief flirtation with Howard Moore, but you completely betrayed her with your Italian floozy—and then you act as if she's the one to blame. Well, I am here to tell you that you are wrong. And when you married Margaret, you said it was for better or worse and in sickness and in health—and all that. But when it gets a little rough, you just take off like a—"

"Do I get to respond?"

She glared at him. "I'm not done."

"Fine." He held up both hands. "Have at it."

"Margaret is in a lot of pain because of you. Yes, she's made her mistakes, but she has apologized to you. And she has offered to forgive you. She even understands about you wanting to finish school. But when you completely neglect your son—you don't even come to visit him during your spring vacation. You don't bother to send him a card for Easter. And you totally ignore his mother on Mother's Day and—"

"Mother's Day?" He frowned. "When was that?"

"Last Sunday," she snapped.

"I didn't even send my own mother a card," he mumbled.

"You know, Brian, everyone understands that you lost a piece of your leg in the war . . ." She tapped his chest. "But I think you must've lost a piece of your heart too."

He just shook his head.

"Maybe you're finished with Margaret, but you still have a son. You can't just toss him aside. How hard would it be for you to visit him? He's less than forty minutes from here—"

"Less than forty minutes?"

She quickly explained about them staying at her house in Hollywood.

"Well, I didn't know that."

"Meaning you would've gone to visit him?"

Brian pursed his lips.

"Brian Hammond, what is wrong with you?" Colleen narrowed her eyes. "It's as if you're hiding out from life. When did you become such a coward? I never knew you to be like this."

"There's a lot you don't know."

"Oh, I'm sure there is. And I don't need to know everything. But Margaret deserves to—and you have a responsibility to talk to her. If you can't talk to her, maybe you should just move forward with your divorce plan." She shook an angry finger in his face. "But just be warned—besides alimony, you will be paying child support—*times two!*"

"Times two?" He blinked. "What do you mean?"

"I hadn't meant to spill the beans, but someone should. Margaret is expecting."

"What? How did this happen?" He looked blindsided.

"Seriously? You should know how these things happen by now. Her first name may be Mary, but I assure you it was *not* immaculate conception."

"Well, no, of course not."

"Her due date is the third week of September.

You're an educated man, Brian—you do the math." She stood and donned her dark glasses. "Now, I'm on my way to the South Pacific for a USO tour. Margaret will be caring for Peter and Mary Ellen at my house in Hollywood for the next three weeks." She handed him a card that she'd written her address and phone number on. "I think it's time for you to man up to your responsibilities. And if your marriage is really over, you need to let Margaret know. She's been hanging in the balance for long enough." Colleen squared her shoulders. "Good day."

Margaret didn't regret encouraging Colleen to participate in the USO tour, but the prospect of being home alone with two small children for three long weeks did make her feel a bit lonely. At least she was in a lovely home, and she did have neighbors—although many of them were celebrities who seemed to appreciate their privacy.

After a few days of feeling a bit lost and alone, like a rudderless boat floating around on the sea, Margaret decided to establish and stick to a daily and weekly routine. She hoped that would help her to pass the time with less stress and more grace. And for Peter's sake, she decided that one part of the daily routine must include a swimming lesson. Not only had he been begging to get into the pool, she discovered that it proved a great incentive and reward for good behavior.

As reluctant as she was to squeeze into a swimsuit since she was almost six months pregnant, she was willing to do so for her son's sake. She'd brought an old suit from home and opened the side seams to accommodate her expanding waistline, but she still looked like an overstuffed sausage. Naturally, Peter didn't care, and Colleen's backyard was blessedly private. So each afternoon, after all three of them had taken a good nap, she would give Mary Ellen her bottle then place her in her playpen in the shade while Peter and Margaret splashed around in the pool. After the first week, she realized that she enjoyed it almost as much as Peter. And his skills seemed to be improving daily.

"Auntie Colleen is going to be surprised," she told Peter after he dogpaddled all the way across the width of the pool. "You're a regular little fishy. Now come on back to me." He giggled as he turned around, dogpaddling back to her and splashing so hard that her hair and face got wet. "Good job!" She caught him in a soggy hug.

"Daddy?" Peter's eyes grew wide as he pointed over her shoulder.

"What?" She slowly turned, expecting to see the pool guy, but was shocked to see Brian standing on the patio. At least she thought it was Brian. He looked strikingly suave and sophisticated. He had on sleek dark pants, a crisp white shirt, a neat striped tie, and a jacket hanging over his shoulder, dangling by one finger, as if posing for an advertisement.

"Daddy?" Peter squinted into the sunlight.

"You're right, Peter," she quietly confirmed. "That is your daddy."

"I knocked on the front door," Brian told her. "When no one answered, I figured you were out. The door wasn't locked so I let myself in, thinking I'd need to call for a taxi to take me back to campus." Brian studied her with what seemed a slightly smug expression, a stark reminder of her less than attractive appearance.

She carried Peter over to the pool's side, setting him on the edge of the patio. "Go tell Daddy hello." Hoping that Peter would distract Brian with a soggy hug, she self-consciously climbed out and hurried over to where she'd laid her terry robe on a lounge chair. As she awkwardly tugged on the robe, sliding her feet into her pool sandals, she could hear Peter bragging to Brian about how he could swim.

"Really?" Brian sounded doubtful. "You can swim all by yourself?"

"Yeah. I a wittle fishy. Mommy said so."

Using her towel to blot her damp hair, she turned around in time to see Peter heading back to the pool. "No, Peter," she called out. "We're done with the pool for today."

"But he wants to show me he can swim," Brian protested. "Why not let him? I'd like to see this."

"He's doing well, but he still needs help," she said with irritation. "And I am done for the day."

Peter looked impishly from Margaret to Brian then jumped into the water and started to dog-paddle in circles, showing off his new skills.

"That's fabulous!" Brian exclaimed. "You're doing great."

"Yeah, just great," Margaret muttered. "Now I'll have to get back in and help him climb out. The pool doesn't have steps, and he can't get out without—"

"I'll help him out." Brian knelt down and held his arms out as Peter dogpaddled toward him.

Mary Ellen was starting to fuss now. "Fine," Margaret told him. "I'm going to take care of the baby." Relieved for an excuse to escape, she scooped up Mary Ellen and carried her toward the house but was barely in the door when she heard a big splash. She turned to see Brian and Peter both in the pool. Peter was giggling like it was the funniest thing ever, and Brian looked thoroughly humiliated—and sopping wet. Margaret couldn't help but laugh at the ridiculous scene. "Need any help?" she asked between chuckles.

"No, thank you," Brian said crisply. "We can handle this."

"Good." She continued into the house, still giggling. "Uncle Brian got dunked," she whispered to Mary Ellen as she took her to the nursery to check her diaper. "Maybe he needed it." After a quick diaper change, she set Mary Ellen in her crib with several toys. "I'll be right back."

She made a quick dash to Colleen's bedroom, where she pulled on her favorite yellow maternity dress and tied back her shoulder length hair with a floral print scarf. As she hurriedly applied a touch of coral lipstick, she wondered why on earth Brian had shown up like this. What was going on? As neatly as he'd been dressed, before his dunking, she wondered if this could be a "professional" visit. Was he here to present her with divorce papers?

Twenty-Eight

Margaret heard the pitter-patter of Peter's feet slapping against the tile floor as he raced to the bedroom. "Daddy all wet!" he exclaimed.

"You're wet too." She toweled him off, pointing him toward the clothes she'd laid out for him. "Get dressed while I check on Daddy." She got a terry bathrobe out of the small closet that contained some of Geoff's clothes and took it out to the pool area, along with a towel. Brian was still dripping, looking dejected as he sat on a lounge chair with his prosthetic leg across his lap.

"Are you okay?" She handed him the towel and robe then sat across from him.

He held up the prosthetic leg with a dismayed expression. "This isn't supposed to get wet."

"We can dry it." She reached for the leg, using a towel to blot it dry then removing the shoe and sock and sitting it out in the sun.

"Why aren't there steps in that pool?" he asked as he removed his soggy tie.

"I don't know, but it drives us crazy."

"It's not safe."

Margaret just looked at him. "Did you really come here to discuss the swimming pool, Brian?"

"No, of course not."

"Why don't you get into something dry?" she suggested. "Then you can tell me why you came." She pushed herself to her feet. "Colleen has some of Geoff's clothes here. I'll go get something for you." She went to the bedroom to discover Peter was dressed but had his sandals on the wrong feet. She told him to switch them around then helped him with the buckles. "Now go talk to Mary Ellen," she said as she gathered some things for Brian to borrow. "Keep her happy for me and I'll give you a Popsicle later."

"Okay, Mommy." He happily skipped off to the nursery. She carried the clothes out to discover Brian, now in the terry robe, using walls and furniture to hobble through the house.

"It figures that I'd come here without my cane today," he muttered as she lent him her arm, helping him make his way to the bathroom. "The one time I could really use it."

"I'm sure your leg will soon dry out." She pushed open the door to the luxurious bathroom, setting the clothes on the bench across from the oversized vanity. "Holler if you need anything."

"Thank you," he murmured as she closed the door. Then, while he got dressed, she hung his garments on the clothesline behind the kitchen to dry. She even emptied his pockets and, laying the contents of his wallet out, she was surprised to see that he still had photos of both her and

Peter in it—and thankfully, no photos of anyone else. Then she went to the laundry room to get a mop, returning to find Brian now making his way out of the bathroom. The tan trousers, which had probably been too long, were rolled up like clam-diggers, but the Hawaiian shirt seemed to fit okay.

"Here." She handed Brian the mop.

"You want me to do some cleaning?"

She laughed. "No, it's a makeshift cane."

He experimented with it as she helped him to the living room. "Sit down," she told him. "And tell me what you're doing here."

He sank into an easy chair with a weary sigh. "Well, I didn't come here to take a dip in the pool."

She smiled. "No, I didn't think so."

He tilted his head toward the front door. "I left something for you on the table in the foyer."

"Oh?" She braced herself. "Should I go get it?"

He just nodded.

Expecting to see a large envelope which would, she felt certain, contain divorce papers for her to sign, she went to the foyer. There on the glass topped table was a long white florist box. She picked it up and returned to the living room. "For me?"

"Happy Mother's Day."

"That was last weekend."

He nodded. "I know."

She opened the box to see a dozen lovely yellow roses. "Oh, Brian . . ."

"Do you still like yellow roses?"

"They're my favorite." She leaned down to smell them. "Thank you."

"The florist told me that yellow represents friendship." He sighed. "I thought maybe that was a good place for us to start."

She nodded, blinking back tears. "If you'll excuse me, I'll go put them in water and check on the kids." So this wasn't about the divorce, she thought as she peeked in the nursery to see that Mary Ellen was contentedly playing with a wobble toy while Peter pretended to read her a picture book. That boy was going to get two Popsicles!

As she arranged the roses in a crystal vase, she wondered if they were simply meant to soften the blow—perhaps he'd come here to discuss the details of the divorce. In that case, she needed to be strong. For Peter's sake, she needed to act perfectly normal. And, really, if he wanted a divorce, maybe it was for the best . . . certainly better than this limbo life she'd been living. Oh, their parents would be upset and the church wouldn't approve, but what could she do?

As she carried the roses out, Brian with his mop-cane came hobbling toward her. "May I get a drink of water?" he asked as she set the vase on the dining table.

"Yes, of course. Or I have some lemonade if you'd rather." She led him into the kitchen.

"That sounds good." He eased himself into the breakfast nook just as Peter bounced into the kitchen, reminding Margaret of her Popsicle promise.

"Take a seat next to Daddy," she told him, "and I'll get it for you."

After they were settled, she went to get Mary Ellen, putting her into her doorway swing in the kitchen. "You keep an eye on her," she told Brian, "while I check on your clothes and things. Maybe your leg is dry by now."

His clothes were still damp, and she moved his shoes to get the last of the afternoon sun then returned with his leg. "The leather straps aren't completely dry," she told Brian. "But you probably don't want it to get too stiff and hard in the sun."

"No, that wouldn't be good," he agreed. "Do you have some kind of oil I could rub into it?"

She got him some vegetable oil and a cloth, then seeing that it was after five o'clock, she decided to get dinner started. "Do you want to stay for dinner?" she asked as she started to cut up some fruit. "We're not having anything fancy. Just franks and beans and fruit salad."

"Sounds like a feast to me."

"And I could make a green salad. One thing about southern California—despite the war rationing, we can usually get good produce down here." She pulled some vegetables out of the icebox.

"Colleen's kitchen is very modern."

"Did you see that she even has an automatic dishwasher?"

"I thought that's what that may be. Very swanky." He set down his empty glass. "This whole place is very swanky. Seems your little sister has really arrived."

She nodded. "And right now she's flying around the Pacific front with Bob Hope."

"Bob Hope . . . I always hoped to see him in a USO show. But we did get Glenn Miller. That was special."

The next couple of hours passed a bit like a three-ring circus, with Margaret feeding the baby, fixing and serving dinner, checking on Brian's clothes, getting Peter to pick up his toys, and finally getting the children put to bed. Although she really just wanted to collapse, she went out to get Brian's clothes off the line. Unfortunately, they still weren't completely dry.

"I suppose you could just wear Geoff's things home." She held out his damp clothes, noticing that he had his prosthetic leg back in place.

He looked down at the overly long trousers. "Yes, I could do that. I'm sure you'd like to get me out of your hair."

"Except that you still haven't told me why you

came." She laid his damp clothes over a kitchen stool then noticed that the kitchen was all cleaned up. "Did you wash the dishes?"

He nodded to the dishwasher. "That thing is washing them."

She blinked. "I haven't ever used it."

"Why not?"

She shrugged. "I wasn't sure how it worked."

"It's simple." He showed her the little booklet that explained everything, which he'd found in a drawer. "And it seems like you should be taking it easier, Margaret." He patted her stomach. "In your condition."

It was his first mention of her pregnancy, and she wasn't sure how to respond. She turned away and, opening the icebox, removed the pitcher of lemonade. "Want some?" she asked. He agreed and soon they were seated in the living room with their drinks. "So, Brian," she said slowly. "Why did you come here today? I'm guessing it was to discuss the divorce?"

"The divorce?"

"Don't you remember that you told me you were drawing up divorce papers?"

He waved a hand. "That was only because I was angry with you."

"Oh . . . ?" She sipped her lemonade.

"I don't want a divorce, Margaret."

"You don't?"

"No . . . but I wouldn't be surprised if you did."

She shook her head. "No, I don't."

He set down his drink and leaned forward to look at her. "Margaret, I am so sorry. I feel that I've made a mess of everything. And it's completely my fault that our marriage has suffered so. I know you said you'd forgive me, but I also know I don't deserve your forgiveness."

"According to Father McMurphey, no one deserves forgiveness. That's the beauty of it."

"I know Father McMurphey also encourages confession." Brian clasped his hands together. "And I need to make a complete confession to you."

Margaret braced herself, hoping he wasn't about to come clean with a list of other women that he'd been involved with. She really didn't think she could take it.

"You know about Vittoria," he said, "but you don't know all the circumstances surrounding that day. It's hard to admit this, but we'd been through a very ugly battle. I'd lost a lot of men, and I wasn't just feeling lonely, like I told you I was, but I was terribly frightened." He looked at her with troubled eyes. "I felt certain that I was going to die in the next battle. It seemed inevitable—and I was truly afraid. So when I helped Vittoria that day, it distracted me from my deep fear. And when we drank wine that night, I let my defenses down."

He ran his fingers through his hair with a

frustrated sigh. "But that's not what I really wanted to say. What I need to tell you is that I blame myself for getting wounded in the next battle. I felt the loss of my leg was the price I had to pay for betraying you. And I felt horribly guilty because after I got home, I knew that I was making you suffer right along with me. And that's when I decided you deserved someone better, and I started pulling away. It just seemed the kindest thing to do."

She took his hand. "You were wrong about that, Brian. That was the cruelest thing to do."

"I know that now." He told her about Colleen's visit last weekend. "I thought about what she said all week long, and I realized I needed to make one last attempt to restore our relationship."

"Does that mean you've been able to forgive me?"

He nodded. "Yes, I have completely forgiven you, Margaret."

"And I've forgiven you."

"Have you forgiven me for thinking the worst of you after I read Patrick's letter?"

"Yes. I understand how that happened. It's all behind us now."

"I was a fool to misunderstand Patrick's letter like that and to react so badly to it. I realize now that he'd simply felt protective of me—probably because of my injury. That letter was his attempt to connect with me." He frowned. "But now I'm worried that I may have said too much to him."

"What do you mean?"

"Well, I wrote a long letter to Patrick—in response to his first letter. I told him that I believed servicemen were mistaken to take a bride before heading out to the battlefield. I told him I had deep regrets and wished I'd never married and—"

"You wish you hadn't married me?"

"It's not that I didn't love you, Margaret. I just realized, too late, that it was wrong to tie you down like that. It was selfish of me. For me to marry you and then bring a child into the world without knowing whether I'd even make it home . . . or that I'd be wounded . . . Well, it was just wrong. I can see that now. And that's exactly what I told Patrick."

"Is that why he broke things off with Molly?"

His brow creased. "He broke things off completely?"

"That's what Colleen thinks."

"But I know he loves her. I'm sure he plans to marry her . . . after the war ends. I think he just wanted to cool things down for the time being."

"Well, he cooled things down, all right. Last I heard, Molly has a string of beaus trailing her around Europe."

"Europe? What on earth is Molly doing in Europe?"

Realizing that Brian had been out of the loop

for some time, she quickly explained. "She's been there for about four months."

"What remarkable sisters you have. Colleen touring with the USO shows, Molly in Europe, and Bridget in the ANC."

Now she filled him in on Bridget's illness and return. "But she's making a good recovery. I talked to her a few days ago, and she hopes to return to nursing as soon as I get back to take over the store, after Colleen's tour ends."

"So, if you're down here for two more weeks, do you think that you and Peter would like to attend my graduation? It's on the tenth of June."

"I'd love to."

He smiled, still holding to her hand. "Do you really think we can make another go of it? Put everything behind us and go forward?"

"I do."

"I do too." He leaned forward to gently kiss her.

"But this time, let's take it slow. Like the yellow roses suggested, I think we should work on our friendship," she told him.

"I agree completely." He looked down at his wristwatch. "I think my dip in the pool killed this thing."

She glanced at the clock above the fireplace. "It's half past eight."

"I should go."

"Or you can stay here if you want. Colleen has

lots of rooms. You can have the guest room on the second floor. Or if the stairs are too much, you could have the maid's room behind the kitchen."

"I can do stairs," he assured her. "And if you don't mind, I'd love to stay over. I want to get as much time as I can with Peter." He smiled. "And with you."

As it turned out, he stayed over on Sunday night too. "I don't have classes on Mondays," he told her that morning. "I'd like to make some steps in the pool today. I think it'd be safer. Do you think Colleen would mind?"

"I think she'd be glad. But how will you do it? We can't drain the pool."

He explained his idea to get concrete blocks and arrange them into steps, drawing a diagram to show her how it would work. "If you don't mind me using a car, I'll see if I can find some blocks at a lumberyard."

"Go for it," she told him. And by midafternoon, before Peter woke from his nap, Brian had completed a set of easy-to-use steps in the corner of the pool. Wearing a borrowed swimsuit from Geoff, he remained in the pool for Peter's swimming lesson and kept him entertained for almost two hours. Sure, it was a small thing, but it meant the world to Margaret. And she felt certain that Brian was finally home.

Twenty-Nine

Early June 1945

The USO tour had been more fun than Colleen had expected, but it was also tiring. She tried not to show her weariness and was still able to smile at Bob Hope's opening joke as he introduced her to the troops. "I know that you boys were hoping to see the lovely Lana Turner up here today," he would always begin. "As much as I hate to disappoint you, I need to tell you she didn't make it." He would then pause, allowing them to express their dismay. Then he would pull a golf club from behind his back.

"I'm a golfer," he would casually say as he practiced a swing. "Would've gone pro until I learned they weren't looking for high scores." The crowd would chortle. "But when I hit a disappointing shot, kind of like when Lana Turner didn't show, I sometimes rely on a *Mulligan* for a second chance." He'd swing again, pretending to watch the ball soar to where she'd be waiting in the wings. "And there she is—the beautiful *Miss Maureen Mulligan!*" And Colleen would stroll out with music playing, wearing one of the beautiful gowns provided for her, and the men would hoot and holler as if she were the greatest thing since sliced bread.

After that, she and Mr. Hope would have some friendly banter, sing a few songs, perform a few dance numbers, do a skit involving the sailors and soldiers, and wrap it up with more music. Although they did some of the same acts and songs, each show varied, which actually made it more fun for everyone. And even when she felt tired and hot and sticky, she kept a Hollywood smile on her face and did her best to be cheerful and fun and entertaining. She knew her reason for being there was to bolster the spirits of these servicemen. And she knew they were probably more tired than she was.

But as the tour wound down to an end, she couldn't help but feel dismayed that she still hadn't seen Geoff. Their second to last show was in Guam, and then they would proceed to Hawaii for a final show. But after Colleen heard reports from a friendly admiral that Geoff's aircraft carrier was stationed near the Philippines, she had given up hope of connecting with him. She tried to conceal her sadness as she played along with Mr. Hope, smiling at the troops and just wishing this show would quickly end.

"So I see we've got a mixed crowd out there," Bob Hope said. "Sailors and soldiers on the same island and so far no fights have broken out." They laughed. "But I want to know, who kisses better?

Sailors or soldiers?" He turned to Colleen as the troops began calling out answers. "You look an expert. What do you think?"

She laughed. "I'm happily married to a navy pilot, so you can probably guess my answer."

"Well, I think we should have a little contest—and I'll need some sailors and soldiers to volunteer." As men yelled and waved with enthusiasm, a variety of soldiers and sailors were invited to join them on the stage. The crowd grew loud with excitement, their competitive spirits getting lively over this little contest. Mr. Hope waved for one of the female assistants to come over. "To conduct this experiment fairly, we'll need to blindfold Miss Mulligan. Okay, kiddies, let's get this clambake going."

Colleen continued to smile brightly as Dorothy tied a blindfold over her eyes. This was a new skit, and although Colleen wasn't excited to exchange kisses with strangers, she was determined to be a good sport. After all, she'd had screen kisses before. Why would this be any different? Besides that, it was nearly time to end the show. She would soon be on her way to Hawaii and then home.

The crowd was hooting and hollering, and Mr. Hope was making funny comments, eliciting even more laughter, until finally he announced that the first serviceman was ready. "Let the games begin. Bring on Kisser Number One."

The crowd cheered loudly and she waited. Someone came up and gave her what was actually a rather tame little peck. Nothing like what she'd been expecting. But she simply smiled and nodded as the crowd clapped and whistled, waiting for whatever came next.

"Now for Kisser Number Two." The crowd got even louder now, but she just waited. Suddenly this fellow swept her into his arms, pulling her close to him, then really laid one on her—a long, passionate kiss that made her toes curl. She ripped off her blindfold to see Geoff in front of her and the crowd going wild. They kissed again and when he stopped, she noticed that someone had made a placard that read, I AM MISS MULLIGAN'S HUSBAND!

"Oh, Geoff." She touched his face, trying not to cry. "It's really you."

"I think the navy won this one," Mr. Hope said sagely. "Let's give Miss Mulligan a big hand. And let's allow her to go do some catching up with her handsome husband, naval aviator Geoff Conrad. Glad you could make it." He tipped his hat as Geoff led Colleen from the stage to the cheers of the audience. "Thanks for your service. Thanks to all you men. *We're going to end this war!*" The crowd roared.

Colleen broke into happy tears after they were off stage. Geoff explained that he'd been trying to get to her, but complications kept arising. "I can't tell you the details, but it's looking good for our side. I just felt bad for almost missing you."

"You're here now." She wiped her eyes. "That's all that matters." More kisses were exchanged, and then they were escorted to a nice little bungalow where a seafood dinner was waiting for them. They tried to stretch every minute for as long as they could, but morning came too soon. After a long, passionate good-bye, Geoff headed west on one plane and Colleen headed east on another. Her one consolation was that Geoff had a leave coming up. He promised to be home in about a month's time. "This war will probably be over and done with by then," he'd said in his usual optimistic way. "Then you'll be stuck with me for good." While that was somewhat comforting, she knew that the worst part of the Pacific war could be right around the corner. From what she'd overheard during her USO tour, the Japanese forces were throwing everything they had at the Allies.

Mid-June 1945

Bridget was overjoyed when Margaret, Peter, and Brian came home to San Francisco. Not only because it seemed that Margaret and Brian were happy and solidly back together, but also because it meant she could hang up her store apron and return to nursing. And to her added relief, they had no interest in living in the apartment above the store. She'd been preparing herself to give up that sweet little nest.

"We plan to stay in Mrs. Bartley's house," Margaret explained as they went over the store books. "Now that Brian's passed his bar exams, he's going to work for his dad's attorney. And the law firm—Holmes, Laxton, and Snyder—is only about eight blocks away from there. So he can actually walk to work."

"His leg can handle that?" Bridget closed the ledger that she'd just been showing to Margaret. "You know it's a little bit hilly."

"He's been walking all over USC," Margaret told her. "A couple of miles a day, he told me. He's in great shape."

"That's wonderful to hear. I'm happy for him. And for both of you." Bridget laid down her pencil.

"And Colleen and Mary Ellen are going to remain in Hollywood. She was barely back from the USO tour when her agent called with a new movie contract offer."

"And she's taking it?"

Margaret nodded. "According to Colleen, it's a great job. The movie has what she calls an ensemble cast. A whole lot of big names. And she only has a supporting role, which means she won't even need to go to the studio that much."

"Who will watch the baby?"

"Colleen hired an older woman named Belle. She'll watch Mary Ellen when Colleen's at the studio and be her live-in housekeeper the rest of the time. I met her, and she seems very sweet. And she came with great references."

"That's wonderful." Bridget felt another wave of relief. Colleen wouldn't want the apartment back either. And when Molly came home, whenever that might be, she would probably want to live in Mrs. Bartley's house. After all, it was really *her* house. This was all working out just fine.

"Mam says you'll be working at Letterman soon."

"Yes. I just passed my physical exam to get readmitted. I've been assigned to the therapeutic rehabilitation department. I start work on Monday."

"That's where I used to take Brian."

"I know. Mam reminded me of that."

"You're really sure you want to work there?"

"When I was nursing overseas, I liked helping patients through their rehabilitation process. Of course, that was so they could return to the field, and those soldiers didn't have serious injuries. Serious injuries were sent home, to be treated at facilities like Letterman."

"So you won't have difficulty with all that?" Margaret frowned. "I mean, I remember how gruesome a lot of those patients looked. Brian's injury, compared to some of those poor men, seemed rather minor. I hate to admit this, Bridget, but I had to look away a lot of the time. Seeing some of them made me feel sick inside."

"I *want* to do this, Margaret. I *asked* to be assigned there."

Margaret's smile looked strained. "Well, they are lucky to have you. I'm proud of you. And I'm sure you'll do a fantastic job."

Bridget hoped she would, but she also knew that Margaret was right. The patients she'd observed the other day, after her interview with the head nurse, had left her feeling a bit overwhelmed. Burn victims, men with multiple missing limbs . . . It wasn't easy to see them suffering like that. But she knew it was simply a fact of war. These men had survived the battlefront. Now their big challenge would be to survive the home front. Bridget wanted to help them, to equip and prepare them to return to some sort of normal life. She prayed she was strong enough.

Late June 1945

Colleen felt almost completely happy as she drove to San Diego to pick up Geoff from the naval base. Their plan was to spend their first night in the beach house while Belle took care of Mary Ellen. Then they'd spend the rest of his two-week leave in Hollywood. However, her balloon burst shortly after she picked him up.

"My leave has already been cut short," he informed her as she drove toward the beach. "I have to report back on Monday morning at 0700."

"Oh, Geoff. I thought you'd been promised two weeks. Why can't you—"

"You know I can't tell you *why,* Colleen. Suffice it to say we've got big plans. Something that we hope will put an end to this war once and for all. You know how badly I want to be home with you and Mary Ellen. But it takes time."

"How much time?"

"I can't give specifics." He leaned over to kiss her cheek. "But everyone is predicting it won't be long. Maybe even before summer is over."

"Well, I'm sad you won't be here for Independence Day. I got us tickets for the Hollywood Bowl."

"I'm sorry, babe. That would've been great. But you know the most important thing for me is just being with you and the baby."

"Maybe we should go back to Hollywood tonight." She counted the days in her head. "You'll only have four nights there. Then I assume we'll come back here on Sunday night, so you can report in the morning."

"I want you all to myself tonight." Geoff ran

a finger down her arm. "We'll go to Hollywood first thing tomorrow morning."

Colleen didn't question this. As much as she wanted him to see their new house, she'd been looking forward to this night alone too. She didn't take their time together for granted. In fact, she'd done some calculating, and since their relationship first started—back on December 7, 1941—they'd spent a total of about seven weeks together.

Sometimes she worried that they'd have difficulty getting used to being together all the time after the war finally ended. What if they'd both gotten so independent that they'd resent having to share responsibilities? Or what if they got tired of waking up to the same face every morning?

But during their few days of his shortened leave, these questions were far from her mind. They started out with a nice evening at the beach house. And then when they got to the Hollywood house the next day, Geoff was suitably impressed with everything. But mostly his daughter. "Look," he said with excitement, "she can stand up all by herself."

Colleen laughed. "Yes, she's learned lots of new tricks. I wouldn't be surprised if she was walking soon."

Geoff tried and tried to get Mary Ellen to take her first steps, but she just wasn't quite ready.

Even so, she was adept at getting to wherever she liked by crawling. And it was hilarious to watch Geoff lying on the floor with his daughter climbing all over him like a jungle gym.

Colleen and Geoff packed as much as they could into every waking minute of every day. And when the baby napped in the afternoon, they would swim and lounge by the pool, sometimes snoozing too.

"I feel like I've been staying at a fancy hotel," he said as they toweled off after a morning dip in the pool. "I've been so spoiled that I'll never want to go back." It was his last day in Hollywood, and Colleen was trying not to feel too downhearted.

"What's the penalty for going AWOL?" she teased.

"Just prison." He stretched out on a lounge chair. "I'm sure US military prisons are like summer camp compared to the Japanese hellhole I was stuck in, but count me out." He sighed. "When I think of the men languishing in Jap camps right now—well, I gotta go back, Colleen. I have to do my part to get those poor suckers out of there."

"I know you do."

Geoff had really seemed to bond with Mary Ellen this time. It was as if he saw her as real person now. It touched Colleen to see him playing with her and unwilling to give her up for her nap when it was time for them to drive back to San Diego.

"I'll see you soon, princess." He kissed her one last time then relinquished her to Belle. "Take good care of my girls."

"You know I will," she assured him. "And you take good care of yourself, Mr. Conrad. Come home safe. Your little girl needs you." She winked at Colleen. "Your big girl does too."

As he drove them to San Diego, Colleen expressed her desire to return to San Francisco after her current movie wrapped. "But I don't really want to stay at Mam and Dad's. And I'm not sure I want to stay at Molly's house with Margaret and Brian and Peter. And I—"

"Go stay with my family," he urged her. "Mom and Grandma and Grandpa would love to see Mary Ellen."

"Oh, I don't know."

"Please, Colleen," he begged. "Do it for me. It would make me so happy to think of you and Mary Ellen being at the farm with my family. When your movie's done, please, tell me you'll go visit them."

"Okay," she agreed. "You win. I'll go."

"Great. I'll call them as soon as we reach San Diego. They'll be over the moon."

Their last night at the beach house was more somber than the first one had been. Colleen didn't usually allow her mind to go to the negative places, but she was aware—just like she always was in their final moments together—that this could be their last farewell. Geoff's job as a fighter pilot was extremely dangerous. According to statistics, it was pretty much a coin toss as to whether he'd make it home again. But she was an actress and knew how to keep a smile on her face, even if her heart was aching.

When she told him good-bye the next morning, she concealed her fear and anxiety. "I pray daily that God and his angels will keep you safe," she reminded him. "Come back to me, darling."

He kissed her one last time, promising to return. And then she watched as he boarded a plane and disappeared into the cloudless blue sky.

Thirty

Early July 1945

Bridget had asked Mam and Margaret to collect donations of sugar ration coupons from store customers during the past several weeks. The plan was to bake special Fourth of July cookies for all her patients in the rehabilitation department. Although they hadn't scheduled therapy sessions on Independence Day, the men were still in the hospital, and Bridget had gotten permission to host a little party for them. She'd posted several notices in her department, inviting the men to come celebrate the Fourth with her. Whether or not they would come remained to be seen.

But for two evenings, Margaret and Mam helped Bridget mass-produce about a hundred big beautiful sugar cookies iced in red, white, and blue. The next day, Bridget took everything to the hospital and set up a party table topped with a banner that she'd painted that said: HAPPY INDEPENDENCE DAY. THANK YOU FOR FIGHTING FOR OUR FREEDOM! She arranged the festive cookies as well as coffee and fruit punch, put on some lively music, and then waited to see if any of her patients would show. She knew this was just a tiny token of appreciation, but she hoped that it would lift the spirits of the men she was working with.

Before long, the room was filled with patients and, instead of hearing moans and groans of therapy treatment, laughter and good will echoed throughout. The cookies and her party were a hit, and Bridget couldn't have been happier as she went around the room, visiting with the men and thanking them for their service.

"This was a lovely gesture," Dr. Stillwell told Bridget as the party was in full swing. "Thank you for doing it." The elderly doctor had given up his retirement to lend a hand with this rehab therapy unit. Although he cared deeply for these patients, Bridget knew he wanted to return to retirement as soon as he could be replaced. "Several doctors have just arrived from the field," he quietly told her. "I hope you don't mind that I invited a couple to stop by here today. Thought it may be a good way to get acquainted with the patients."

"That's a great idea." Bridget set a fresh pitcher of punch on the table. "Does that mean your time here is coming to an end?"

"You know how I've missed my leisurely mornings and fishing on the bay. I wouldn't complain if some young, energetic doctor wanted to kick me out of this place." He grinned. "Speak of the devils, here comes one now." He nodded toward the door. "Be nice to him, Nurse Mulligan, and maybe we can talk him into staying."

Bridget smiled, glancing over to where a tall figure had just entered the room. But her smiled faded as she recognized his face.

"Not a bad looking chap, eh?" Dr. Stillwell gave her a good-natured elbow. "Say, Nurse Mulligan, is something wrong?"

She felt her heart in her throat as she dumbly shook her head. "I need to make some fresh coffee. Please excuse me." She turned away, hurrying toward the staff area where she pretended to be busily brewing another pot of coffee, but her hands trembled as she measured the grounds, spilling some on the counter.

"Careful there," a familiar voice said. "Can't be wasting precious coffee."

Bridget turned to look into Cliff Stafford's face. "What are you doing here? I thought you were in Europe."

"I asked for a transfer after VE Day." He used a paper napkin to capture the spilled coffee grounds, dropping them into the metal basket.

"But why here?" Her hands were still trembling as she poured water into the pot.

"Because I hoped to find you here." He put a hand on her shoulder, turning her around to face him. "Bridget, I've missed you so much. You have no idea."

"Really?" She set down the water pitcher, staring into his eyes with disbelief. Was this really happening? Or was she having a malaria attack, becoming delusional?

He pulled her closer to him. "We should've gotten married when we had the chance, Bridget. I was a fool to let you slip away like that. I'm so sorry."

She felt her eyes moistening. "I missed you too, Cliff." Still, she almost wondered whether this was a dream. "I almost wrote to you . . . so many times . . . but I stopped myself."

"Can we start over?"

She nodded, blinking back tears. "Yes, of course."

And then he kissed her—and she decided that even if this *was* just a sweet and delightful dream, she was going to make it last as long as possible. But when he finally pulled away, using his handkerchief to blot her tears, she knew it was real. Blessedly and wonderfully real.

Mid-July 1945

After her part in the film was finished, Colleen entrusted the care of her Hollywood house to Belle then drove to San Francisco, where she and Mary Ellen spent a week with Mam and Dad. During that time, her family gave her a small birthday dinner. Not that she'd been particularly inclined to celebrate. It wasn't because twenty-two was so old but simply because she was missing Geoff. She hadn't heard from him since June and felt a bit dismayed that he'd forgotten her birthday.

To be fair, Geoff had his hands full with the war. Just last week she'd read how the Allied forces had sent out a thousand planes in the biggest bombing spree in history. She had no doubt that Geoff had been involved. And she'd hoped and prayed that the Allies' relentless pounding would bring Japan to its knees. But Hirohito still refused to surrender.

Keeping her promise to Geoff, after her visit with her family, Colleen drove to his family's farm, where she and Mary Ellen were warmly welcomed. Geoff's mother and grandparents couldn't have been more thrilled with little Mary Ellen. Between the three of them, Colleen barely had to lift a finger for her care. In fact, it turned out to be a rather relaxing time and the country-side was beautiful.

With Mary Ellen's first birthday a few weeks away, Ellen had just asked Colleen if she would remain with them long enough to celebrate. They were dining outside, under the shade of a big oak tree, watching as Mary Ellen attempted to take her first steps in the soft green grass, tumbling down again and again.

"I'm sorry," Colleen told her mother-in-law, "but my sister Margaret is already planning her birthday party. She made me promise to be home for it."

"Perhaps we could have a pre-birthday party for her," Geoff's grandmother suggested.

"Yes, that's what we'll do," Ellen agreed. "We'll have a cake and everything."

"And I'm going to get her a pony," Grandpa Conrad declared.

Colleen laughed. "That's very sweet of you, but I don't think she'll be ready for a pony—not for quite awhile."

"That's true, but I'll need plenty of time to train the pony. We want it to be nice and calm by the time she's old enough. And Geoff rode his first pony when he was only two."

"With help," Ellen clarified.

"He could ride alone by the time he was three," Grandpa bragged.

"Well, that boy was always a risk taker." Grandma smiled.

"He still is." Colleen wanted to ask if any of them had heard from him lately but knew it was a sore subject. Geoff had never been much of a letter writer, and what few letters he wrote usually went to Colleen.

"I'll be so glad when that part of the war ends," Ellen said glumly. "Every time I listen to the news, I hope they're going to announce that it's over. But day after day, it just drags on."

"Geoff felt certain it wouldn't last much longer," Colleen told her.

"Really? Did he tell you anything specific?" Grandpa Conrad asked with interest.

"No, he can't do that. He just seemed to feel it wouldn't be long now."

"Let's all pray that he's right," Grandma said.

Just then Mary Ellen started to toddle toward Colleen. "Keep going," Colleen urged her, getting down on her knees and extending her arms. "Come on, baby girl. You can do it." They all clapped and cheered as Mary Ellen completed half a dozen good solid steps. Then just as she started to stumble, Colleen caught her in her arms. "Oh, Daddy is going to be so proud of you!" She kissed her. "I'll have to send him a letter tomorrow morning!"

Late July 1945

Molly's honeymoon stage with Paris was finally over. Oh, she definitely loved the beautiful old city and felt certain she always would. But she'd grown increasingly weary of the deprivations and even wearier of the mundane office work. Ever since most of the press had fled to the Pacific Front—where the real action was—the press office was shorthanded. As a result, Molly had been talked into remaining in the European office for a few more weeks. “Just until we can find someone else,” she’d been told.

Before the press evacuated, they’d all enjoyed a big celebration—partly for the victory in Europe and partly for Mick and Mazzie’s wedding. Once again, Molly had stood up as maid of honor, reconfirming her suspicion that she’d always be a bridesmaid. But she was glad to see them tie the knot. Perhaps she’d been just a tiny bit jealous, wondering what it would’ve been like if she’d been in Mazzie’s shoes—which were actually Molly’s shoes since she’d loaned them to her. But Molly didn’t love Mick. Not like that anyway. She loved him like a big brother. Like what she’d written to Patrick in her last letter. Not that Patrick was writing back.

Molly suspected Patrick had his hands full with the war still raging over there. Just days ago, the Allies had called for unconditional surrender of the Imperial Japanese armed forces. Everyone had felt very hopeful, assuming this would bring an end to the madness in the Pacific. The document was called the *Potsdam Declaration* and left little room for debate. Plus, the Allies had offered only one alternative to signing this agreement—“prompt and utter destruction.” And, based on everything Molly had been reading lately, the Allies had the means to deliver it.

To everyone’s disappointment, the obstinate

Japanese Imperialists had decided to ignore the declaration. Really, it hadn't been surprising. Molly expected that Hirohito was even more stubborn than Hitler had been. The arrogant leader would probably rather be ground into ashes than give up.

Early August 1945

Molly was no stranger to startling news on the UPI telex machine. Lately, all the flashes had been relevant to the war in the Pacific, and part of her job was to pass any important messages along to the few editors still in the office. But on July 30 an announcement had really knocked the wind out of her. The USS *Indianapolis* had been sunk by Japanese torpedoes somewhere near the Philippines. The cruiser had 1,196 crew members aboard and had sunk in just twelve minutes. Rescue attempts were underway, but it was unknown if there were any survivors in the shark-infested waters. According to the telex, it was destined to be the "greatest single loss of life at sea from a single ship in the history of the US Navy."

Molly had felt numb as she'd passed the news on to her superiors along with her official resignation. "It's not that I haven't enjoyed my time here," she'd explained to Mrs. Warren, the current office supervisor, "it's just that I want to go home."

"We appreciate that you stayed on with us after your team left," Mrs. Warren had told her. "We knew it wouldn't be for long. We appreciate your hard work."

Molly had finished out the week, and Mrs. Warren had made her travel arrangements. Now Molly was on her way home with only one suitcase thanks to the flight's weight limit. But she'd been happy to leave many things behind, sharing various greatly sought-after items with her grateful female friends at the UPI office. It had been like Christmas there on Friday.

As she flew over the English Channel to London, she was eager to get home to her family. But as much as she missed them—and she certainly did—she missed Patrick even more. Hearing that news about that ship being torpedoed . . . the loss of life . . . it had all been a stark reminder of the danger that Patrick was in. Possibly more now than ever before. The Japanese were relentless and even though they were obviously losing this war, they were determined to take down everyone with them. It almost felt as if they would rather destroy the entire globe than surrender. More than ever, Molly felt seriously worried that Patrick's submarine would be one of the numerous casualties of this never-ending war.

In England, Molly was informed that she would

have to wait until Monday for the next available flight. While staying in a nurses' dormitory over the weekend, she sent a wire to her family, informing them that she hoped to be home in about a week. On Monday morning, she boarded a passenger plane with her single suitcase. And after a bumpy flight, she landed in New York just in time to hear the biggest news ever.

"First atomic bomb dropped on Japan!" the newsboys shouted in the terminal, hawking copies of the *New York Times* to the crowds that couldn't seem to buy them quickly enough. Molly waited in line to purchase a paper then hurried to the sidelines to read that the United States had dropped a missile equal to 20,000 tons of TNT onto Hiroshima, Japan, and the devastation was unlike anything ever witnessed before. President Truman was now warning of a "rain of ruin" if Japan refused to surrender. Hopefully this really was the end of the end.

The celebrating was loud and rowdy on the train out of New York that evening. The smoke-filled cars were filled with raucous servicemen, and alcohol was flowing freely. Everyone seemed certain that this new "monster bomb" had finally brought Japan to its knees. She was happy for the merrymakers and didn't even protest over several victory hugs and kisses, but she was grateful to escape into a sleeping berth. And even though it sounded as if the servicemen partied all night,

Molly was so tired that she slept through most of it.

The train seemed relatively quiet the next morning. Molly assumed that the other passengers were just sleeping off their long festive night, but when she went into the dining car, she noticed the headline on a morning paper from Ohio: JAPAN REFUSES TO SURRENDER. She felt too dismayed to even read the details as she ordered a cup of coffee, toast, and an egg. And as the day progressed, she could tell that others felt the letdown as well. The general morale had gone down considerably. The evening papers were even less encouraging. Japan was not giving up.

The news on the evening of August 8 was more encouraging. The Soviet Union had declared war on Japan by invading Manchuria and the Kuril Islands. Passenger morale lifted again, servicemen began drinking and singing, and a few hours later, Molly got off the train at the Southern Pacific depot in San Francisco. She'd wired her family that she would be arriving late—close to midnight—telling them that she'd take a taxi home. But to her surprise, Bridget was waiting on the platform, waving with enthusiasm.

Molly ran to her, tossed down her suitcase, and fell into her arms, bursting into tears as they clung to each other. "It's so good to see you," Molly sobbed. "It's been so long!"

"Too long." Bridget held Molly at arm's length,

staring at her. “You’re still pretty as ever. But you’re pale and skinny.” She frowned. “Are you well?”

“Just worn out.” Molly picked up her suitcase. “I feel like I could sleep for days.”

“Then you shall.” Bridget took her suitcase from her. “Allow me.”

“Thanks. And thanks for coming for me.”

“You’re going home with me,” Bridget explained. “I hope you don’t mind.”

“Not at all.” Molly couldn’t stop crying as they walked through the depot. She suspected it was probably from just plain exhaustion . . . or maybe relief . . . or they could be tears of joy. Mostly she was glad to be home.

Thirty-One

August 14, 1945

Colleen's departure from the Conrad farm was softened by the news that Japan had just surrendered—unconditionally. "Thank you for everything," she told Ellen and Geoff's grandparents as she loaded her things into her car. "We had a wonderful time. And Mary Ellen's pre-birthday party was purely delightful." As she reached for Mary Ellen, she kissed Geoff's mother on the cheek. "Thank you for your kind hospitality."

"I wish you didn't have to go so soon," Ellen said sadly. "I hope you'll come back again before you return to Los Angeles."

"Yes," Grandma Conrad said. "Please, come back soon, Colleen."

"I'll do my best." Colleen set Mary Ellen in her car seat, giving the miniature steering wheel a little toot before she turned around to hug them all good-bye. "Geoff will soon be home," she assured them. Of course, she had no idea when he'd be home—or even if he was still alive since none of them had heard anything from him. But in her heart, she believed he was alive and she believed that he'd soon be home. He just had to be. Not only for her sake and Mary Ellen's sake . . . but Colleen felt fairly certain that she was expecting. And, although there was no way to know, she felt certain that it was going to be a boy. A little Geoff Junior.

As she drove toward San Francisco, she thought about this morning's news—that the war was over. They'd all danced around the living room, celebrating. Grandpa Conrad had even opened a bottle of champagne, insisting on mixing it with their orange juice for breakfast. And it had felt wonderful to celebrate. Especially after the last week, when they'd all been on pins and needles, closely following every newscast. Grandpa Conrad had kept the radio tuned to his favorite news station, hushing everyone in the house each time a news announcement began, turning the radio's volume up so that not a word would be missed.

It had started with the atomic bomb being dropped on Hiroshima, Japan just over a week ago. They'd all thought the war was over then. But no, it dragged on. Then on August 9 a second bomb had been dropped on Nagasaki, Japan. Still, Japan had held on. Then finally today, it was official—Japan surrendered. Life would start returning to normal. At least that was what they were telling themselves. Suddenly, Colleen knew she needed to be with her family. And then, if she got word from Geoff, she would gladly make the drive to San Diego and meet him there.

After several weeks, Molly still felt somewhat like a displaced citizen at home. Oh, she'd been glad enough to see her family. And happy to hear that the war was ended. But she just wasn't sure what she wanted to do. She knew that she could work at the photo studio again. At Lulu's wedding reception last weekend, Bernard had begged her to consider returning. Molly had kept her promise to be maid of honor, smiling happily as Lulu and Tommy repeated their vows. And, really, she couldn't have been happier for them. But a small part of her had felt sad and wistful, like they had found something that she had lost.

Molly had stopped by the *Chronicle* a few days ago and, although she'd been offered a clerical job, Jim in the photography department had warned her it might be temporary. "Servicemen are popping in right and left," he'd divulged, "and the newspaper promised them priority for employment." She also considered going back to school and, thanks to Mrs. Bartley, she could easily afford tuition. But it was too late for registration—not to mention that, according to Mick, who'd just returned from the Pacific, classrooms would be packed thanks to the GI Bill. "Although my chances of getting a professorship just got a whole lot better," he'd confided. And then Mazzie had shared her good news. “I’m expecting,” she’d whispered in Molly’s ear. “Can you believe it? Mick and me, parents at our age? Will wonders never cease?”

Molly had congratulated them both. And she truly was happy for them. But once again, she felt displaced. As if she were on the outside of life looking in. And the truth was that she really didn’t want to work at the photo studio or the *Chronicle* or even go to school. She wasn’t sure what was wrong with her—except that she didn’t seem to fit in anywhere.

Even as she puttered around the victory garden, which had been sadly neglected in her absence, she felt no connection to it. Oh, she remembered how much she’d loved it here before, planting seeds, watching things grow, harvesting. She pulled out an overgrown weed, tossing it on the small pile she’d started. That was exactly how she felt—as if she’d been pulled out by the roots and cast aside. She didn’t belong here.

She glanced up at Mrs. Bartley’s house. Margaret, Brian, and Peter were nicely settled in there, just like Molly had encouraged them to do last winter. Although now that Brian was working, they’d insisted on paying rent. They’d asked Molly to come live there with them, but she just wasn’t comfortable crashing in on their recently restored little family. She knew they were still working things out, trying to fit themselves back together . . . and she didn't want to do anything to disrupt their progress. Especially since they were about to welcome a new baby into the mix. No, they didn't need Molly there.

Then, when Colleen stopped here after her visit at the Conrads' farm, they'd all decided Dad didn't need a noisy toddler underfoot, so she and Mary Ellen had stayed upstairs at Mrs. Bartley's. Although now that the birthday party was behind them, they'd probably be going soon. Even so, Molly didn't want to live over there. And then there was Bridget. She was happy as a clam up in the apartment above the store and planning what was sure to be a beautiful fall wedding with Doctor Cliff.

Molly hated to admit it, but she felt slightly trapped, stuck in her childhood bedroom in her parents' home. She would tiptoe about and try to act like everything was just fine, all the while feeling like she just didn't fit in anywhere. Maybe she never would again. Maybe this was simply part of growing up.

She'd read about displaced servicemen returning home and experiencing difficulty in the transition, unable to assimilate back into civilian life. Maybe something like that was happening to her. She'd discussed it with Bridget and, although her sister claimed to understand and had gone through similar challenges, she was so happy about her engagement and upcoming wedding, plus she loved her work at Letterman . . . She had clearly moved past any feeling of displacement. She assured Molly that she would too, but for some reason, Molly still felt stuck.

It didn't help that Patrick had never responded to her last letter—her feeble attempt to reopen the communication between them. No one had heard from him in months. Sometimes Molly would wake from a dream where she'd seen him walking in a bright light, wearing his naval uniform, but completely out of reach. As if he were dead. But she hated to think about that.

"Can we join you?" Colleen asked as she and Mary Ellen emerged from the back door of Mrs. Bartley's house.

"Of course." Molly forced a smile, waving her hand toward the small, unkempt yard. "Although it's not too pretty out here."

Colleen set Mary Ellen down, watching as she toddled toward a pile of dirt, squatting to dig her fingers into it and squealing with delight.

"Looks like a natural-born gardener." Molly gave her a small spade to dig with. "This place could've used her help last spring."

"Maybe in a few years." Colleen sat down on the bench. "Right now we're getting ready to leave. I was just offered another supporting role in a big movie. I need to get down there and get ready to go to work in a week."

Molly nodded glumly. “Yeah, I figured you’d be going soon, now that the big birthday bash is over. That was quite a gathering.” Mary Ellen’s birthday party had turned into a victory celebration too, with a number of neighbors stopping by to enjoy the festivities.

“Margaret really outdid herself.”

“I hope she’s not too worn out. Isn’t her due date only about a month away?”

“Yes, but she still seems pretty energetic.” Colleen sighed. “I think she likes having Brian around to help.”

“I’m sure you’re right.” Molly tugged out another weed, staring down at its long, scraggly roots.

“Come to Hollywood with me,” Colleen said suddenly.

“What would I do down there?” Molly tossed the weed to the pile.

“I don’t know. You could play with Mary Ellen. Or just do nothing. Or work on your tan by the pool.”

“You have a pool?”

“Sure.” Now Colleen started to describe what sounded like a very posh house. “And I’ve even got a housekeeper-nanny, so I wouldn’t expect you to work or anything.”

Molly considered this. “That’s actually rather tempting.”

“Then come with me.” Colleen grabbed her

hand. “There’s no one—well, besides Geoff—that I’d rather have down there with me, Molly. Come on, please, say you will.”

“What about when Geoff gets discharged? After all, the war’s over.”

“Then we’ll all celebrate till the cows come home.”

“But you two would probably want to be alone. I’d hate to be in the way.”

“Then you could go to the beach house in San Diego. You could take up beachcombing or something.”

“I have Mrs. Bartley’s car,” Molly said suddenly. “I could drive down there. That way I’d have my independence.”

“Yes.” Colleen nodded eagerly. “Do that, Molly.”

“When do we leave?”

“Is tomorrow too soon?”

September 2, 1945

As Colleen drove south the next day, with Molly following her, she had the radio tuned to a music program when it was interrupted for an important announcement. She turned it up and listened with interest as the newscaster described the formal surrender of Japan.

“President Truman has declared today as

VJ Day. Victory over Japan. The formal surrender took place aboard the USS *Missouri* in Tokyo Bay. Officials from the Japanese government signed the *Japanese Instrument of Surrender*, thereby ending the hostilities. During this momentous and long-awaited occasion, a thousand carrier-based planes flew overhead, the sound of their engines echoing across the Pacific in a celebratory roar of victory."

The newscaster continued to ramble about the history-making day, but all Colleen could imagine was a *thousand military planes* soaring majestically and victoriously over Tokyo Bay. She felt certain that Geoff's plane must've been among them. And even more certain that he'd be coming home soon.

Late September 1945

Molly had thoroughly enjoyed her time with Colleen. Not only were her home and pool absolutely beautiful, it had been like a haven for Molly. And Belle was a dear, sweet woman who clearly loved Mary Ellen and was kind to Molly too. And she hadn't resented it when Molly had spent time with her niece.

Colleen's supporting role had required her to go to the studio several days a week, but never for the long hours that she'd put in for starring roles.

All in all, their time together had been relaxing and enjoyable and just what Molly needed to start feeling like herself again. She couldn't thank Colleen enough for inviting her down there. But when Geoff had joined them in mid-September, Molly had welcomed him home then hopped in her car and headed for San Diego.

Colleen had encouraged Molly to stay in the beach house for as long as she liked. "Make yourself completely at home." And Molly had done just that. She'd been there for two weeks and felt in no hurry to leave. Although she still had no idea what was next for her, she no longer fretted over it. Instead, she would walk on the beach, take a daily swim, and do some beachcombing. She'd also managed to take some rather amazing color photos of sunsets and wondered if someday she might return to a career as a professional photographer. Although there was no rush. And no rush to return to San Francisco either.

Even when Margaret had her baby last week—John Riley Hammond—Molly hadn't felt inclined to dash back to San Francisco to see her new nephew. She'd assured Margaret that she and Colleen would be back the week before Bridget's wedding in late October and that they'd meet the new baby then. And to her relief, Margaret hadn't even seemed to mind. Maybe they were all growing up.

Molly had just finished a morning swim in

the ocean. Toweling herself off, she studied the thick layers of dark clouds swirling in from the Pacific. The weather forecast called for a storm that would last several days, so she knew this might be her last swim for a spell. She shoved her feet into her old rubber sandals and headed back toward the house, wondering if she would beat the rain but not particularly caring whether she did or not since she was already wet.

As she walked, she noticed someone coming her way. Thanks to the early hour and the weather, the beach had been fairly deserted, so she was surprised to see anyone else out. But this person seemed to be coming directly toward her. The morning sun was still shining through a thin layer of white clouds in the east, forcing her to squint to see the figure better. It was a man dressed in white, and for a moment, she thought perhaps this was an apparition or hallucination—because it reminded her of a dream she'd had a number of times. Something about his stride looked familiar, and as he got closer, she could see the formal white navy uniform. *Patrick.*

"Molly!" he called out, quickening his pace.

"Patrick?" She started to run, stopping just a few feet short of him and staring in wonder as she clutched her towel around her. "What are you doing here?"

"I came to see you."

"But how did you know I was here?"

"I called your house. Your dad told me." He smiled, opening his arms wide. Without thinking or questioning herself, she ran straight into them.

"I can't believe you're really here," she said. "I thought I was seeing things."

"Oh, Molly." He stroked her damp hair as he held her. "We have so much to talk about."

She hated that she was crying, but there was nothing she could do to stop the tears. "Yes," she muttered, using her sandy hands to wipe her tears and picking up her discarded beach towel. "We do have a lot to talk about." She nodded toward the house. "Let's go inside before it starts to rain."

He peered up at the sky. "Good idea."

"Are you on a pass or on leave?" She led him into the house, kicking off her sand-encrusted sandals by the door.

"Neither. I'm done—honorably discharged." He kicked off his shoes too. "A free man."

She blinked then nodded. "Congratulations. Welcome home."

He stared at her, and she suddenly realized she was in her bathing suit. "I must look a mess." She reached for her hair.

"You've never looked more beautiful, Molly." He shook his head with an expression of disbelief. "You are a vision."

She didn't know what to say. "Well, uh, thanks, but I'm also cold. I better get dressed."

He nodded to the dark fireplace. “Want me to build you a fire?”

“Sure. Thanks.” While he attended to the fire, she put the coffeepot on the stove then hurried to the bedroom for a quick cleanup. She pulled on a pair of white pants and a soft cable-knit pullover. As she ran her fingers through her damp, wind-blown curls, she remembered his words. He’d called her a *vision.*

Before long they were sitting by the fire with mugs of hot coffee, and Patrick was trying to explain about what happened between them the last time they were together. “I attempted to write to you about it a number of times, but the words just never came out right. And then I got that letter from you that made me believe you were done with me. I sent you that Christmas card . . . then never heard back. And then you seemed to vanish. Brian wrote that you were in Europe, but I didn’t know how to reach you, and I figured you didn’t want to hear from me. And, really, it just felt like the whole world was going crazy.”

“My world was pretty crazy too,” she admitted. “I thought you had given up on me . . . on us. I thought the best thing I could do was just move on.”

He told her about exchanging letters with his brother. “Brian was adamant. He continually warned me that it was a huge mistake to get engaged or married while actively serving overseas. His warning made sense to me at the time. The idea of tying you down to me, not knowing if I would survive or come home with injuries . . . Well, it did seem wrong to me. It seemed selfish. Especially after I saw how much the war had hurt Brian and Margaret. It nearly destroyed their marriage. Well, that and other things. I realize that both of them made some serious mistakes."

"But did you really think I would make those same mistakes?" she asked. "I felt like you compared me to Margaret—as if I may betray you."

"No, I never thought that. Not once, Molly. I've always trusted you. I had been ready to propose to you that night. I had the ring in my pocket. But in the back of my mind, I was thinking about Brian and how he'd come home injured and the toll it had taken on him and Margaret. And then you told me about Margaret, and . . . and I just didn't know what to do. So it seemed prudent to wait."

She nodded. "That actually makes sense. As much as it hurt at the time, I'm glad you decided to wait."

Now Patrick looked worried. "Does that mean you've changed your mind about me? Have I've lost my chance with you? I can't tell you how many times I've braced myself for a letter from my parents or brother, telling me that you'd married someone else." He ran his fingers through his hair. "I know you must've had multitudes of chances."

She smiled. "My feelings toward you haven't changed, Patrick."

He let out a sigh of relief. "So can you forgive me?"

"Forgive you for what?"

"For hurting you. I know I hurt you. I'm really sorry. I kept telling myself that I was trying to protect you by distancing myself. But I think I was just being a fool. You didn't need my protection. You were stronger than I realized."

"I meant what I said. I'm really glad everything went the way it did." She set down her coffee mug. "It gave me a chance to really grow up and stand on my own two feet." Now she told him a little about her time in Europe, including the story she'd written about Eva Braun and how it had been picked up by the UPI. "And I actually hope to return to photography or journalism someday."

"That'd be great. You're such a talented writer and photographer."

"But that whole time, Patrick, you were always in the back of my mind. You were always in my prayers." She took in a slow breath. "And I'm so very, very thankful you made it home safely." She touched his cheek and smiled. "Not even a scratch on you."

He reached for her face and, taking it with both

his hands, soundly kissed her—with the same sort of passion that he had kissed her with the time before that awful conversation. And she kissed him back. The fire crackled and the rain pelted against the windows and Molly had never been happier.

"I love you," Patrick told her. "I think I've always loved you."

"I love you too." She reached under her cardigan, showing him the strand of pearls. "I only take them off to swim or bathe."

He kissed her again and then he reached into his pocket, pulling out a worn looking blue box. "This has been through the war." He handed the little velvet box to her. "Kind of like us. But I've always dreamed of this day . . . of giving it to you."

Her hands trembled as she lifted the lid on the box. There, nestled against the dark blue velvet, was a gleaming platinum ring, but the solitaire was not a diamond. "An aquamarine." She stared in wonder, knowing the glittering pale blue stone was more rare and expensive than a diamond.

"Remember when we helped Brian pick out Margaret's ring back in 1941, how you told me you wanted an aquamarine for your engagement ring?"

She nodded happily, blinking back tears. "It's perfect. Absolutely beautiful."

Patrick got down on one knee. “Molly Irene Mulligan, love of my life, will you please do me the honor of marrying me?”

Molly couldn’t stop the tears as she slid the ring on, but she didn’t care because they were simply tears of joy. “Oh, Patrick.” She wrapped her arms around him. “Yes, yes, yes!” she cried. “A million times yes!”

By that evening, after much discussion, Patrick and Molly both decided that neither of them really wanted a great big wedding. And neither of them particularly wanted to wait too long either. With Bridget and Doctor Cliff getting married in a few weeks, it seemed impractical to try to plan anything too close to their date.

“Let’s just do it,” Molly said suddenly.

“What do you mean?”

“Let’s just get married at the little church we attend down here. We can let our families know after the fact. If they want to have some sort of dinner party to celebrate, fine, but we don’t need a fancy wedding to be married.”

“Are you certain?” Patrick looked surprised but happy.

“I’m positive,” she assured him.

“Well, I’m glad that I got your dad’s permission this morning.”

“What?”

“When I called to inquire as to your whereabouts, I just happened to ask your dad if he would mind if I proposed to you. And you know what he said?"

"What?"

"He said, 'What took you so long?' "

They both laughed.

"So you really don't want a traditional wedding with all the bells and whistles?" he asked with a concerned expression.

"I'm tired of weddings, Patrick. I've been in too many, and there's still Bridget's in a few weeks. I just want to be your wife."

He laughed and hugged her. "You are, and always have been, a girl after my own heart."

So it was that Molly, wearing a stylish sky blue suit, and Patrick in his officer's uniform, with Geoff and Colleen by their sides, repeated their vows before a San Diego priest. After a quiet but wonderful ten-day honeymoon in the beach house, they headed north to where the Hammonds and Mulligans had put together a big celebration for them. They also got to meet their new nephew, John Riley Hammond, as well as attend the festivities surrounding Bridget's upcoming wedding.

And what a wedding it was! Old Saint Mary's was filled with autumnal blooms and about three hundred guests, including many of Bridget and Cliff's patients from Letterman. Bridget's gown of white taffeta and lace was sophisticated and beautiful. Margaret, as matron of honor, had worked hard to get her figure back, determined to have a slimmer waistline than Colleen. Of course, Colleen didn't care since she was four months pregnant and just glad that she could fit into the apricot colored satin gown. Molly was just glad that she'd finally broken that "always a bridesmaid" spell.

Cliff was handsome in his army officer's uniform and grateful for the groomsmen provided to him by Bridget's family. Brian, Cliff's new good friend, stood up as best man, wearing his army officer's uniform, with young Peter beside him as the ring bearer. Geoff was next in line, wearing his navy officer's uniform, and finally Patrick, also in a navy officer's uniform, finished off the line. They made a fabulous looking wedding party.

Sitting in the front row, on the bride's side, were Mam and Dad, holding little Mary Ellen, and next to them, their best friends the Hammonds, holding the newest addition to the family, John Riley. It was the first time they had all been together since the beginning of the war in 1941.

The reception was held at the VFW hall. Dad officially welcomed everyone to the festivities by lifting his champagne glass in a toast. "Here's to the lovely bride and the handsome groom." He looked around the crowded room. "And here's to our great big, beautiful, and ever-growing family. We thank the Good Lord for bringing the war to an end and for bringing our remaining children safely home. There were many times when we were unsure, times when we almost gave up hope, times when we thought that it may never happen . . . that we would never all meet again. But here we all are together. And here's to Bridget and Cliff. God bless!"

The bride and groom opened the dance floor with their favorite song and many of the guests joined in the singing. *Don't know where, don't know when . . . but I know we'll meet again . . .* By the time the dance ended, there was hardly a dry eye in the crowd.

But they were tears of joy!

Books are produced in the United States using U.S.-based materials

Books are printed using a revolutionary new process called THINKtech™ that lowers energy usage by 70% and increases overall quality

Books are durable and flexible because of Smyth-sewing

Paper is sourced using environmentally responsible foresting methods and the paper is acid-free

Center Point Large Print
600 Brooks Road / PO Box 1
Thorndike, ME 04986-0001 USA

(207) 568-3717

US & Canada:
1 800 929-9108
www.centerpointlargeprint.com